Rue's Rapture

Divergent Omegaverse: Paranormal Gay Romance - Book 5

JP Sayle

Contents

Rue's Rapture

Rue's past haunts his present, but is there a happy ever after in his future?

Lane and Derick Starling adopting Rue may have saved him, but his subsequent therapy fails to make him believe he is worthy of love. More than a decade later, Rue faces a personal crisis.

One night of passion with his PA Monty is enough to tell Rue that one man can't meet his needs. A trip to Bayfield offers Rue a moment to be open about his sexual preferences. Monty and Kendrick are perfect for him, but a week just isn't enough. Then Kendrick comes up with an unusual offer...

Rue grasps the chance, but the deeper the emotional connection gets, the harder it is for him to preserve the shields he uses to keep his past at bay. As they crumble, can Rue accept he is worthy of Monty and Kendrick's love?

Rue's Rapture is book 5 in the Divergent Omegaverse series, where sometimes three times the love is what's needed to make someone believe love always wins no matter what.

Prologue
Lane

Twelve Years Ago

The ringing phone roused Lane from sleep. He rubbed at his bleary eyes, blinking twice before realizing it was the middle of the night by how dark the room was. His hand moved automatically to nudge his husband, who could sleep through a hurricane, only to find cool cotton. His stomach dipped as he recalled that Derick was away on business. All sleepiness fled, and Lane uttered a curse word his husband would have called him on as he rolled to the edge of the bed to reach for the lamp. His hand was not quite as steady as he'd have liked, the persistent ringing clearly signalled nothing good as far as he was concerned.

He blinked in the sudden brightness, reaching for the phone sitting on the bedside cabinet.

"Hello?" The breathy quality of his voice revealed his nerves.

"Lane, I'm so sorry to be ringing you at such an ungodly hour, but I'm desperate," a familiar voice said causing Lane's heart rate to further accelerate. Though now, hearing uncontrolled sobbing in the background, it was for a different reason.

"What is it, Ewan?" he questioned in a hushed tone, figuring whoever was crying needed someone calm to help him.

This wasn't Lane's first rodeo with Ewan and children who had been rejected by their families. Lane's gaze landed on the family photo sitting next to his bed. Laken, one of their adopted sons, came into their family via Craigend House. The smile on his face spread warmth through Lane's chest. It had taken eight months to see that smile, but it was worth all the patience and nurturing Laken had needed to trust Lane, Derick and their other sons.

"Can you come to the house? It's better if I explain in person," Ewan said over the increasing sounds of distress.

Oh gods!

Lane's blood ran cold, and an image of a broken boy flitted through his mind. A shiver ran down his spine, and Lane would have sold his kidney to feel his husband's strong arms around him. He struggled to hold on to the sob trying to choke him, so much that he needed to swallow twice before he had enough control to reply.

"Give me an hour." It would take that long for him to dress and drive the forty miles to where Ewan lived.

"Thank you."

The call ended, and Lane was up in the closet, pulling out random clothes and throwing them on. He barely shoved his feet into the sneakers sitting by the door of the walk-in closet. His mind racing, he messaged Bessy, their housekeeper, who had a small cottage on the grounds of their home, to let her know he had to go out. He knew she was a light sleeper and would come up to the house to be here for the boys. She was a part of their family, and Lane didn't know what he would ever have done without her or how he'd have managed seven sons. Although the boys were of ages that didn't need to be watched, Lane wasn't comfortable leaving in the middle of the night without a word.

He left the lamp on for Silas, their eldest son, which illuminated the passageway as he sent a second message to Derick letting him know something was up.

He shoved the phone into his jeans and raced down the stairs to find his car keys. On his way barely a minute later, Lane conjured up reasons as to why the child in Ewan's care was sobbing so hard.

Ewan was married to Lester, the owner of Craigend House. The man had come into their lives when they approached Derick looking for sponsorship for an outreach programme some four years earlier. Lester had turned his home into a safe place for divergent children cast out by their families. Lester, himself a divergent, was fortunate enough to be able to support himself due to some talents he had with computer software. It was just that he wanted to help more children, and though he used his earnings to help others, he didn't have the resources to do everything he wanted. That's why he had contacted Derick. Lester and Ewan's personal story endeared them immediately to Lane.

Derick was a lot more reserved, and he'd only relaxed after he'd had their head of security do a background check on both men. Satisfied they were genuine, Derick had invested heavily in their divergent outreach programme, which had become so much more to them when it had allowed Laken to come into their lives.

Lane's mind wandered to the lost boy with trust issues after living on the streets for two years. Lester had come across him begging for food, half starved and heavily bruised, and had offered him a bed at Craigend House. They may have created a supportive environment for divergent children, but Laken, ever wary, had not accepted it initially.

Lane had gone out with Lester, having started doing a volunteer shift once a month, and one look at Laken's grubby, gaunt face and huge wary eyes hurt Lane's soft heart. He wanted to help, and what followed was months of gaining Laken's trust. Derick had sighed resignedly at what was coming, Lane recalled, his lips tugging into a smile. His husband had no willpower against Lane. They both knew it, but never talked about it.

The streets were mostly deserted, and Lane had nearly reached his destination when his cell phone rang. He pulled over to the curbside and tugged it out, pressing to answer Derick.

"Hang on, love." Lane placed his phone in the cup holder before continuing.

"What happened?" a sleep-roughened voice questioned at the sound of the car moving.

"Not sure." Lane saw the turning up ahead, slowing. "Ewan called. There was someone crying in the background. He didn't say much other than he needed my help."

"You made me a promise," Derick groaned, in such a way that a smile appeared. "No more, Lane. You hear me?"

Lane said nothing.

"I mean it. It's hard enough to control seven boys and run the business as it is."

"Derick, my love—"

"No, it won't work."

A chuckle escaped at Derick's pleading. "I'm here. I'll call you back once I know more."

"Seriously, Lane—"

"Yes, love," Lane replied, cutting the engine outside the large house that had around twenty divergents at any one time. He ended the call hearing Derick's frustrated sigh.

The door opened, and light flooded the outside area as the security lights came on. There were two minivans sitting on the driveway, along with a Corvette that belonged to Ewan. It was very much his baby.

A man stood at the top of the steps leading into the house. Tall at six foot four, his wiry build made him appear taller. Black shaggy hair hung around startlingly pretty features. Although it was his pale gray eyes that held Lane's attention. Sadness seeped out of him, soaking Lane before he'd taken more than a few steps towards the three-storey home. The wrap-around porches on both the first and second stories were littered with bicycles, bats, balls, baseball gloves and other toys.

Lights illuminated only the bottom windows, and Lane could see Lester in the main room, which they usually used as a group room. Lane mounted the stairs. He couldn't see who Lester was talking to. His lips were moving, and he wore a look that sent a spike of fear through Lane.

"Thank you for coming." Ewan looked drawn and tired, older somehow, when Lane returned his attention to him.

"What happened?" Lane preferred the direct approach.

Ewan stepped out and closed the door behind him. His gaze went to where Lane had seen Lester. A deep furrow appeared as he ran a hand through his messy hair. "We got a call from a friend asking us to take a child"—his gaze moved to Lane—"*to hide him.*"

Lane tasted bile at the back of his throat. Swallowing, he wet his lips. "Hide him?"

Ewan nodded so slowly he appeared to be in slow motion. "His parents were murdered... in front of him."

Lane's knees buckled at such an atrocity, and he became forced to lock them out to keep standing, fearing this wasn't the worst of it by Ewan's grim expression.

He was right.

Ewan treaded quietly over the porch as if he was unable to stay still for a second longer, showing an awareness of those in the house despite the lost look he wore as he continued.

"They were divergent, Rue's parents, and he isn't. As part of a crash—"

"A crash? God, I didn't think any existed anymore?" Archaic sprang to mind, and that added to the worry burdening Lane's thoughts because that meant ultra-crazy fanatics. The belief about divergents—those who couldn't shift into their animal spirit—and those who could shift, became warped if both parents were divergent and conceived a shifter child. Then the hocus-pocus nonsense got spouted about them therefore being a stronger and superior species. Utter crap as far as Lane was concerned because there was no evidence to support any such theory except in the mind of those who hated divergents.

"Unfortunately, they do! And this one is real old school. It seems they wanted Rue but not his parents. They allowed them all into the crash, acting like they accepted the mall," he said, his voice filled with pain.

So much pain that Lane rested back against the porch to keep himself upright as Ewan stared unseeingly into the night.

"From what I can gather from Rue, though he's still in shock and won't let anyone get too close to... to clean him up, they accepted the whole family six months ago. Not sure where they moved from, but they landed in Martha, Texas, after having issues relating to having a son who could shift when they could not." Ewan's hands repeatedly clenched and unclenched at his sides as he returned his attention to Lane.

"Fuckers drew them in with fake platitudes and lulled them into a false sense of security." He shuddered, his eyes glistening in the porch lights. "Rue got out of the house somehow and found his way to one of the safe homes we have scattered about. He hasn't said how he knew about them, and right now, that's not what's important."

It was a familiar story, one Lane had heard more than once, of children running to safety houses. Except the children were divergent, not shifters.

"How did his parents end up in this crash?" Lane asked with a growing sense of trepidation for Rue's family and their misguided beliefs.

At the brusque head shake, Ewan glanced into the house, his expression revealing the devastation he clearly felt. "Rue hasn't said, but clearly it was a ploy to get their hands on Rue. They have very few young, strong males and..."

"They saw his potential to..." Lane couldn't bring himself to say it. Someone like Rue would be considered a prize in this type of situation. It was the thing nightmares were made of. If they'd managed to contain—imprison—Rue, his life would have been all about crash life and not his own.

"Of course they did. I don't think they counted on him being concerned about what they had done. The boy is devastated, and they wouldn't understand that when they don't see any value to his parents at all," Ewan whispered, eyes blinking rapidly as the tears sheened his eyes.

Whatever they needed, Lane would do it, and he'd deal with his husband. "What do you need from me?"

The tension in Ewan's jaw released as he stepped to Lane, relief evident in his eyes. "Come meet him before I say anymore."

Lane's chuckle was wry. "I know your ploy."

Ewan gave him a sideways glance, a hint of a smile forming as they walked towards the front door. "Whatever works, right?"

"Then you can deal with Derick."

Ewan rolled his eyes. "You have that man wrapped around your finger, heck, your whole body. You won't need me."

Conscious of the time and the children sleeping, Lane didn't voice a protest but shook his head, casting his gaze at Ewan and raising one brow. Ewan shrugged, and Lane witnessed the grim expression return as he opened the door leading into where Lane had seen Lester.

In the room, Lane's sole focus was the teenager sitting on what looked like bath towels. Lane gasped in shock and shuddered at the brown stained clothes. The stains had dried, looking stiff, and flaking blood covered the boy's face, hands and bare feet. It looked like he'd been bathed in blood from head to toe. Nothing was untouched that Lane could see. His imagination ran wild with awful visions of how so much blood could cover a person.

How close had he been to his parents to get this much blood on him?

Pain in his chest alerted him to the fact he hadn't taken a breath when black-rimmed, gray eyes met his and held him captive. Flakes of dried blood clung to long eyelashes, and the boy's gaze was filled with terror. If it could live and breathe, then it lived in this boy, and Lane knew he would move heaven and earth to take it away. Derick often said his capacity to love and love quickly was his greatest gift and biggest curse because once Lane felt love for someone, he would do anything for them no matter the cost to himself. It was why they had four adopted boys besides the three Lane had given birth to.

"Who are you?" Rue's voice was rough and raw, signalling the boy's need for Lane's strength in a way he couldn't ignore.

"Lane." He took a step closer, praying his legs would hold him up, continuing to hold the boy's terrified gaze, and keeping his own expression open. He crouched down in front of Rue, giving him his entire focus.

"I'm Lane Starling, and I help Ewan and Lester from time to time. They rang me asking if I could help you, Rue." Lane knew honesty was the only way forward and was grateful his voice hadn't cracked under the immense strain that what he had to offer wouldn't be enough to save this boy. Because saving was what he needed when Lane caught the dejection and vulnerability as he worked not to inhale the now overpowering scent of death.

The question was back. How close had he been to the destruction of his family?

Two large hands, so big that Lane wasn't sure how he missed them initially, balled together, causing flakes of red to flutter in the air before landing on the rug.

"Why would you help me?" His nose wrinkled, making it look like he was wearing face paint when the blood creased into the grooves. "You don't know me... don't know what I did," he finished, tears forming in his pain-filled eyes before they leaked out, creating a macabre picture as they ran down his cheeks.

Going with his gut, Lane came closer and placed a hand on top of Rue's, feeling the iciness of his bloodied skin. "I might not know, and it's up to you if you want to share that with me, but it won't make a difference to me and my family if you chose to come and live with us."

"You can't say that," Rue replied, the hands beneath Lane's trembling. "Not really."

Lane searched his gaze. "You don't know me, but if you come and stay with us, I'll show you, you're wrong. Just give me a chance," he pleaded, sending a mental apology to Derick. He would move heaven and earth to protect this boy. He was part of Lane's family now, whether the boy realized it or not.

Chapter One

Rue

Rue had a moment to acknowledge how fortuitous it was that their PAs weren't with them. A decision Taylin and Booker, his brothers, were fully on board with. Rue certainly didn't want to be distracted by the level of distress Monty, his own PA, had shown after their last visit. Memories of the last time they had come to the Design Detailing & Co factory did nothing to prepare him for this time. The stench, fuck, it was worse with the way they'd ensured they—who were doing fuck knows what to the omegas working for them—weren't aware they had bought the factory and would come today.

Surprise being the best element of attack. And right now, his rhino half pushed hard enough that Rue visibly trembled, resisting the desire to shift and stomp the alphas facing off with Taylin into the ground until they were nothing more than a stain on the concrete.

"I have the emails from Starling Enterprise advising you had no interest in working with us. Your loss," Amatus sneered. He was the alpha who ran the factory—or had, because he was done as far as Starling Enterprises were concerned.

"We had a better offer." He came closer to Taylin and spat, "Divergent."

Booker's growl was ominous, echoing in the cavernous room. Rue had tracked where the security team they had brought with them were in the room as he and Booker prowled closer to Taylin. Divergent 'haters', they must be, and it all made horrible sense to Rue when the damage the omegas suffered was evident in rail-thin bodies, bearing marks of abuse a divergent wouldn't be able to heal.

"You're trespassing on private property, you need to leave now, before..." An armed alpha came up behind Amatus, lifting the gun in their direction.

They moved together to flank Taylin, Booker on one side while Rue stood on the other, close enough to shift to protect Taylin. These fuckers would not be the first to draw blood. Rue's experience in the army meant he was no slouch when it came to defending those he loved. He'd failed once; he'd never do that again.

"The only people trespassing are you and those fuck-tards aiming guns at the omegas." Taylin stepped closer to

Amatus, and they followed. "You're all fucking fired, every damn one of you, *now get out.*"

"Totally professional, bro," Booker muttered, sounding extremely amused. Rue wasn't amused, he was furious when Amatus didn't move, but the omegas did.

"We don't mean you guys." Booker walked towards the work benches and approached the nearest, trembling man, keeping his voice soft. It had taken Rue six months of living with Booker to know the soft side to him wasn't an act. The bear had the biggest heart, he just used a grumpy exterior to hide it, but it was on full show now.

"Listen to me. Every omega here, if you wish to stay and work for a company that will take care of you, then you can. No one is going to be forced into anything." Taylin infused warmth into his voice that had been lacking when he spoke to Amatus. "I know it is hard to believe right now—"

Rue was moving before the scream fully registered, but Oakland beat him to it.

Oakland had a whip-wielding alpha by the throat, effortlessly dangling him a foot above the ground. The sheer power displayed brought with it an unnatural silence.

One side of the alpha's face swelled, and blood dripped from a cut over his eyebrow down the skin where a bruise formed. Oakland held the whip in his other hand, looking ready to attack anyone who moved.

Rue had never seen the man in action, but was impressed, along with aroused. He closed off the uncomfortable reality.

"Brier, get the Medi pack from the Hummer for me," Oakland demanded with total authority. His gaze on the omega and the damage to his face from the whip wielding fucker Oakland held. "We'll take care of you, little one," Oakland murmured, almost sweetly to the dumbfounded-looking omega.

"You will?" the omega squeaked.

"Yes," Oakland answered, his gaze shifting to the alpha, who dangled and kicked out, struggling to escape his hold. "Move again and I'll snap your fucking neck."

Ice coated his voice, and Rue knew Oakland was deadly serious.

Except Amatus wasn't getting that. "I don't know what the hell is going on here. You can't come in here and threaten my men when they are only protecting the omegas."

"Bullshit," Booker rumbled out.

Amatus raised his hand and made a circling motion with his finger.

Whatever that signal meant, it didn't get the desired effect. Moments later, he spun around, looking up, only to come to a stop with a gasp.

Oakland's men were there, their guns aimed at the heads of the alphas, who were minus their weapons. Rue grinned wide and dangerous.

Taylin reached into his suit jacket and pulled out two envelopes. "This terminates your employment effective immediately and that of all the assholes wielding weapons."

"You can't fire us!" Amatus blustered, fear shining in his eyes that made Rue's heart happy.

"You should have read the small print, dickhead. We can, and we have. The company buyout contract," Taylin held up the second envelope, "gives a large percentage of the profits to the omegas who have worked to build up the reputation of this firm."

Taylin waved it high in the air, ignoring the man foaming at the mouth and going a shade of red that clearly wasn't healthy. "We will compensate you all for the distress you've endured while working here. We'll pay your bills for any medical care you require, assisting you in recovery. It's all written here, and I've copies for all of you."

"Noooo," Amatus cried out.

"Yes," Booker replied, grabbing the ass by the throat and lifting him effortlessly. "Just be fucking thankful getting fired is all you're getting today." Booker threw the other man towards the door. He landed in a heap, hard enough to rattle his teeth. "Now get the fuck off our land."

"Oh, and one last thing," Taylin said with such glee, Rue found himself amused. "There's something else in the fine print that you should be aware of. It's a standard clause in all Starling contracts, but it's one of my favorites. It's buried in there, amongst all the boring legal mumbo jumbo, but basically it says that if we discover any kind of foul play perpetrated by the previous owner...that would be you...then all monies involved in the deal are forfeit. So, not only are you not going to get a single cent, what would have been your money is actually going to go towards righting all the pain and suffering you've inflicted here."

There were whimpers, sobs, and giggles coming from everywhere, and Rue blinked furiously because of the ache at the back of his eyes.

Taylin grinned happily at Rue, paying no attention to the protesting alphas. "This is a fucking good day!"

All teeth, Rue smiled at his brother. "No, this is a great day." One he prayed the omegas would cling to when he suspected they'd had very few with the motherfuckers treating them like possessions rather than people.

"Time to clean this place up!" Booker marched to the alpha who'd stood behind Amatus. "You aim that thing at me for a second longer and you'll be wearing my fucking fist." He snatched the gun from the alpha's limp hold. Then, hands shifting into great enormous paws, Booker crushed it like a twig, throwing it back at the alpha, who stood stunned. "Scram," he growled.

Chaos ruled as Oakland's men dealt with protesting alphas.

"Come on, Mr. Unprofessional," Booker called, shaking his head at Taylin, who looked to be filming what was happening. Was that for the PAs? Monty had asked Rue before he'd left if he could let him know the outcome.

"There's work to be done, so stop staring at yourself on camera and start figuring out who needs what." Booker shook his head at Rue, eyes rolling.

Taylin gave him a salute and walked to the nearest omega. "Hi, I'm Taylin Starling. What's your name?"

Rue paused, willing the omega to be brave, like he'd been once when a Starling had offered him a lifeline. The comparison wasn't lost on him. The gift of unconditional support. And for him, love. Moments like this were rare, he got it. It was why it could still take him by surprise at the oddest moments, how fucking lucky he'd gotten when Popi had walked into his life at the worst possible time.

He'd been taught that he could repay a little of the kindness shown to him, and he tried. Thoughts of the past fled at the bone-chilling exchange between Taylin and the omega.

"Will... will we have to stay... in the basement... when you leave?" Big green eyes ate up the tiny face of the omega. "I'm frightened of the dark."

Rue's legs buckled, and it took sheer will to keep him standing as he met Taylin's horror-filled eyes.

"No one needs to stay anywhere they don't want to. Can you show us the basement?" Rue asked gently when Taylin remained quiet.

If Rue thought the smell in the factory was bad, what was in the basement had his stomach heaving. The cavernous space was icy cold despite the warmth outside the building. Iron cot beds with chains attached told a story all of their own. Buckets filled with excrement were scattered about, some nearly overflowing. Threadbare blankets rested on soiled mattresses that were barely thick enough to support a toddler. Rue's nails dug into the palms of his hands to prevent himself from unleashing his burning rage at such a fucking injustice.

His icy stare met Oakland's, who'd come with them. "Stop your men from kicking out the alphas, they need to detain them, and we need the authorities in here...now," he voiced in a flat monotone that he used to hide his despair. His fury.

The suffering of those moving around the filthy space was the only reason he held his rhino in check. Prison was too fucking good for the shit-fuck-bastards who'd inflicted Rue could only imagine what.

Chained.

Held prisoner.

How many had endured this? How long had they been doing this?

An icy shiver ran down his spine as he met the terror-filled gazes of those brave enough to look at him. It took genuine effort to keep his expression soft. "I'm Rue Starling, and we are going to do everything in our power to protect you. I swear it."

That's when he heard Booker roar, and Rue ran.

Alphaholes

> **Taylin:** *Jupiter, what the fuck have you been doing with my mate at a sex club? You better fucking answer me, or I won't be responsible when I get my damn hands on you.*

> **Silas:** *Why are you messaging at one in the morning?*

> **Silas:** *Forget I asked, now I've got my eyes to wake up.*

> **Booker:** *Why would Jup take Hollis to a sex club? I'm confused.*

> **Kodi:** Not the only one, bro… are you guys home?

> **Rue:** It's too sordid a story for now, will catch up tomorrow. But yeah, we got home an hour ago.

Rue found his sense of humor, despite what he'd just typed. He dropped his phone on the bed, hearing it ping as he stripped out of his clothes, desperate for another shower. He couldn't rid himself of the feeling of despair that clung to him worse than the stench from the basement.

Having Taylin as a distraction was far better than his morbid thoughts. Taylin had moved in with Hollis after the 'heat incident' on a business trip. They'd all known Taylin had lusted after Hollis. What seemed to have passed them all by was just how deep Taylin's feelings were for the pygmy loris. Their enforced return to Hazardville gave Taylin his chance with Hollis, and he'd taken it. Rue was happy for Taylin, despite ripping the back out of him. That's what brothers did to each other, he'd learned.

Naked, he picked up his phone when it finally stopped pinging to see what Jupiter had to say for himself. The group chat, aptly named 'alphaholes' by Jupiter, always made Rue chuckle. His chuckle died a few moments later as he read the thread of chat.

His mouth dried and his eyes narrowed.

Taylin: *Jupiter, answer me!*

Jupiter: *Keep your fucking hair on, I was busy…*

Taylin: *I'm not in the fucking mood Jupiter. Why did you take Hollis to a sex club tonight? What the fuck were you thinking? Did someone touch him? He reeks of sex.*

Jupiter: *I did no such thing! They were all there at Sinful. Hollis and the other PAs getting drunk and having fun watching what goes on in there. And I wasn't paying attention to what they were doing, I was preoccupied.*

Silas: *All of them?*

Booker: *What's this shit?*

Laken: *Why is it that I'm figuring preoccupied means having someone bounce on your balls in a public place?*

Jupiter: *Don't knock it till you try it bro.*

Kari: *We aren't all as kinky as you.*

Jupiter: *You sure about that… Daddy…*

Kari: *Fuck you!*

Silas: *We don't care what y'all get up to. More importantly, what were the PAs doing in the club, Jupiter?*

Jupiter: *How the hell would I know? Having a good time, I suspect, away from you boring alphaholes. Now leave me the fuck alone because whatever they were or weren't doing has nothing to do with you lot. Or me!*

Taylin: Hollis is my mate!

Jupiter: Then if you take a damn second to pull your head from your ass, you'll know he's incapable of doing anything because you're mated! Now if you lot have finished the Jupiter bashing part of the night, I'm going to finish living my goddamn life the way I choose.

Booker: Anyone know if we could find out if the others got home safely?

Kari: I'll reach out to Bowie, he'll have been sensible.

Taylin: You couldn't be more wrong. He was as drunk as Hollis when he was here.

Kari: Is that right?

Kodi: What's with you, bro? Something I'm missing here?

Silas: We're all fucking missing something... our damn sanity since we got assigned these PAs!

They'd all gone to a sex club! The rest of the conversation was lost on Rue when he couldn't get past why they—Monty—would go to a sex club like Sinful. Rue had been once and though he had different desires from the traditional, a sex club offered little titillation for him. Although he often wished he could be more like Jupiter, he wasn't uptight or cared about what others thought about his sexual preferences.

Rue read the chat again, like a masochist, imagining the PAs getting fucking frisky with alphas in a sex club. Rue agreed with Silas. They had lost their minds, because what he was contemplating was utter madness. Despite the bone weariness invading his whole body, Rue went and showered in record time, dressed in the first clothes that came to hand, and grabbed his car keys.

Was it wrong to go into the HR database to find his PA's address? Possibly, but fuck it... he needed...

Rue shut off his head, creeping out of the silent house with determination. He never gave himself any time to think about what he was doing as he drove down familiar empty streets. He gripped the steering wheel until it creaked under his white-knuckled grip, hyperventilating as his sneakered foot pressed hard on the gas pedal.

Outside Monty's home, Rue stared up at the windows, seeing that a light was still on. Someone was clearly home.

Was Monty alone?

Fuck, this is stupid. If he's home with someone... what then?

I'll make the fucker leave.

Rue blanched at the violence of the thought, which had no place between him and Monty. They were work colleagues who cuddled once. That did not justify this kind of behavior.

It didn't.

He comforted Monty, which was reasonable after Frey had talked in the restaurant back in Drinkwater after the disastrous factory visit, upsetting Monty.

Then what's this?

Fucked if he could answer it when deep down, he knew that whatever it was, it would never be enough for him, for Monty, when Rue needed something the omega wouldn't want. He'd tried coupledom, and it had failed miserably.

So why wasn't he waiting until Monday to talk to Monty?

Turn the car around and head home, it's what he should do. The emotional upheaval from the discovery at Drinkwater left him... vulnerable, old wounds exposed. A position he avoided at all costs, usually.

Why had he opened the group chat?

Fuck it, I'm here.

Do you want me to point out the obvious? His rhino side remained pissed at him for holding back in Drinkwater. It didn't matter that the omegas remained scared. For his rhino—and if Rue was honest, for him too—those atrocities needed addressing. Except the six of Oakland's men holding Booker back increased the stink of fear. Rue worked extra hard to hold his rhino in check, not wanting to add to the distressed tension flooding the factory.

No, he snapped at his rhino.

Exhaling sharply, he stomped up to the door leading to Monty's apartment and pressed the bell, waiting.

"Hello?" came the wary reply, quickly enough to suggest Monty hadn't been entertaining someone naked.

He rubbed his nose, feeling ridiculous. "Monty, it's Rue."

The door buzzed open, no questions asked. It was one of the many reasons he liked Monty; the man knew not to question, even when it was called for.

Standing in his doorway wearing nothing but sleep pants, Rue kept his gaze from traveling over the slim, honey-colored torso. Rue could smell liquor, but Monty's eyes weren't unfocused as he stepped back to allow Rue to pass.

This is a fucking mistake.

Even as he acknowledged it, he walked inside. The click of the lock engaging got him turning.

The burning anguish that had accompanied him, which he'd refused to admit to, pressed on his chest, forcing him to gulp in air. Only it didn't help. Didn't stop him from floundering in a well so deep he couldn't find his footing.

Go now. This is a mistake, his brain screamed.

Monty, wordlessly and without hesitation, wrapped his arms around Rue's waist and buried his head in his chest. "Was it that bad?"

Shudders wracked his body, and he clung to Monty for reasons he just couldn't explain, not even to himself right then when Popi was the person he should have gone to.

"Worse," he rasped out through a throat so tight the word ripped at his vocal cords.

Fingers slid over his T-shirt making soothing motions. It felt nice, but it just wasn't what he needed. He'd known why he was here, and so did Monty. The attraction had simmered like a pot on a stove, waiting for someone—or something—to turn it up.

When Monty looked up at him, Rue couldn't fight the desire to let go after pretending it wasn't there between them. Denial was futile when his heart hurt. Bled inside him, bringing back memories of a past he worked to out-run.

Just this once, he promised himself, dipping to taste the cherry red lips. *Fool*, whispered through his mind as he sank into the kiss. One he could admit, in this moment of madness, that he'd wanted for a long time.

He lost himself entirely when Monty parted his lips and kissed him with a hunger that matched his own. He prayed he'd be able to find himself after.

Just this once won't change anything.

Chapter Two

Rue

Tired and tense, Rue drilled holes into Silas as Ethan, Darling Ranch's manager, spoke.

"So, you and Silas will share this cabin, Ziggy," Ethan stated, looking at the sheet of paper he held as he stepped off the porch. "Jupiter, you're next door with Wilder."

Just this once won't change anything. Those words rang like a bell tolling his doom with what was about to go down, when he'd been struggling for weeks to keep his distance from Monty after his return from Drinkwater.

"Say fucking what?" Jupiter growled, and Rue bit back a groan, rolling his eyes to the blue sky, knowing this would not go down well. How could it when he knew what Ethan's announcement meant for him to.

Ethan didn't so much as blink at the challenge in Jupiter's gaze when the two faced off. Ethan nodded in a measured way. "You heard, darlin'. You and Wilder are in there." Ethan pointed to the cabin next to the one that he'd allocated to Silas and Ziggy.

"He's not my PA anymore, Ziggy is!" Jupiter spat out.

"No one told me you guys had swapped." Ethan shrugged, seemingly unconcerned by Jupiter's behavior. His baseball cap shielded his eyes, making Rue wonder if Silas had indeed not given Ethan the updated information. Silas, like all of them, had a fucking lot on his plate... but Rue's gut—which he always listened to—said Silas was up to something. "You worked with Wilder, so what's the issue?"

Silas remained inside the cabin, possibly staying out of the bomb blast.

"I've no issue with who I'm sharing with." His gaze shifted to Taylin, who grinned widely.

"You're mated, why would you care?" Rue questioned, unable to stop his eyes skipping to where Monty stood looking unconcerned. *Why wasn't he pissed?*

Monty lounged against the railing of a cabin on the other side of the one Ethan allocated to Jupiter.

"Are we all sharing with our PAs?" Kodi asked with an icy control he wasn't known for.

"Yep," Ethan replied with a wide grin, his gaze sweeping over the group of men. "I emailed y'all with how this works. How many of y'all actually read what I sent?"

Isley was the first to put his hand up, then Lennon, Hollis, Frey, Bowie, and Monty followed.

Monty knew.

He knew we'd be sharing.

Fucking great.

Ziggy looked sheepish, whereas Wilder's head shake came with a sniff and a puppy dog expression.

Ethan chuckled and shook his head, a gleam of unmistakable interest appearing as he stared at Wilder.

Wilder, the cheekiest of the bunch, had dressed to impress in painted-on skinny jeans and a T-shirt that stated he 'likes to ride a cowboy'.

"Never mind, although it looks like this is your first lesson. Read shit you're sent when it pertains to you," chuckled Ethan.

"Silas, get your fucking ass out here," snarled Laken, which caught Rue's attention.

Silas appeared in the doorway looking unconcerned, arms crossed as he leaned against the door frame. "You bellowed, Laken?"

Laken pinned Silas with a hard stare. "Why didn't you say something about this plan?"

"You think I've got time to fucking spoon feed you?" Silas brushed past Ziggy, striding down the steps, his cowboy boots clacking on the wood.

Rue was already over this shit when he'd avoided sharing with Monty after...

Don't think about it!

"I'm not. I don't have time for that shit, and neither does Ethan. This is a working ranch." Silas's stormy gaze traveled over all of them. "You're here to work. To learn what the true meaning of being a team is. Here, everyone pulls their weight because it's the only way to get everything done. Sunup to sundown, there is shit to do, animals to be taken care of. Y'all will learn how to do that, together. That was what was in the emails you failed to read. Sharing a cabin will be the last thing on your minds when your body is aching and all you want is some food, a hot shower, and a bed to sleep on."

"Now if we're done with the hissy fit part of the day, drop off your gear and I'll show you around the ranch." Ethan sent an arched look at Jupiter, before his gaze swept the group of men.

There were grumbles and mumbles, but no one said anything more about their sleeping arrangements as Rue moved his head from side to side to release the tension gathering across his shoulders.

Rue wasn't sure whose ass he wanted to kick for finding himself in this damn predicament, but it was most definitely one of his brothers'. Silas for sure, except the alphahole group chat everyone used to bitch and moan in meant it could be any of them. Himself included.

Why hadn't he kept his goddamn thoughts to himself?

Rue dropped his bag onto the single bed nearest to the door in the rustic cabin and did his best to avoid looking at the silent man sharing with him. It wasn't the basic accommodation that annoyed him. Being in the army, he'd put up with much worse. In fact, the cabin had a bathroom, which was a luxury not afforded to him for five years of slogging through rainforests and deserts.

The issue was the man quickly emptying his things and taking his wash bag into the bathroom. How would he keep the element of professionalism between them when they were fucking sharing breathing space at night?

Monty was too fucking tempting, and after the once he'd given in to his emotions, he'd worked hard to put the professional boundaries that he should never have removed back in place.

By Rue's estimation, as he looked at the gap between the beds, they were barely three feet apart. Monty's aftershave was subtle, sweet almost, with a sexy under-tone that was all Monty and impossible to avoid in such a confined space.

Could he find a way out of this situation?

Dad had been clear; they all needed a reality check, and Rue got it. But this? Why did it have to be this? Rue wasn't sure whether he believed Silas hadn't done this to them. The only upside was that Jupiter—who absolutely had the blame sitting on his doorstep for this crap shoot—had to share with Wilder. Rue hoped the cheeky raccoon tormented Jupiter.

Rue might be the youngest brother, and not aware of Jupiter's backstory, but he wasn't blind to the effect Wilder had on Jupiter. As the youngest, he'd been the butt of many a prank, and Jupiter had been the worst. Rue wouldn't suggest Jupiter was spiteful or after causing hurt, just that he liked to keep shit light by causing mischief.

In the beginning, Rue hadn't...

"Shake a fucking leg, daylight's a wastin'." Ethan's shout brought groans loud enough Rue heard them through the wooden walls.

He masked his frustration and walked out of the cabin, looking at his surroundings and ignoring Monty. Before Silas became the face of Starling Enterprises, the family fashion business, he had split his time between Darling Ranch, which he owned, and his job in the company. A part of Rue understood why Silas became pissed at having this taken away from him. There was something about the vastness of the land, the rocky mountains reaching skyward to a blueness that didn't seem real, that spoke to Rue's restless soul.

"Jupiter, haul ass," Ethan grumbled when everyone appeared except for Jupiter.

"You miss me already? How sweet," Jupiter fired back in a sickly sweet tone that belied the scowl he wore as he stomped down the wooden steps, causing dust to billow around his cowboy boots.

Jupiter encroached on Ethan's space, and Rue compared the two men. Similar heights, but that was where the likeness ended. Jupiter was willowy whereas Ethan was solid, lean muscle. The cowboy was sex on legs, with ruggedly dark good looks. His skin was the color of caramel and a stark contrast to Jupiter's pale, golden skin and flawless complexion. The lines around Ethan's eyes, despite the baseball cap, were sunbaked deep from working outside. There was much about Ethan that Rue found appealing, and the way Jupiter casually placed a hand on the other dude's arm suggested he was laying claim before anyone else.

Rue found his humor returning at just how bad that would turn out for both men if they tangled in the sheets.

Ethan glanced at the hand, chuckled and batted it away like swatting a fly. "This is a working ranch..."

Rue followed behind at the back of the group, listening with half an ear as Ethan explained expectations for their stay, and who was in charge—him.

Silas remained silent, and Rue figured it was because he was too preoccupied with Ziggy by the way he kept casting glances in his direction every three seconds. Rue counted.

Coming home and living with his brothers was like stepping back in time. The angst that came from having eight alphas—seven now that Taylin had moved in with Hol-

lis—under one roof vying for attention was unexpected. They were all grown men, and yet they'd somehow
slipped back into old behaviors. One scroll through the
group chat revealed they might have aged in years, just
not in mental ages. He couldn't discount himself in
that. They all could rile each other up when in close
confines. He supposed he should count himself lucky
that he wasn't sharing a cabin with one of his brothers.

One quick glance at Monty, who was the ever-atten-
tive suck up—alright he wasn't that bad—made Rue
reconsider. Sharing with one of his brothers had to be
better than Monty.

A nudge on his shoulder brought his attention to
Laken's grim expression. His jaw was tight with tension.
"What?" Rue questioned, giving Laken an arched look,
slowing to match his brother's stride.

Laken was probably the brother that Rue spent the
most time with outside of work. The one brother who
had come into the Starling family through the same
route as Rue, though not in the same circumstances.
As far as Rue knew, Laken's family was still out there
somewhere.

"You believe this shit?" Laken hissed through his
teeth, keeping his voice low.

"Yep." Rue swept his arm out toward the paddock of
horses they were passing. "Not like we get horses in
downtown Hazardville, is it?" he replied with sarcasm.

"Ha fucking ha." Laken pinned Rue with eyes sharper than daggers, and Rue's lips twitched in response. "Taylin and Booker are the only two that fucking win in this situation," he grumbled louder this time.

Booker shot them both a smug grin and tugged Frey closer to him. His mate. Taylin was the first to mate, but now Booker had fallen down that rabbit hole.

Except Rue was envious of Booker's situation. It differed from Taylin's situation with Hollis. First, Booker had become a father before he'd mated with Frey. Second, Booker had shown no interest at all in wanting anything more than keeping things casual when he dated. How fucking wrong Rue had been on that score?

The big bear, fuck he was like a bear with three damn dicks.

Back to thinking about three dicks? his animal half scoffed.

And your point is?

"Over there is the bunk house where you'll find food pretty much all day. Breakfast gets served up at five-thirty—"

"A M?" Jupiter interrupted, looking aghast.

"What other time would it be?" Ethan's dark eyes held a wealth of amusement and didn't wait for Jupiter to reply. "Lunch is anytime from eleven to two. After that, there's food in a cooler that you can heat up if something happens to delay you..."

Rue stopped listening when Monty stepped closer to Ethan, his gaze lingering on the guy's wide, mobile mouth. Monty chewed his lower lip between white, even teeth, a habit he had when something interested him.

The conversation was boring as fuck.

Did Monty find Ethan attractive?

The second the question leapt to the front of his thoughts, Rue squashed it.

Working colleagues, that's all you are.

Bullshit.

Chapter Three

Monty

Monty wasn't one to play games. He preferred a straightforward approach to life. His animal side was the one who could be a chaos-causer. Only it wasn't his otter side who'd gotten naked all those months ago and...

He bit his lower lip and toed off his cowboy boots, looking for a distraction. With each passing day they spent on the ranch, in the confines of the tiny cabin, it got harder to ignore the attraction. He'd known, when he'd opened the door to Rue, that he was inviting trouble in. It hadn't stopped him. He could have blamed the cocktails he'd drunk, or the sex club where he had found it entertaining and gotten horny. But Monty didn't lie like that.

He'd found himself attracted to Rue, and initially he had no issue managing it. Drinkwater had changed that when he'd seen Rue's very unanticipated vulnerable side. Then,

Rue had shown up at his apartment wearing a devastated look, and Monty's resolve to keep his distance had crumbled.

But the next morning, Rue had run, quite literally, out of his apartment and refused to talk about the unmistakable intimacy between them. Monty hadn't imagined it, he'd felt the connection, so had his animal side. He refused to believe that Rue was so dense he had missed it. And his avoidance of any personal conversation since suggested he was hiding from what they'd done. Monty had no issue with regrets, if that was what Rue felt, just fucking alpha up and say so.

Dirty and aching in places Monty hadn't thought possible, he wasn't in the mood for whatever this was, which Rue avoided. With the growing sexual tension buzzing intensely in the room, Monty was having to act oblivious.

This is what happens when adults don't talk to each other.

Don't act like the sensible one, Monty argued back with his animal side. *I have tried to talk to Rue, but it's like speaking to a brick wall.*

"You can use the shower first," Rue rasped, not looking in Monty's direction, which was an achievement given how close they were to each other. Monty could feel the warmth radiating from Rue. The guy was a heat factory, a delightful smelling one even after spending hours cleaning out horse shit.

Was it the best thing to be thinking about how good Rue smelled? Absolutely not. Did that stop Monty?

"Fine," Monty replied moodily, peeling off his sweat-drenched shirt to drop it at his boots. Next, his hands went to the belt buckle at his waist, uncaring that he was stripping in front of Rue. It wasn't like he'd not seen him naked before, and Monty wasn't shy.

Not overtly muscly, his lithe frame had gotten a solid workout the last few days. He was feeling a little buffer. His cum gutters were definitely more defined. Despite that, Monty had always thought his best asset was his eyes. The blue was so pale it appeared colorless, except for the dark ring of black that encased the outer rim. Add in the inky black eyelashes, and the final result was a rather sultry look.

"What the fuck are you doing?" Rue hissed.

Monty bit back his initial response of *"showing you what you're missing"* and instead shifted his attention to Rue with a fake smirk. Was that alarm that Monty could see in his gray eyes?

Rue wore a scary snarl on his full lips that, somewhat perversely, gave Monty the stomach flutters.

"What does it look like?" he quipped back instead, finding no amusement in the situation as he continued to shuck off his jeans. "It's not like you haven't seen me naked."

He was more than a little fed up with what wasn't happening between them.

Rue's violent coughing gave Monty no satisfaction.

He stood and, without preamble, shoved down his boxer briefs. *Take that, you damn prude.* He didn't say it. It was childish, and he wasn't sinking to Rue's level, he just wasn't.

"You're playing with fire," Rue snarled, his whole body so still he appeared to be made of rock. Whatever training the man had in the army, he put it to good use. For such a big person, he could be light on his feet and blend with his environment. It was a knack that Monty envied when Rue caught him unaware.

"I don't see how? You don't want more than what went down in my apartment. Or that's the only assumption I can come to when you treat me like a leper and refuse to discuss what happened like *adults, after you ran away.* I can accept that you don't want more. It happens, but why should I feel embarrassed now about my nakedness when you've seen everything I have to offer?" Monty waited a beat to see if Rue would talk to him.

When he met Rue's impenetrable stare, Monty shook his head and stomped past him, realizing the discussion was a waste of breath when it would once more remain one-sided.

Rue was...

Monty threw up his arms inside the bathroom, then kicked the door closed. He blew out a breath and shut his eyes, rubbing at his temples to rid himself of the pounding that came from his frustration. It had been months, and yes, Monty continued to harbor an attraction to Rue. Oh, he'd tried to push past it, and to an extent it had worked. He'd even gone on a few dates and had sex—once. Then he'd recall Rue's large, work-roughened hands dragging down his thighs, stroking his cock, his gaze warm with affection, and Monty was right back to questioning what made Rue put so much distance between them.

Rue's brothers were clearly not worried about being intimate with their PAs, so Monty couldn't see what the issue was.

Stop persecuting yourself! Berating himself as he got in the shower, he came to a decision. He would get laid *tonight* because enough was enough. The last few days proved one thing: Monty should cut loose any attachment he had to Rue and have fun—in town with the cowboys!

Yes, siree. Tonight, he was going *to get laid* and move on with his life.

Determination made him pay extra attention as he washed. He primped and groomed his body until he was happy, using all the hot water. Dried and with a towel around his slim hips, Monty sailed out of the steamy bathroom, not once looking at Rue.

He heard movement behind him as he went through the clothing options he'd brought with him. The door snapping shut behind him added to his conviction. He dressed with purpose, grabbed his wallet and headed out of the cabin to go in search of the other PAs, who were finding out how they were getting to town.

Monty couldn't recall if Cassidy, or Cass as he liked to be called, one of the ranch hands they'd spent time with, was taking some of them in his truck. They'd yet to go into town to Ranch-Down, the bar that Cass had mentioned once or twice when he'd talked about what there was to offer locally.

"There you are," Wilder called from his porch as Monty walked down the steps, squinting in the low-lying sun. "I thought you'd changed your mind 'bout coming."

Monty eyed the cheeky raccoon, who had been very vocal about the fact that Jupiter had moved from their cabin up to the big house after only one night. So instead of explaining why he took an exceptionally long shower with his plans for the evening, he pointed out, "There's two of us having to share a bathroom in my cabin."

Wilder gave a dramatic eye roll. "We aren't all divas like Jupiter, so I can't help it if I get to have a cabin all to myself." The level of miffed Wilder displayed said he was unhappy to be alone, rather than pleased.

Hooking his arm through Wilder's, Monty grinned. "Jupiter was born a drama llama. Whereas you are such a saint."

They both lasted all of two seconds before they fell about laughing because it was so far from the truth. Wilder was such a drama llama, he had Monty, Lennon, Bowie and possibly Isley's share too.

"What are you two laughing at?" asked Bowie, who walked up from his cabin.

Monty continued to giggle as he pointed his thumb at Wilder. "Just how saint-like Wilder is."

Bowie frowned, then his lips twitched. "You're joking, right?"

"I am." Monty hooked his other arm through Bowie's, who had a tendency to take everything too literally, and tugged both men off toward Cassidy's cabin.

"Let's go see if Cass is ready, I'm in the mood to get laid," he announced unashamedly.

His friends never judged him.

Bowie tripped and Wilder groaned, "I think I need to find someone that I can—"

"Noooo! Please don't say whatever is in your head," Bowie begged, eyes wide as he glanced about to see if anyone was listening.

"It wasn't bad..."—Monty and Bowie looked at Wilder—"alright it was." He shrugged, wearing an impish smile. "Can I say in my defence, you guys know what I've had to put up with. So a little payback is called for."

"You've got a cabin on your own," stated Bowie. "How can that be bad?" Bowie was always the logical one.

"What if Kari had moved out of your cabin up to the big house? How would you feel?" Wilder questioned. Monty caught the uncomfortable look on Bowie's face before he looked down.

"Look, there's Cass," said Monty to distract Wilder and give Bowie breathing space from whatever had made him uncomfortable. "I hope he's got enough space in his truck for all of us."

He did, and twenty minutes later, Monty strolled into a busy bar alongside Frey and Isley. First impressions were of how nice the place was. It was cowboy heaven.

Folks looked at them as they entered, but there was nothing that suggested they weren't welcome. The music came from a jukebox, and some people were already dancing on a wooden dance floor that sat in front of a small, empty stage, bar a mike stand.

"Do they book bands to play here?" Monty glanced at Cassidy as he spoke, but the other man was paying more attention to the bar area.

"Let's get a drink," Wilder encouraged, when Cassidy didn't reply.

Frey wiggled his butt. "Great idea. As I've no baby to get up for, I'm gonna cut loose." Frey, much to everyone's amazement, with maybe the exception of Ziggy—who had become confidant to most of the PAs in the group—wasn't the flirt he'd pretended to be. In fact, it turned out Frey had not dated before Booker, like he'd led them all to believe. Since he had adopted his daughter, Emmy, he'd opened up about his past. The group of PAs, at Lane's request, had met and talked about how to help with Emmy, and they'd created a work rota. It was neat because they all got to spend an hour of their day playing with a baby. She was a total sweetheart, and the circumstances of Emmy's birth were so horrific it made Monty and his friends just want to take away the bad stuff.

A shudder ran through Monty as it did every time he thought about the events leading up to Emmy's birth and the poor omegas in Drinkwater.

"Will Booker be happy 'bout that?" Bowie's question gave Monty an escape from where his thoughts had gone wandering without his permission.

"I'm sure he'll be real happy with a flirty Frey," Monty said, tongue in cheek.

Heck, Booker had surprised them all, including Monty, when he'd made a move on Frey. The big bear had acted so indifferent to Frey—in fact, to them all—then, bam, everything changed. Before anyone could recover, Booker and Frey became a couple, and Emmy completed the package. *Frey and Booker were parents and mates.*

There was always hope...

Monty's gaze clashed with the huge guy wearing a check shirt that looked custom made to accommodate his massive chest. Monty's train of thought derailed right off the tracks when the guy's gaze clashed with his. He heard Frey laugh, but what he said didn't register when his attention stayed right where it was.

A flare of desire took his breath away. Gray cropped hair allowed the guy's face to be the focus. Striking tiger eyes held Monty's attention for several seconds before he noticed lush lips surrounded by scruff. The flare turned into a downpour, a heavy one, when the guy inclined his head in welcome. A sexy, enticing grin—even with the distance between them—offered more than just looking.

Monty's earlier determination to find someone to fuck became more of a tangible opportunity when witnessing the heat in the guy's tiger eyes as they swept over him. Heart rate picking up, his body hummed with a level of arousal similar to what Monty experienced for Rue.

As that registered, it left him a little disconcerted when he got a sudden picture of Rue and the barman entwined around him.

Someone stepped up to the bar and blocked his view, breaking the spell and giving him some breathing room to process the random thought.

Frey's nudge to his ribs gave Monty a welcome interruption, only noticing how his friends were all staring at him. "What?" His cheeks burned with embarrassment when Frey shook with laughter, and he recalled they were supposed to be going to the bar for a drink.

"Something or someone interesting behind the bar?" Wilder questioned with quivering lips.

Cassidy gave Monty a worried look, one Monty didn't get. Unless... Cassidy was interested in the guy who'd caught all of Monty's attention.

Crap!

He debated with himself for a second before deciding he didn't want to waste his time if Cassidy already had a thing with the giant behind the bar and had laid claim. He'd never poach, even for a one-night stand.

"Who's that behind the bar?" Monty nodded in the direction of the man mountain, who had moved on to serve another customer, continuing to wear the sexy grin.

"Which one?" Visibly stiffening, Cassidy lost his friendly tone.

"Huh?" Was there more than one big guy behind the bar?

Monty glanced from Cassidy to search behind the bar and felt the heat in his already hot cheeks increase at missing seeing another big guy serving. Not as big, but still unmissable if one was paying attention!

"The one with buzzed gray hair," Monty explained, to remove any confusion, when he glanced back at Cassidy.

He witnessed Cassidy visibly relax, giving Monty the idea that he was indeed interested, just in the other man—*thankfully*. "That's Kendrick. He runs the bar with Trey, the owner."

"Trey, is he your boyfriend?" asked Frey, wearing a coy smile when Cassidy didn't hide the possessiveness.

Cassidy shook his head, but his expression suggested he was fibbing. "No... we're..."

Looking a little lost and understanding his friend, Monty threw himself under the taxicab. Cassidy clearly knew Kendrick. "Is Kendrick single?"

"As far as I know." Cassidy glanced about cautiously. "Though you might wanna steer clear of him 'cause I've heard he's more into threesomes," he continued, keeping his voice low.

"Really?" Wilder wore the same wide-eyed look that Monty was fairly convinced matched his own. His pulse skyrocketed as the earlier unbidden image of him sandwiched between Rue and Kendrick popped right back into his head, seeding itself with no watering on Monty's behalf. Except his cock had taken notice. He dropped his gaze to check he wasn't making a show of himself.

"So I've heard," Cassidy answered, unaware that he'd hooked Monty's interest better than someone deep-sea fishing for fun.

"Let's go get a drink," Wilder hadn't finished speaking before he was marching up to the bar, "and introduce ourselves."

Monty gave chase.

We saw him first, his otter pointed out.
And Monty didn't argue. They had!

Chapter Four

Kendrick

The unmistakable interest coming from the guy, Monty, who'd arrived with Cassidy and then sauntered to the bar, giving him a sultry-eyed once over, had given Kendrick a solid hum of desire he hadn't felt in a while. His interest increased as he spent a few minutes listening to Monty banter with his friends.

When his friends headed towards the dance floor, Monty lingered, his fingers running up the side of the beer glass as he held Kendrick's stare.

"I'm only here a few more days in Bayfield,"—he traced his tongue over his lower lip making it glisten in the overhead lights and drawing Kendrick's attention—"I don't suppose you're interested in getting to know each other *in a more private setting*?"

His sexual preferences fell into dominating a couple rather than just one guy. He got off on watching—directing—before he joined in. He also liked to fuck hard, and though omegas and betas could hold their own, he struggled to let go the same as he would with an alpha. Hence why he preferred couples, so he could fuck the alpha while he was buried balls deep in an omega. A win-win for him.

Yet the arousal he had going on suggested Monty would be enough of a challenge for a night or two while he passed through.

Kendrick inclined his head, a dirty smile appearing to reveal his wild side. "Yep, private works for me. I gotta close up at midnight. That work for you?"

Monty glanced toward his friends. "I'll make it work." When he returned his attention to Kendrick, an ache formed in his balls at the downright playful expression he wore. "'Cause I'm sure you'll make it worth my while."

His desire kicked up another notch, and only the need to head to a customer got Kendrick moving after nodding and growling, "That's a promise."

Good at compartmentalising, he served the customers with ease, only occasionally letting his gaze stray to Monty. He hung with the group he'd arrived with, laughing, drinking and dancing, and occasionally eye-fucking Kendrick.

Moving down the bar, seeing Trey, the owner and his best friend, busy enough not to notice his interest in Monty, was definitely a bonus. Kendrick wanted it to stay that way. His friend would only give him shit as it had been a while since he'd last bothered to get naked with a lone out of towner.

A cowboy tapped the bar and Kendrick strolled over. "What can I getcha, Cranny?" Kendrick's gaze swept the bar and, finding that Zippy wasn't in, the sudden tension across his shoulders released.

Cranny's often repeated verbal battles with Zippy were legendary in these parts. The two worked on Darling Ranch and had a love-hate relationship that spilled out in the bar a time or two. Kendrick was not in the mood for dealing with that tonight.

"Beer, thanks."

Cranny wore a look of misery, and Kendrick debated a second before asking, "What's got you looking like you lost a hundred dollars and found a nickel?"

"Don't ask." Cranny shook his head and left the money on the bar. Taking his drink, he slipped through the crowd towards the pool table.

Kendrick had no time to dwell on it when a guy stepped into the bar, once more giving him a solid kick of arousal to his balls. Linebacker's shoulders narrowed to a trim waist. Powerful thighs flexed under soft denim as the guy strode to the bar with purpose. He ticked every damn requirement Kendrick had for an alpha. Big, strong and nearly as tall as him. The guy was classically handsome, with a lean face, strong jawline, pouty lips and beautiful eyes that scanned the room, assessing everything. Military training, he would bet his life's savings on the guy having been in the forces.

A 'fuck off and leave me alone' expression went with repressed tension, visible in the way he moved. He was all kinds of wound up, and Kendrick groaned under his breath, adjusting himself quickly at how he'd like to bend the guy over the bar and help him release the tension—with Monty pinned beneath them both.

One look into the gray eyes and he let his fantasy slide; no way the guy would be up for the fun and games Kendrick had in mind. He was a realist, tonight would be no different.

Pity.

Although Ranch-Down was one of the busiest bars in Bayfield, and attracted some out of towners, like tonight, it was mostly those who worked on the surrounding ranches that populated the bar. Two guys in one night, both out of towners, what were the chances of them knowing each other? They both looked like they were playing cowboys.

The alpha took a seat, alone, and Kendrick appraised him, a part of him still clinging to the dream of enticing the alpha to play. Only, something about the guy said he didn't look the type to give up his ass. Kendrick knew most alphas preferred to keep their asses to themselves.

Most of the time.

His bear's opinion came out of the blue and caused Kendrick's pulse to skip a beat.

You picking up something I'm not?

Continuing with what he was doing, Kendrick side-eyed the big guy to see what he was missing that his bear side hadn't. Beneath the polished veneer was something untamed. *Dangerous.*

More intrigued than he suspected was healthy for him, Kendrick finished serving, moving towards the alpha unhurriedly. They didn't have any additional staff manning the bar tonight as there was no band, just the jukebox, which meant Kendrick got to serve the guy.

When he first felt those intriguing gray eyes land on him, Kendrick's senses vibrated with an awareness that set off something in the pit of his stomach. He couldn't say exactly what it was, but there were shadows behind those pretty eyes that suggested past trauma. His gut clenched when something told him he was right, and it plucked at Kendrick's senses like a violinist.

He's only gonna be here for a few days—possibly.

He shook off the weirdness and gave the guy an enticing smile, one he'd been told could charm the pants off anyone, and called out, "What's your poison, honey?"

There was a bark of laughter, which sounded bitter, then the guy's attention roamed over to where Monty stood with his friends, and he muttered, "Monty."

As he was looking away, he missed Kendrick's jerk of surprise.

What were the fucking odds?

One quick glance at Trey, who was busy at the other end of the bar, assured Kendrick his friend wouldn't notice what he was up to. Kendrick felt this was too good of an opportunity to miss. Fuck, the pair would look glorious together, their contrasting sizes...

A worm of guilt snuck in at the promise he'd have to break to get what he wanted. Trey had no issue with his finding someone, or a couple, to take home. He would have an issue with Kendrick picking up two single guys in the bar when there could be fallout if things went pear-shaped. It had happened once, and it hadn't ended well when the men weren't compatible and started a fight in the bar over who would take Kendrick home.

Trey had made him swear he'd not do that again. Except this was too good an opportunity to miss... wasn't it?

Hadn't Cassidy mentioned something about there being a bunch of PAs from Starling Enterprises up at the ranch? Maybe there were some other folk with the PAs? It wasn't beyond the realm of possibility, when they offered cowboy experiences to city folks.

Kendrick leaned on the bar, letting the seconds tick by. As they passed, his belief that the guy sitting at the bar was most definitely interested in Monty, despite the sour look he now sported, continued to grow. Had there been something between the pair?

His intuition played to them having had sex... but whether it was more than that, he wasn't sure. There was something in the vibe he was picking up from Monty, who chose then to glance toward the bar. The smile that graced his pretty mouth remained, but something about his eyes clashing with the guy said they had unfinished business of the sexual kind. Monty was most definitely not looking at Kendrick when he witnessed the challenge the guy threw down.

Motherfucker.

Kendrick had to take a moment to get his damn libido under control before he could speak.

"Someone caught your attention, honey?" he rasped huskily, adding enough innuendo the guy wouldn't miss his interest when he turned his gaze from Monty and back to him.

He flexed his biceps for effect and witnessed the guy's gaze drop, then hood just a second too late to hide the interest.

Bingo... full house, baby!

Kendrick was nothing if not an optimist in going after what he wanted, despite the odds of success of having this guy and Monty in his bed tonight being pretty slim. As a bear shifter, he was as big in both forms. Bigger than this guy, by just the right amount. Kendrick inhaled deeply, familiarizing his bear with the scent, having done the same earlier with Monty.

He's something...

Yes, he is, Kendrick answered his animal side.

He wasn't quite sure what type of shifter he was, but he suspected big as he eye-fucked him over the bar, continuing to make his interest known when the man appeared to forget how to speak. The guy's skin darkened, and his nostrils flared, clearly picking up on the signals Kendrick wasn't subtle about.

Fuck, he was adorable. "What'll it be, honey?"

When the guy coughed, eyelids dipping to hide his thoughts once more, large hands clasped together on the bar.

"IPA if you have it," he finally murmured in a smooth voice that ran over Kendrick's skin like a piece of silk.

Kendrick's mind ran wild with possibilities of how to get Monty interested in some threesome fun. Could he persuade this guy to join if he knew Monty?

Cool your jets!

The imagery that floated through his mind enticed him. The couple, naked and fucking in his bed, got his system revving harder than a Corvette. He went to grab a bottle of IPA from the cooler. With one quick adjustment to move his now painfully crammed cock, he grabbed a glass, placing both on the bar.

"Here you go, honey." He made sure their fingers brushed together.

He felt a bolt of electricity shoot through him at the hissed curse and the startled, wide-eyed look he got for his effort.

The hand got snatched away, and the urge to demand he put it back caused Kendrick to bite the inside of his cheek.

I don't know his name.

Why is that important?

Trust his fucking bear half. *It is.*

A twenty appeared on the bar next to his hand, one the guy avoided, getting Kendrick to zone back in. He collected it and went to the cash register, taking another moment to adjust the monster dick crammed against his zipper.

Fuck, it was going to be a long night if he couldn't get his dick to take a chill pill.

His name being called by a regular made it impossible to do more than give back the guy's change. Dropping it on the bar when the guy kept his hands balled at the edge, which caused Kendrick no end of amusement. Like that would stop him. He had his scent, and the desire wasn't one-sided. Far fucking from it, so all bets were off.

What Kendrick needed was a minute with Monty to assess whether he was whistling the wrong tune. His frustration grew when the guy who collected the glasses and washed them left him with no reason to leave the bar area, and Monty showed no signs of returning fifteen minutes later.

Grabbing a cloth from his back pocket, Kendrick wiped up the spills on the bar top, an automatic move he'd done a thousand times, as he caught Trey's worried expression. Had he noticed Kendrick's interest in the two men?

"What's with you?" Kendrick's gaze narrowed on Trey when he turned to the cash register, working on keeping any of his nerves out of his voice. "You look like you swallowed a hornet, and it's stuck in your throat. It don't have anything to do with a certain someone who is getting lots of attention, does it?" Kendrick quickly glanced to where Cassidy was and his lips quirked up. The blond cutie—Frey?—in the group had gotten very flirty and handsy with Cassidy.

"I don't know what you're talkin' 'bout," Trey muttered crossly.

"Liar," Kendrick fired back. "That color green ain't never suited you."

Trey nodded to where Cassidy stood at the side of the dance floor. "Who are they?"

"How would I know?" Kendrick's powerful shoulders shrugged, doing his best not to reveal his amusement or that he was aware who the men were. Before he could say more, he got distracted when *his* hottie signaled for another beer.

"You're the gossip," Trey called, loud enough to be heard over the music.

"Might be so,"—Kendrick grabbed another IPA and opened it before the guy could ask, offering a filthy smile that hinted to all the naughty things he wanted to do to the dude—"but where would be the fun in telling you when I can watch you sweat over Cassidy?"

Kendrick caught Trey lifting his middle finger when he took the cash off the guy, giving him a flirty wink, holding his gaze for a second before going to the cash register before continuing, "After Friday, isn't it time you fucking admit there's something real goin' on between you two?"

Trey didn't so much as look at Kendrick, not bothering with a reply. He was used to it. Kendrick continued to move up and down the bar serving customers, except his attention didn't stray far from the guy at the bar who was watching Monty dance. He was worth watching with the hip action he had going, a slow, sensual grind that kept in time to the beat of the music.

Movement caught Kendrick's attention when the hottie slid off his bar stool. Was he leaving?

Kendrick frowned when the hottie stopped next to a stunningly beautiful guy perched on a bar stool at the other end of the bar, near Trey.

He had moved before he could think better of it. Although the other guy was dressed similarly in cowboy clothes, he looked to have stepped out of a top fashion magazine.

Kendrick swallowed back a growl of possessiveness he had no right feeling, catching the name, "Jupiter Starling," aimed at Trey.

Then Kendrick's hottie snapped, "Jup, there you are! Why the hell didn't you wait for me?"

Damnit to hell and back.

Kendrick wasn't blind to his own appeal, but he looked nothing like the stunner with the most enticing smile Kendrick had ever seen. Except Jupiter ignored the angry demand and took Trey's offered hand.

What was his issue? How fucking dare he treat the other guy like that!

Tension thickened the air and Kendrick grew wary for reasons he didn't want to reflect too hard on. Cassidy's appearance at the bar made the tension increase.

Kendrick wasn't sure if he was going to have to crack some heads together when Jupiter replied, "Because, Rue, you were fussing about having a cold shower and I was in need of a *stiff* drink!" Jupiter's strange green eyes were on Cassidy when he emphasized the 'stiff'.

The man was playing with fire, something Kendrick realized Jupiter was aware of. Kendrick couldn't figure out the dynamic when... *Rue* just rolled his eyes at Jupiter's behavior. If they were dating, surely Rue would become pissed at the obvious flirting with Trey—Cassidy?

Kendrick wasn't sure who the fuck Jupiter was interested in.

Kendrick didn't have time to dwell on that when Cassidy made a noise in the back of his throat that sounded decidedly threatening. "If you can let go for a moment," he snapped, his aquamarine eyes swirling with an unusual temper, "I'll have a glass of water. I'm parched."

Jupiter chuckled and dropped Trey's hand, his gaze shifting between them. "It seems you are. Care to join me for a glass of wine?"

Kendrick eyed his friend with some amusement when he could read exactly what was on his mind, even though the 'fuck no' didn't leave his lips as he went to get the drinks.

Rue stomped to his seat, only to scowl at the group of omegas when, not more than a few minutes later, Jupiter and Cassidy joined them on the dance floor.

This would not end well. Kendrick knew it with how much testosterone was floating about—his included. Jupiter was asking for a punch to the throat!

The thought had barely taken root when he heard Trey growl low and mean, causing the hairs on Kendrick's arms to rise. Instinctively, he prepared to stop Trey from ripping Jupiter's head from his body, stepping towards his friend. Only his lips flapped open at seeing Trey vault the bar in a move any world-class gymnast would be proud of.

Kendrick was both impressed and concerned he was going to have to clean up blood before the night was through.

When Trey marched Cassidy off the dance floor and out of the bar, towards the stairs leading to Trey's apartment, he cursed. "Well, fuck me! How am I supposed to manage the bar alone?"

"Do you need a hand?"

Kendrick's attention shifted to Rue, his pulse picking up speed at the unexpected offer.

Why had he offered?

Was this to do with making Jupiter jealous?

Kendrick immediately shut off that line of questioning and nodded before he could think better of it.

"I most definitely wouldn't say no…" and under his breath he muttered, "to you naked, riding my dick while you fuck Monty like you want to."

Rue, who had stood at Kendrick's initial response, froze like a statue, clearly having better hearing than Kendrick expected.

Yeah, like you didn't want him to know what was going on in your head.

Of fucking course he had!

It would have been comical if Rue's head, when it swung in Kendrick's direction, hadn't pinned him in place with naked desire better than a knife-throwing act.

Kendrick groaned under his breath and struggled to use his lungs for their intended purpose with how snug his jeans became, imprisoning his hard shaft.

Seconds passed and the bar noise became more of a distant hum as Kendrick followed his instincts, moving to the end of the bar to show where Rue needed to enter. When he brushed past, his body taught with unmistakable tension, Kendrick whispered in his ear.

"Nice to meetcha, Rue. I'm Kendrick. Interested? 'Cause if you are, I'll see if I can make that fantasy a reality for both of us."

Chapter Five

Rue

Rue really couldn't have said if Kendrick had said anything else of note after whispering in his ear. It could have been double Dutch, Chinese, and Russian combined in an impressive show of languages. He was totally clueless, his usual attention to detail simply vanishing.

Only one thought remained lodged right at the forefront of his mind, like a landmine. One wrong step and his world would disappear in an explosion.

You naked, riding my dick while you fuck Monty like you want to.

Had Kendrick really said that to him? Implied he could play out his kinky fuckery desires beyond his head?

Yes, he did!

There was no escaping his rhino. Ever since they'd arrived in Bayfield, the damn thing wouldn't stop going on about what it wanted.

Monty alone wasn't enough for Rue, though he hated to admit that even to himself. Their one encounter had absolutely proven that they had sexual chemistry, but something was off with the dynamic, and Rue had run. It was cowardice. He knew it, but he had no wish to hurt Monty, and continuing would have led Monty to believe they could have more.

You left him without explaining. Don't you think that hurt him?

He groaned internally, unable to deny he had when he couldn't explain himself.

It wasn't like you were the one who had to do the talking, so stop being so fucking righteous.

Sharing the small cabin left little room to avoid the small otter with puppy-dog eyes begging for answers. He'd made sure to maintain a distance between them, wishing he could undo what had happened.

Lying won't fix it.

Fuck you.

No, let the bear and our little Monty fuck you. That's what you want.

His teeth ground together, knowing he couldn't deny it as much as he wanted to. For most of his adult life, Rue kept his needs hidden after one encounter seven years earlier had given him a reality check about his sexual desires. He'd found himself drunk with two of his alpha army buddies, and things had gotten more than a little out of hand with a game of truth or dare. It irrevocably changed how he saw himself sexually, and nothing worked to suppress his desires once he'd let the lid off the fucking pot and all the steam escaped. He'd tried to put it back on, but nothing worked to make his head switch off when he was alone with one man. Wrong. Wrong. Wrong, is how it felt.

His rhino chuckled, pushing forward images of him sandwiched between two big alphas. *You weren't that drunk, so stop kidding yourself! And there is nothing wrong with wanting more than one man in your bed.*

A shudder ran through his body. Patience. He just needed to have a little patience. It was hard when his head was a fucking mess. Why else had he opened his big mouth to offer to help when it meant getting closer to the bear?

Except, what had he revealed to Kendrick to make him offer?

Okay, he could admit he'd been staring at Monty and let slip his name when Kendrick had asked what his poison was. It was true, Monty was it. He was slowly killing him when the attraction between them—though very real—was just not enough to satisfy Rue. And no fucking way was he going to explain what he liked to the omega, *no.*

Even if it gets you what you want? his animal said slyly.

He couldn't argue with that, except it didn't answer how Kendrick knew he liked...

God, he couldn't even admit it to himself.

He swallowed, doing his best to concentrate on serving customers. It had been a few years since he'd worked at a bar. It was much better than thinking about why he was half-hard at the idea planted in his head. One he'd never contemplate voicing to his PA.

Kendrick is voicing it.

Change your damn tune.

Rue wasn't ashamed of his needs, more embarrassed than anything at admitting aloud he liked to be pinned down and fucked hard by an alpha or an omega—at the same time—or any variation of that. So long as he wasn't the one in charge and there were three of them.

There, he'd admitted it and not gotten struck down by lightning!

"Sorry, mate, I asked for Bourbon," a deep male voice broke through his inner turmoil.

"Shit... sorry." He offered an apologetic smile at seeing the clear liquid in the glass he'd placed on the bar.

His face warmed, but not just because he'd fucked up. The guy's nose twitching and his gaze lowering to the bar top were quite obvious. Thankfully, the bar top also prevented the cowboy from seeing what action he sported in his jeans.

Was he giving the dude the wrong impression?

Christ, get it together!

He strode to the back of the bar, grabbed a bottle of bourbon and a clean glass, adding two fingers of liquor before taking it back. "On the house," he said, not meeting the questioning glance, and swiftly moving to the next customer.

He was doing okay until Kendrick upped the ante, taking every opportunity to remind Rue how close he was.

His breath hitched, and his skin buzzed with tiny aftershocks as possessive fingers brushed over the nape of his neck. It was too much with how his body responded, and it fucked with his mind when any of the PAs, or his brother, could see what was happening.

Rue was a private person, reserved in public. Yet his brain could more than imagine how Kenrick would look and feel naked, with his body pressed against him for all to see, begging for cock. His feelings had him doubting his sanity, and Kendrick's proximity made his head fuzzy with bizarre thoughts.

He was never going to explain this to his brothers—especially Jupiter—when they questioned his reasoning for working behind the bar after a grueling day on the ranch. Also, he'd need to get up at the ass crack of dawn tomorrow for more *bonding*.

Aren't I in enough trouble? he groused to himself.

A gusty exhale followed when he spun around and miscalculated how close Kendrick was. Their chests bumped together, and Rue staggered, getting just how much bigger the bear was than him.

Damnit, am I panting?

The man was a behemoth.

A mountain of muscle—hard muscle.

As if he'd not just knocked Rue sideways with the touch, Kendrick gripped his shoulder to steady him, his full lips tugging into a devil-may-care grin that shot straight to Rue's balls and made them ache.

I'm in so much trouble.

Isn't it marvelous?

Rue's rhino side might think that, but he didn't with how fucking horny he was.

"I can't wait to see you come apart." Back was that dirty fucking smile, now combined with a husky drawl that made Rue wish he was naked, even when he'd agreed to nothing.

Haven't we?

He barely resisted the need to argue. He shouldn't have left it so long between fucks, he thought, unable to do more than give a jerky nod in response.

Sending up a silent thank you when someone shouted, "Is anyone serving?" Rue took that as his cue and all but jumped to get to the guy to have something to do with hands that wanted to... *don't think about.*

"Yep, what can I get you?"

The busyness of the bar and Kendrick appearing to understand he needed a bit of space gave Rue a chance to calm his fucking ass down. Until Monty strolled up to the bar looking good enough to eat. "What's this? You looking for a new career?"

The softness of Monty's voice could still be heard despite the music, loud laughter and voices shouting. He had a way of always making himself heard.

Rue swallowed to wet his mouth, meeting Monty's unusual pale blue eyes, which were a little unfocused. Only the sexy smirk that graced his red lips made the attempt futile when Rue's mouth dried up faster than a desert after a severe drought. Thirst trap, he'd heard Jupiter use the term, and it fucking applied to Monty.

Out of all of them, Monty fitted in more with the cowboys. The clothes gave him a rugged appeal. Dark scruff on his chin, which appeared after a few days of not shaving, gave him a bad boy appearance when combined with the look he was aiming at Rue.

The press of an enormous chest against his back came right as Kendrick's hands landed on the bar, trapping Rue between it and Kendrick. The underlying arousal ramped up from a steady five to a fucking ten.

His startled gaze held Monty's and Rue witnessed the way his eyes hooded the same way they had when they'd had sex.

He isn't turned off...

The thought bedded in as Monty's heated gaze roamed over both men.

He's not repulsed.

He's interested... Christ, he's interested.

Everything around them faded into a haze of lust as Rue worked to determine what—if anything—he should do.

"You still planning on sticking around after closing?" Kendrick's voice rumbled out, vibrating through Rue, and it took a moment to register what he'd said.

Monty nodded without hesitation. "Yeah, I can help clean up, if you like?" His gaze held Rue's. "If there's a reward?" His voice wasn't quite steady as he perched on the seat Rue had vacated, looking all kinds of tempting.

"*Fuck*... yes." Kendrick rolled his hips, branding Rue's ass with the steel pipe he sported in jeans that left little to the imagination. Rue battled to control himself. The desire to beg to be the reward was there, despite the audience they had. It was shocking—scarily so.

He bit his inner cheek hard enough to fill his mouth with the coppery taste of blood. That didn't stop him meeting the next roll with a hip tilt, so it pushed the dick between his ass cheeks. He clenched, hard.

What was he playing at? He wasn't Jupiter, who liked an audience when he played.

I've lost my goddamn mind, is what.

Kendrick's hot breath touched the rim of his ear, as he murmured, "That ass of yours is ours later."

Rue's thoughts whipped away like leaves in a storm, and he felt a keen sense of loss as Kendrick stepped away.

Strolling off down the bar, he left Rue breathless and hurting with how hard he was. He didn't know which way was up.

"When he fucks you, I'm gonna suck your cock till you scream my name."

Rue growled in distress and spun around to avoid anyone seeing him come in his fucking boxers. Sweat coated his top lip as his head dipped between his shoulders and his hands trembled with the need to stroke his dick. *What in damnation was that?*

The power of two!

Heart hammering against his ribs, Rue could only agree with his animal side and let the truth seep in.

I'm in so much fucking trouble.

Chapter Six

Delicious & Vicious

Frey: *Are we missing something here?*

Wilder: *What are you talking about? You're not making any sense, how much have you had to drink?*

Isley: *Not as much as you have!*

Frey: *Rue's working behind the bar with the gigantic bear…*

Ziggy: *You have a gigantic bear of your own… and why are we group messaging when we're all together?*

Frey: *'Cause I don't want Jupiter to know we're talkin' bout his brother, of course!*

Lennon: *Is Monty getting a round of drinks?*

Wilder: *He looks like he's drooling over Kendrick. You heard what he said when we got here. I think he's gonna get his wish. I'm so jealous, that guy can toss me around any day.*

Ziggy: *I think Monty's gonna get a whole lot more than he wished for with the move Kendrick just pulled!*

Frey: *What move? What did I miss? Being short is definitely a disadvantage.*

Isley: *Ask Booker if you can climb on his shoulders. You forget I'm smaller than* *you, and you aren't the only one missing the action.*

Frey: *He lets me climb…*

Hollis: *Please, no! I do not want to know what my future brother-in-law likes in the bedroom! Haven't I said this before? And Monty, remember we have an early start in the morning.*

Frey: *Stop being a party pooper. I'm sure Monty will manage to get… up!*

Chapter Seven

Monty

How he acted normal through the following couple of hours, Monty couldn't say. He was conscious of his phone having buzzed repeatedly, meaning the group chat was blowing up. He'd not chanced taking it out because he really wasn't ready for what he might read. They had all looked suspiciously eager to chat after meeting Kendrick. Monty had gone back and forth on whether he should let on that he had gotten an invitation to Kendrick's place after the bar closed, but in the end he'd caved and told them.

Monty got it, the guy was sex on legs, and he had said he wanted a playmate for the night. He wasn't doing anything except what he'd said. Then Rue got added to the mix, and Monty didn't want to have to explain any of that to his friends.

Hell, no!

He'd kept the one sexual interlude they'd had to himself. Yes, he liked to gossip, same as the rest of them, just not about real personal stuff. Especially when it came to Rue, who was a very private person. He might have hurt Monty's feelings with the cold-shoulder treatment, but that didn't mean he'd spill his guts over it.

Was it wrong to direct any conversation towards Cassidy? He liked the guy, but 'needs must' and all that jazz. They had all seen Cassidy leave with the bar owner—they couldn't stop talking about the move Trey executed!

"Are you sure you're gonna be okay here if we leave?" Ziggy's question came with a searching glance in Rue's direction.

"I'll be fine, I'm not worried 'bout Rue. My extracurricular activity away from work *is none of his business.*" He held Ziggy's gaze, hoping that he didn't notice how fast Monty's pulse was beating at his throat. He had never been great at lying. Evading, he was a pro at.

"I'll leave my cell on, just call if you need me." Ziggy was all heart.

Monty nodded. "Thanks, and don't worry, I'm sure I can handle Kendrick,"—he winked slyly—"if you catch my drift."

Ziggy rolled his eyes, chuckling. "If you think so!"

Monty didn't breathe easy until all his friends had gone and he couldn't see any sign of anyone else staying on the ranch.

Having stopped drinking, Monty chugged a gallon of water to ensure he was less tipsy than he had been. He wanted to remember tonight for a very long time!

As he'd offered to help, he moved about the emptying bar, picking up glasses and wiping tables, filling time as his excitement grew. Monty didn't care about how late it was or getting any sleep. The way he felt, he was sure he could bounce off the walls for hours with the reward Kendrick was offering. Rue naked... or that's what Monty thought he was suggesting with the 'fuck... yes'.

A vivid recollection of Rue's reaction to Monty's bold statement. Yeah, that was going to fuel many nights when he was alone. Because the second Kendrick had crowded in behind Rue, meeting Monty's gaze with a heated one, Cassidy's earlier warning about threesomes wandered through his mind and sat begging for attention. Until that moment, Monty hadn't fully believed his brief fantasy could be a reality.

Did he feel bad about Kendrick being the conduit to getting more of a naked Rue? Whatever this was they were doing, they were consenting adults, Monty reminded himself.

Time ticked by in slow motion and Monty felt his skin burn and crawl, every nerve ending firing at the possibilities of what was to come. The desire was so over-whelming it left Monty momentarily scared of the 'what if's' that would come afterwards, when they had to leave.

Stop it. We talked about this, we're doing it.

The lack of music made the click of the lock ring loudly, bringing the empty bar into full focus. Kendrick turned to face the bar, and his expression held a wild-ness that sent shivers of desire through Monty.

Everything about the large shifter spoke of re-strained power. Would he unleash it on Rue? On him?

Monty shivered once more in anticipation. He didn't look at Rue to see what he was thinking. It was point-less; the man could mask his emotions far too easily, even when aroused.

"My truck's out back." Despite his size, Kendrick moved through the bar with a fluid grace, seemingly uncaring that there were still dirty glasses on the bar top.

Monty wasn't going to argue and hot-footed it be-hind him, watching how his bountiful ass flexed in tight denim. Would he let Monty lick his ass?

Lost in his thoughts, he stumbled at Rue's presence right behind him. A shovel-sized hand took hold of his arm, steadying him. He glanced over his shoulder, the 'thank you' dying in his throat at the taut features and intense desire that burned in reckless gray eyes.

Monty was consumed by the passion and they weren't fucking naked. Monty worried how he'd survive. How would he survive intact?

There was no chance to let the worry sink in and take hold as Rue guided him outside into cool, refreshing air after the warmth inside the bar. Monty gulped greedily, getting his first real, untainted whiff of Kendrick's scent. Where Rue smelled like rich spices, Kendrick's was woody, earthy even, with an undertone of citrus. They conjured a picture of a wooded area, maybe an orchard with orange trees.

Out back, in the darkness, Kendrick set the alarm while Monty's pulse hammered through his veins in expectation. Having never experienced anything like this, he wasn't sure if jumping onto Rue and kissing him like he really wanted to was the done thing.

He hesitated when he recalled how Rue had reacted after sex. Was Rue interested in what Monty offered, or was it Kendrick?

You could smell the scent of his cum when you told him you were gonna suck him off while Kendrick fucked him.

He couldn't deny that. But could that be more what Kendrick had done to Rue prior? Monty wasn't blind to the hip-rolling action happening behind the bar. If anyone else noticed, Monty couldn't have said. His attention had been on the couple in front of him, giving him a show.

Kendrick strode to one of the mean-looking trucks parked up. Black, with big wheels and fancy chrome, it fit the big shifter. Lights flashed as the locks disengaged, and for a brief moment, Monty caught something flicker in Kendrick's expression that looked somewhat like doubt.

His heart sank at the possibility he had changed his mind, crushing Monty's hope of a repeat with Rue.

"Now we're alone, I wanna check we know what's happening here."

"The three of us getting naked and fucking," Monty said hopefully, and with a touch too much enthusiasm by how Kendrick's laughter filled the quiet.

"Yep, I suppose that sums it up. With a few extras thrown in," Kendrick replied, between snorts of laughter.

"Extras?" Rue, to Monty, sounded as if someone was strangling him.

With how dark it was, despite the stars filling the sky above, he couldn't see Rue properly to gauge what was going on inside his head, not that he had any practice at that.

"We can talk here, or head to mine and lay it out where there's no chance of being overheard—or seen."

Monty's answer was to hop into the back of the truck and buckle up.

Rue muttered something that sounded decidedly like, "fuck, am I doing this?" before he climbed in the front passenger seat, giving his answer.

The drive was made in silence, like they were all contemplating what would happen when they got to Kendrick's. That was what Monty was doing. He played it over and over, him pinned between the two men. He also wasn't sure he'd last more than a minute when they touched him. Ten minutes later, his pulse beating so fast with all the positions he hoped he'd get to try, Kendrick parked in front of a large, two-storey home in the typical clapperboard style.

Painted white, with flower boxes on windowsills, Monty's eyes widened when they landed on the picket fence. This was a family home in a neighborhood that was bound to be filled with children. The guy gave off a vibe that said this was the last type of neighborhood he'd live in.

Kendrick got out of the truck and waited until Rue and Monty did the same. In the house, way too big for one person in Monty's opinion, Monty glimpsed large, comfy furniture as Kendrick led them through the house and upstairs.

They passed a closed door before Kendrick opened the next one and stood back, allowing Monty to pass first. The focal point of the room was the humongous bed. Draped with throws of fur and a mountain of pillows, the covers were a dark brown and orange.

"Fuck, that's the biggest bed I've ever seen!" Monty exclaimed in his nervousness.

"Had it specially made. I like to have room to... stretch out."

Monty bet his tiny ass he liked to do a lot more than that. The bed most definitely was made for three.

Rue hadn't taken more than two steps inside the room, whereas Monty roamed around touching the dark wood furniture that matched the bedframe. There was an enormous chair sat at the end of the bed. Its position was at odds with the rest of the furniture in the room, unless...

Kendrick went and sat in it, stretching out his jean-clad legs in front of him.

Monty eyed the man who looked to be eyeing them both with lazy interest, just the light in those hooded eyes spoke of a predator, and they were his prey. Monty's chest rose and fell rapidly, his lower body vibrating with a flood of desire.

The chair had a purpose, and with Kendrick's ability to view the bed in his current position, it didn't take much to figure out what Kendrick might want.

"Do you know what a voyeur is?" A sound came from Rue, but Monty didn't look away from Kendrick as he nodded. "It's my biggest kink. That and directing a couple to do as I bid before I join in. Do either of you have a problem with that?"

"What do you mean by that?" Monty wanted clarity now, before he combusted on the spot with what he imagined. He didn't want to be disappointed, fuck that.

Kendrick glanced at Rue, and Monty's hand pressed hard against the throbbing cock between his legs, chugging in air so fast he could have run six miles without a breather.

At the naked desire swirling in those tiger eyes, Monty's breathing became even more erratic.

"Drop the hand," Kendrick growled, without taking his gaze off Rue.

Monty whined in distress but did as he was told.

"Good boy. Are you verse?"

Monty wasn't sure if that was meant for him or Rue, but he answered. "I am."

"You fucking would be," Rue rasped.

"Are you?" Kendrick persisted, and Monty's lungs seized, waiting for the reply.

If there's a goddess, let it be a yes!

Monty thought he could hear a clock ticking. Maybe it was his pulse buzzing in his ears as he counted off the seconds.

He got to ten before Rue murmured, "Yes."

"Do you want what I'm offering?"

Again, Monty was the eager otter. "Please."

A strangled sound came, but before Monty's gaze had moved to Rue, his lips got claimed in a searing kiss. It burned him alive. Heat poured off him with the same desire he'd experienced from Rue the last time. Yet as familiar as this was, it was different. Frantic even.

Rue tore at his clothes to get to his skin. The urgency far surpassed their last sexual encounter by about a fucking thousand times.

"Off. Take them off," Rue demanded against his mouth, his tongue shoving back into Monty's mouth where it slid and twisted around his tongue before sucking so hard that it sent pulses right through him.

Desire, potent and devastating, settled low in his groin, making Monty's dick and ass leak in tandem, soaking his boxers and probably his jeans. The knowledge that Kendrick was watching somehow added a dimension to the lust. It expanded the feelings into the room and they moved freely, carried by the weight of their desire.

A hand gripped the base of his neck, fingers flexing and digging in enough to make Monty aware it wasn't Rue. In a daze, he watched Kendrick murmur next to Rue's ear, "Who's in charge here?"

If Monty hadn't witnessed with his own eyes, he'd never have believed the submissive dipping of Rue's gaze and the following stain of red that graced his cheekbones as he whispered, "You are."

Biting his inner cheek to keep himself in check, Monty waited not so patiently for what was coming next.

It was as if the devil had come out to play when a wicked smile graced Kendrick's plump lips. "That's right, I am." He kissed the corner of Rue's trembling mouth. "Now, let's see exactly what you're packing in those designer jeans. Strip for me." His gaze flipped to Monty. "You too, honey."

Released, Kendrick moved to sit back down. Monty couldn't look away from the impressive bulge, which surpassed Rue's, housed in denim as his legs stretched out in front of him yet again, thighs parted.

Oh, goddesses, thank you.

Quickly naked, Monty didn't feel self-conscious as both men's gazes hungrily raked over his body.

"I believe Monty needs to present that bubble butt of his, then we can see exactly where your cock will be when I slide inside you, Rue, and fuck you both *hard*. For that to happen, let's use that tongue of yours to get Monty nice and loose, then Monty can return the favor."

Monty liked detailed people, and he absolutely fucking loved how detailed Kendrick got, especially when Rue kneeled behind him after he leaned over the end of the bed. Spreading his legs wide, he presented his ass, as directed by Kendrick.

"Part his cheeks, reveal that pretty hole. Oh, now lookie there. Slick and shiny, ready for your tongue..."

Don't come.

Don't come.

Don't fucking dare come!

Chapter Eight

Kendrick

Kendrick stretched out the kinks in his back as he walked buck-ass naked to tug open the curtains, allowing the rising sun to cast a glow over the two men wrapped around each other in his bed. The covers were snagged around their legs, leaving their upper bodies exposed. The difference between them appealed to Kendrick. Rue's broadness and thick, corded neck were a thing of beauty. Strong, veiny forearms. So different from the slender—no, lean—musculature of Monty. Rue had his face pressed against the gentle curve of Monty's neck, almost like he was seeking his scent.

Entwined as they were, whimsical thoughts of contrasts, dark and light, reflected what was inside of each man. Rue held a dark shadow within. Kendrick couldn't rationalize why some part of him believed this, it just was.

Monty's contrasting light—whether or not Rue realized it—balanced the other man.

Kendrick had witnessed it when Rue let go and submitted to his attraction for Monty. *Beautiful. Intoxicating.*

Kendrick wanted to bask in the glow from both men. Feel its warmth against his skin, let it sink inside...

Whoa there!

What kind of thinking is that?

The damn kind that only brings heartbreak.

The sound of his hands running over his bristly chin was the only noise in the room. Neither stirred, but Kendrick wasn't surprised when it had barely been three hours since they'd crashed after two hours of vigorous sex. There had been very little talking, except for his kinky demands, and he was usually fine with that.

Except... a lingering sense of disquiet at how he wanted to get to know these men was the reason he had gotten out of bed. He could have explained away the early rise as knowing both men needed to get up to return to Darling Ranch, but he wasn't one to lie to himself.

The disquiet came from his allowing Rue and Monty to stay. More to the point, he'd encouraged it. His usual behavior was 'get them out the door the minute the fun was over'.

There had been no one serious in his life for more years that he wanted to consider. He did like his own space and the ability to come and go as he pleased. Yes, the time between being intimate with someone, or getting his freak on with two someone's, could vary a lot with how small Bayfield was.

Also, he knew most of the cowboys that were regulars at the bar and lived in the surrounding ranches. It limited his options when he didn't do messy. It's why he usually preferred out of towners as bed partners. They were easy, and there was little chance of finding it becoming complicated.

Then why hadn't he followed his own rules when the attraction went beyond the normal for him?

It was fucking.

He tried out the lie and felt a punch to his gut.

Unable to get his gaze to shift from the couple, a frown marred his brow. Whatever was going on with the two men, neither—possibly just Rue—acknowledged it wasn't the first time they'd had sex. There was a level of intimacy between them that spoke for them.

Years behind a bar gave him an interest in watching others, not just in the bedroom. No, Kendrick was genuinely interested in people. What made them tick. What drove them to behave the way they did. Was this all it was?

"What time is it?" rasped Rue, his eyes barely slits as he glanced at Kendrick before he looked away, moving to untangle himself from Monty.

Kendrick sensed the withdrawal. The barriers being put back in place that he'd removed last night.

That wasn't working for Kendrick, not one fucking bit. "Time to see how tasty that mouth is when it's full of my come." The deepened, gruff tone caught Rue's attention when he gave Kendrick a startled look, but as the seconds ticked by, he didn't say no.

Monty stirred, and Kendrick suspected it was because of the erection poking at his back. "Is that a firefighter's pole or are you just happy to see me?" Monty murmured sleepily.

"Shall we find out?" Kendrick chuckled, amused at how Monty was already wriggling up to get Rue's arousal someplace better.

"What about work?" Monty replied, though he lifted his leg and stuck a hand between his thighs to bring Rue's cock between them.

"I'm sure work can wait." Kendrick tilted his head to the side and arched his eyebrows. "Except, I think you're forgetting something, Monty."

Rue released a strangled moan, and impish eyes met Kendrick's, delivering a heady buzz with how responsive his body was, already tingling at the feast laid out before him.

"And what's that?" Monty demanded cheekily.

"Who's in charge."

Rue stilled, ever so watchful, all traces of sleep gone as Kendrick stepped to the edge of the bed when Monty answered sassily, "I'm not sure."

Kendrick held back a smile at how he was enjoying the game, especially when Rue's cheeks reddened and his breathing accelerated. "Then let me remind you."

"Get your ugly ass out of bed," Kendrick called from outside Trey's apartment, too pissed to stop hammering on the door because his friend hadn't rocked up to open the bar—*like he should have.*

The low-level hum of arousal added to his frustration when it wouldn't quit.

"Fuck off," came Trey's shout through the door, not sounding at all like he was moving his ass to do what Kendrick wanted.

He seldom used the key Trey had given him, but he didn't care about Cassidy's sensibilities, or Trey's for that matter. Neither had shown the common fucking decency to get up in time to stop anyone hassling him.

Having so easily persuaded Rue and Monty to stay, they'd barely gotten started when he'd received a call from a delivery driver sat outside the bar. He should have ignored it, but hadn't as he seldom got a call that early. He'd discovered that Trey hadn't responded to the pounding on the back door of the bar. To make matters worse, Kendrick didn't miss the sound of disappointment Rue had made before he'd slipped on a mask of indifference, acting like his cock wasn't dripping and so hard he'd battled to get his fly done up.

Monty, on the other hand, had gone with the flow and been the one to ask if they could finish what they'd started later. Wanting to use Kendrick's phone to add his information, Kendrick didn't miss Monty adding both his and Rue's contact details. Kendrick loved his boldness, it matched Rue's reticence. The balance was appealing when it was also challenging, and Kendrick had thrown caution to the wind and agreed.

Outside the bar, where he'd dropped them when Rue had refused the offer of a lift to the ranch, Kendrick had gone about his business with the knowledge Monty decided *they* would come to his after supper tonight. He wasn't sure Monty would easily sway Rue, but no matter what, Kendrick would wait at home because Trey owed him the evening off.

Three days, that's all the time he had before they'd be gone. He was going to fuck them senseless—if they let him—then let them go. It was for the best. Fucking, no ties. It worked for him.

Then why did the thought leave him feeling hollow inside?

He exhaled sharply. Going inside, he could hear Trey moving around his bedroom. Going to the kitchen gave him something to do with his hands when they trembled at his sides. *Three nights, it is all about fucking. Nothing more than that.*

Is there any need to shout that?

I was expressing my fucking opinion... to myself. Was he shouting at himself? His bear seemed to think so.

It was more like you were trying to convince yourself of it, loudly.

Can't you fucking shut up! Kendrick forgot all about his own honesty vow.

Harsh, much.

"What part of fuck off don't you get?" Trey called out from the other room, giving Kendrick the perfect target for his frustration as he rummaged for what he needed to make coffee.

Bare feet stomping to where Kendrick was filling the coffee machine gave him a perverse sense of pleasure.

"You better have brought breakfast."

"It's nearly lunchtime, you ass." Kendrick measured out coffee beans while Trey went to the cupboard where he kept his cereal. He dragged out the box and grabbed a bowl, milk and a spoon.

Bowl filled, he leaned against the counter and ate, watching Kendrick way too closely.

Kendrick didn't need to look at his friend, they'd known each other for two decades. They knew each other's moods, so he wasn't at all surprised when Trey pointed out, "You're pissed."

"I shut the bar down last night when you did a disappearing act. I was hoping to get a fucking lie in only Des rang me 'cause you hadn't shown up to set up for opening."

The sound of chewing ensued as Kendrick felt the weight of Trey's gaze on him as he worked on filling the machine in front of him.

"You had company."

Kendrick didn't deny it. "I did, and thanks to your lazy ass, I had to leave when things were just getting interesting."

Again!

"Sorry."

Kendrick pointed a stirrer at him, looking at him for the first time. His lips parted, the next tirade fleeing when his eyes dropped to the collar of Trey's old sweater.

He was mated... to Cassidy. *Holy fucking chickens!*

Trey had been fucking Cassidy for the best part of two years, and Kendrick had thought Trey was too stuck in his ways to lay claim to the little chick.

He took a step towards Trey, eyes stretching wide, and to his horror he let rip a strangled noise that, fuck him, was all jealousy.

"What the ever loving fuck! Did hell freeze over? Did fancy pants at the bar last night steal your fucking sanity?"

Kendrick rasped, sounding winded as he continued to stare, fighting his own emotions.

"Just stop—"

"Stop what? You let Cassidy claim you!" he exclaimed loudly, the shock at how much he wanted that for himself left him reeling when it came with double the impact after his epic night with Monty and Rue.

One night changes nothing.

Yes, it does. His bear laughed—loudly.

"That's none of your business," Trey snapped back.

Kendrick stomped off towards Trey's bedroom to glance inside. He needed to shake off the weirdness of his own… anxiety, after how he'd woken this morning. This day was too fucking much when it came with a ride on a bucking bronco of his emotions.

Tonight, he was canceling.

"Where is he?" He looked back at Trey, his nose wrinkling at the heavy scent of sex. A wave of concern washed over him when he realized Cassidy wasn't anywhere to be seen. Had Trey claimed him without consent? The dive over the bar Trey had executed hadn't happened because his friend was feeling rational. "Tell me it was consensual?"

"How fucking long have you known me?" Trey fired back angrily. "He fucking bit me first!"

"He did?" Kendrick questioned, not at all convinced. Cassidy had never been pushy, ever. Kendrick went back to the counter, searching Trey's expression for answers. It was better than admitting to his mixed emotions.

"Yes, he did." Trey plonked his spoon into his half full bowl of cereal and placed it on the counter. "Now, if you've finished havin' a go, you can leave."

The coffee machine started to spit and bubble as the scent filled the kitchen. Kendrick went back to the pot, shaking his head. "Nope, I'm not going anywhere until you explain how you went from never wanting a mate—only last week—to being mated."

Trey groaned and took the doctored coffee Kendrick offered him. "What's to say? You know I was interested in Cassidy—"

"Fucking is what you kept saying you were doin'," Kendrick pointed out sharply.

Trey ground his teeth together, and Kendrick just gave him a hard stare. "That might be so. But I ain't fucked anyone else in more than a year."

Kendrick nearly laughed aloud at how his friend thought he was fooling him; it was closer to two years. Kendrick was observant, but didn't argue over that. He sipped the dark brew and eyed Trey over the rim of his mug. "You ain't had sex with anyone since Cassidy"—his eyes narrowed over the mug—"have you?"

Trey sagged against the counter. "No, I tried once, and I just couldn't..."

"Get it up," Kendrick finished, smirking because his friend was being too ridiculous for words.

Trey gave him the finger. "Smug asshole."

"Always. So what you gonna do now?"

"What do you mean?" Trey questioned, his brows pinching together.

Kendrick sighed and rolled his eyes at him over his coffee mug. "The mating bit is easy. But Cassidy lives up at the ranch. You live in town above the bar. He works at the ranch. Early mornings mostly, from what I see. You work here, late nights typically. So how is all that gonna work?" The comparison was there as he laid it out, only Rue and Monty weren't from these parts, meaning Kendrick had no opportunity to figure out if the intensity of the attraction was all there was between them.

If it freaked him out how interested he was—*after only one night*—no one had to know.

I know.

Shut it!

He was too long in the tooth to change now—to move somewhere else when he was happy with his life here.

"We'll figure it out."

Kendrick blinked in confusion at Trey's response. Then it registered, he was answering him, not the unspoken shit having a party for one in his mind that meant canceling was out of the question.

"I'm sure you will, but whatever you've got going, I ain't working this evening 'cause you owe me." If he didn't meet Trey's inquisitive stare, who gave a fuck?

Chapter Nine

Alphaholes

Booker: *If we have to get up this damn early, then so should fucking you, Rue!*

Taylin: *Can't you give it a rest?*

Laken: *Tay, I heard you moaning this morning…*

Jupiter: *Nice comeback, Laken.*

Kodi: Did anyone see where Rue went, cause he ain't in his cabin, and neither is Monty.

Jupiter: They were at Ranch Down last night. In fact, Rue decided to go back to his old job.

Dad: What are you talking about, Jup?

Jupiter: Don't worry, Dad, I'm sure it ain't a permanent change. He did a spin around the back of a bar to help the big bear when the owner vaulted the bar after a little experiment I did.

Booker: What did you do, Jup?

Jupiter: Nothing much.

Laken: Your 'nothing much' is usually a whole heap of something.

Jupiter: I'm offended. I was helping one of the ranch hands out, I'll have you know.

Taylin: It wasn't out of his clothes, was it? I thought you were interested in Ethan.

Silas: Fuck Jup, are you fucking with my staff?

Jupiter: Eye rolling over here. I have no idea why you always go for the worst possible scenario.

Silas: I know you. Now stop fucking around and tell me what damage control I need to do?

Jupiter: None!

Kari: As long as you can keep that kind of interfering—helping—away from your family!

Jupiter: *Now Kari, why would you be worried?*

Dad: *Isn't there work to be done? Rue, when you see this, please call me so I know you're… okay.*

Chapter Ten

Rue

Kendrick had offered to drop them at the ranch, but Rue had refused, feeling it was a more obvious 'walk of shame' after the ease with which he let himself get persuaded to stay last night and this morning! It spelled trouble in so many ways, he couldn't fathom where to unpick this fucking disaster.

His phone buzzed repeatedly as he stood at the curbside waiting for whoever showed up to collect them from outside the bar. Ethan was pissed at them, and Rue got why. He was in denial; he could admit it. Last night—this morning—he'd lost his mind. Allowed lust and sensual paradise to...

What?

"Are we going to talk about this?" Monty asked quietly.

Talk about how spending his time in Kendrick's bed with Monty was a much better idea than team building with his brothers?

We were team building. The snark from his animal was unwelcome when he didn't know how to answer Monty. More talking would bring questions. Because in Kendrick's home, talking had not been on the agenda.

Like you wanted that!

He visibly cringed at the truth when he was damn sure it should have been top of the list before he'd stuck his...

"Are you seriously gonna pretend like I don't exist?"

The snapped-out comment reluctantly brought his gaze to the man seething next to him. Sexily mussed up, hair all over the place, skin flushed, eyes sparking with temper, Rue wanted him so bad he fucking ached.

"How can I pretend you don't exist when... when..."

Fuck, he couldn't say it.

"When what? You had your cock in some interesting places, directed by another man?" Dark brows rose as he tilted his head. "That?" he hissed, visibly upset with how he clenched and unclenched the hands hanging at his sides like he was resisting thumping Rue. "I'm not going back to playing pretend, I'm not." He stamped his booted foot as a truck slid to a halt in front of them.

The hum of an electric window lowering brought Rue's stormy gaze from Monty to Ethan's unamused stare. "Get in."

Monty climbed in the back without saying a word, looking in the opposite direction as Rue climbed in the cab's front. Using the seatbelt as a reason not to look at Ethan, he noticed just how unsteady his hands were.

They took off and a heavy silence fell in the cab. One that Rue was grateful for when his mind was a fucking mess.

Ethan navigated his way through town, and only after they left the outskirts, heading up the hill towards the ranch, did he speak. "Care to explain why you two couldn't get your asses back to the ranch last night?"

"That is none of your business," Rue muttered angrily, in no mood to answer questions or explain his actions. He was certain seven other men at the ranch would be equally interested. He hadn't bothered to open their group chat and discover exactly what he was going to have to face.

It could all wait fifteen more fucking minutes until he'd showered and washed off Monty and Kendrick's scents so he could get his thoughts out of the gutter.

"If you read the damn paperwork I sent y'all, then you'll find it is. You're my responsibility when staying on the ranch."

"We weren't on the fucking ranch," he spat back.

The truck came to a shuddering halt, and Rue glared as the seatbelt dug into his chest. "What the fuck, man," he exclaimed, glancing over his shoulder to check on Monty, who yelped.

"I've had enough of the Starling brothers' attitude, so fucking can it. If you wanna sleep elsewhere, I don't give a flying fuck. But when you don't rock up at the designated time you're supposed to, and I must come collect your asses when I've got a truckload of other shit I gotta be getting on with, you make it my fucking business. Stick to the damn rules of the ranch experience,"—Ethan jabbed a thumb between them—"then you and I won't have a fucking issue. Got it?"

Rue gave a stilted nod and clamped his lips together to keep in the need to release the anger—that really had fuck all to do with Ethan and was more at himself for the situation he'd gotten himself into.

Ethan dropped them by the bunkhouse with a warning, "Get your acts together! Now grab something to eat, it's gonna be a busy day."

Rue was too wound up to consider eating when Monty's eyes glistened with what looked suspiciously like tears as he remained tight-lipped and strode off in the direction of the cabins before Rue could consider how to broach whatever this was between them.

Sex.

He groaned aloud, taking out his cell phone to check what kind of shit his brothers had been talking because of his absence. His eyes skimmed the thread with a sinking feeling when he saw Dad's comment.

Why hadn't he left last night to avoid this shit? The feel of Monty's warm body pressed to his and Kendrick's chest against his back, cuddling him. A sap. He turned into a sap from getting cuddled.

His brothers would have a field day with that. They would never leave him be. They were all up in each other's business; it had always been that way. In the main, Rue had no issue with it, except now he was going to be the target.

"Fucking great!"

Eyes drawn to Dad's comments, Rue blew out a frustrated breath, reading the annoyance between the lines.

A part of him had known his actions would bring trouble, and yet he'd ignored it, for what? Sex? A chance to see if he was right about the dynamic between him and Monty becoming epic with a third?

He deflated faster than he could blink at how real the fucking issue was, when the night had far surpassed any expectation he had. He trudged over the uneven ground. Skirting away from the paddocks and stables, where everyone would be at this time of day, he admitted to himself that he was in trouble.

He'd fucked Monty after he'd sworn never to do that again, and it had blown his mind. The dynamic changed with what Kendrick offered them.

What was wrong with him? Why didn't he see this last night? It was a mistake to start something that was never gonna work in the 'real world'?

Monty now knew... everything about his sexual cravings.

In the cold light of day, without Kendrick's damn presence clouding his decisions, he acknowledged the fucking enormous error in judgement. The offer of having something that had not felt tangible before Kendrick placed all his desires on a silver platter. One that was impossible to resist. Especially when it contained Monty wrapped in a fucking bow of Rue's need.

Why is this so wrong?

He snorted at his animal side. Kendrick was worse than the lure of a muddy wallow Rue could sink into and let the gooey, cool mud slide over his hide in that delicious way that emptied his mind.

It is fucking disastrous how fast I fell in without looking for crocodiles. Those fuckers will chomp away and take me down for a death roll. Don't you get it!

His life was uncomplicated. He needed it to be like that.

Why?

You know why.

The past is gone. Nothing changes what—

Don't say it. The edge of desperation cut at his frayed nerves. He was in no mood to have them played with right now. Anytime, but particularly when it brought back his inability to change what had happened before Lane rescued him. Being vulnerable was not a state Rue thrived in—it wasn't. After all, it was why he'd gone to Monty's that night and regretted it.

It needs to be said when for the first time in months—years—you allowed yourself to drop those damn shields you use. They are exhausting to you and me.

"Oh lookie here, you finally deem to grace us with your presence now all the hard labor is done." Booker's snarling gave him the diversion Rue needed and a target for his anger as he swung to face his brother, who was charging across the dirt path leading to the cabins.

Kari was chasing after him, looking concerned, his attention swinging between the two men. "No fucking way are you two taking potshots at each other."

"You sure 'bout that?" Rue muttered through clenched teeth, shoving his cell into his jeans pocket to free up both hands.

"Yes!" Kari snapped, getting between them, shoving at Rue's chest while looking at Booker. "Booker, leave it be. You had enough time away from work when things between you and Frey were all over the place, so you ain't got no room to criticize." Kari turned to Rue with none of the anger he aimed at Booker, making Rue's cheeks heat with embarrassment for no apparent reason.

Kari's nose twitched. "I'd suggest you go shower and figure out why Monty appears a little *upset*. I saw him minutes ago heading to your cabin."

The groan was all in his head. He cringed at how he was going to need to talk, address the bear in the room—Kendrick.

"Right!" He stomped off in the cabin's direction, not looking at Booker when he wanted a target. Kari wouldn't stop him if he really wanted to get into it with Booker. The two of them had come to loggerheads a few times when Rue had first moved in with Lane and Derick.

Booker had taken the brunt of his angst because, out of all the brothers, Booker was the only one strong enough to keep him in check. They'd muddled through in the beginning and found an accord that worked for them. Now, Rue loved his brothers—all of them. And that meant he'd need to add Booker to the list of apologizing he was going to have to do today.

First, he was going to need to call Dad.

Reaching into his pocket, he pulled out his phone and dialed home, stopping at one of the paddock fences where no one was close enough to hear.

"Are you okay?" Dad asked before Rue could utter a word.

Rue shut his eyes, feeling them ache with the desire to cry at the concern. The love that came unconditionally and had from the beginning.

Did he deserve it?

"Rue?"

His eyes flickered open to glance about. "I'm not sure," he answered truthfully. Dad and Popi were possibly the only two people on the planet he was completely honest with.

"Is this to do with Monty?"

He released a bitter laugh at being so damn fucking obvious. "Sort of." In a moment of weakness, and several whiskeys, he'd confessed about what happened after the awfulness in Drinkwater and his visit to Monty's apartment when he'd gotten home.

"Son."

The one word held a weight that left Rue struggling to hold himself together. How had one night turned him into a basket case?

"Dad… I'm… fuck!" Rue yanked on his hair and kicked at a rock as he looked forward, seeing none of the beautiful scenery. Just Kendrick and Monty in bed together. "It's complicated."

"Can it be uncomplicated?"

His laughter came out twisted and pained. "I don't see how when I can't even explain why I'm feeling… feeling torn up inside from one night with…" he couldn't say it, despite knowing Dad wouldn't judge his choices. No, he was doing that all by himself.

In three days he'd head home—*back to normality*. The thought left him cold at his core.

"It's okay, Rue. We'll figure this out together, like we always have."

The assurance made it worse somehow, when it would make no difference. What he'd experienced last night was like licking the icing off a delicious cake that had many layers left beneath for him to taste, only to have to throw it away because it was too big to handle. The hint at what it could be like to have Monty in his life, what Kendrick could bring to them if they had time to explore what was between them, gave a bridge to a relationship with Monty he'd not been seeking, yet he'd found anyway.

Life was cruel.

His life, his commitment to his family, to business—it's why he'd left the army. Why he had come home when Dad and Popi needed him—when his brothers needed him. They came first, and that meant what was in Bayfield was only fleeting. It had to be.

"Not this time, Dad."

Chapter Eleven

Derick

Derick sat back in his office chair and stared at the room, not seeing it. The anguish in Rue's voice hurt as much as the words themselves as they repeated in his head. *"Not this time, Dad."* They squeezed his chest at how much Rue believed them.

Recalling vividly his own frustration at Lane breaking his promise of not adopting another lost boy, Derick chuckled at how it fled the second he'd met Rue. One look into those haunted eyes and Derick's heart engaged in the same way it had for each of his sons. Rue was big for his age, so a person could have missed the defenselessness, but Derick had not. Offering truthfulness as the foundation for their sons' growing up, some had struggled more with this than others. Rue had taken more than a year before deciding to allow the adoption, the longest of all their adopted sons. Derick suspected Rue's inability to share with them was a part of that.

The youngest of their sons, he hid his vulnerability behind a protective wall built out of what he believed was necessity. The blood he'd been covered in when rescued might have washed off easily. But his guilt at not protecting his family, his younger brother, left an indelible mark on his soul. Rue had never mentioned his brother, not once.

Derick had discovered, after he'd gotten his investigators involved, that the child, no more than five, had been slaughtered with Rue's parents. There were photos taken in the aftermath, but Derick had never shown another soul, including his husband. The brutality of the attack Rue had witnessed firsthand left Derick gutted to his core.

Rue would cringe at Derick defining him as gentle and kind, but despite the trauma he had a capacity to love bigger and bolder than many who hadn't experienced such loss. He used bluster, indifference and aggression to shield himself.

Rue carried guilt with him. They could tell him a thousand times he wasn't to blame for what happened to his family. His size did not mean he could have stopped the other crash members, of which there were ten, from brutally murdering his divergent parents and brother.

They'd gotten Rue a therapist, like they had for all their sons when they'd needed them, but he was the only one who hadn't benefitted from it. He'd closed himself off from the past and held the guilt like a shield over his heart. Nothing they had done changed that, and Derick felt this keenly, much like Lane.

They loved him. Cherished him. Was it enough?

Derick wasn't sure after the call.

Rue was only truly open and honest with him and Lane, yet he held back anything connected to relationships. The one time he'd spoken about someone had been liquor-fueled.

Derick's love for Lane was something he accepted from the moment he'd figured out his feelings. Rue had strong feelings for Monty, and the liquor freed his tongue. There was no other reason for the guilt he felt after sleeping with him. Not that Derick could find... unless.

The rest of the conversation ran through his mind.

Was it more to do with Rue's other desires?

Blowing out a breath at what that could mean, his gaze narrowed on the phone.

He wasn't the matchmaker; his mate was. He hadn't wanted to interfere, except sending them all to the ranch hadn't just been for team building for his sons. Close proximity could work wonders.

Had he miscalculated, given how miserable Rue sounded?

Derick was sure that Rue was holding back something vital about last night for him to be this upset.

"Did Rue call?"

Lane's question made him jerk his gaze to the man who'd somehow come into the room without alerting Derick to his presence. A feat most never achieved, which revealed the level of concern he felt for Rue.

He frowned at his husband's drawn, worried expression and reached to tug Lane onto his lap, inhaling the familiar scent, allowing it to settle him.

Lane rested his head on Derick's shoulder, slinging one arm around his neck. "That bad?"

"Something is up, and he believes it's not fixable."

"Is it to do with Monty?" Lane stroked a hand up his chest, while the other played with the hair at the nape of his neck.

"Love, I told you, no interfering in this. I mentioned what happened because—"

"You needed my wisdom."

Derick kissed the top of Lane's silvery hair and groaned. "Let's go with that." He was defenseless against Lane when he used his wiles to get what he wanted. They both knew it.

Lane moved to meet his gaze. "He's in love with Monty. You can see it, I can see it. I'm sure Monty can see it, too."

Derick pinched his husband's chin, shaking his head. "Rue can't see it, that's the point here." He kissed Lane's pouty lips, resisting deepening it when he could hear Bessie bustling about in the next room. Of late, it was impossible to resist him, and Derick couldn't trust himself not to shock the housekeeper with his antics.

"I think he needs more," he said instead.

Concern clouded Lane's gorgeous gray eyes. "What do you mean?"

Derick hesitated; it wasn't a conversation he'd had with Lane when Rue had been very drunk when he'd confessed about Monty. Only it wasn't the only thing he'd confessed that night. Derick was pretty sure that Rue had no recollection of the latter part of the conversation as he'd continued to down half a bottle of whiskey. Derick, thinking it unwise to speak about it when Rue was sober, had let it be. Again, he questioned whether he'd made a mistake.

"You know something. Give it up!"

Derick swallowed the groan at the glint in his husband's eyes that threatened retribution if he didn't spill. Torn, he hesitated. He released a resigned sigh when Lane's hand moved to the buttons on his shirt.

"Rue's tastes differ from our other sons. He needs more than one mate," said Derick. And if he considered the reason Rue hadn't come home last evening was because he might have found a third to bridge the gap between him and Monty, in Bayfield, he was keeping that quiet when he needed to do some investigating of his own.

Lane, who had two buttons open, paused, blinking slowly. "Well, I never! Would that be an alpha, beta or omega?"

Trust his husband to get straight to the heart of the matter. "That I can't say, which means you need to leave this alone, love," he warned, already seeing it was futile but felt he needed to try for Rue. "I mean it this time."

Chapter Twelve

Monty

Monty had showered quickly, and he'd managed to avoid Rue thus far, because he was more confused than ever by the recent turn of events. Why had he thought that Rue would somehow be different? No one could give an asshole a transplant personality overnight, could they?

No!

Slipping on his boots, he grabbed his Stetson off the bed and ran out the door. He was eager to face up to the music and then move swiftly on. The sun blinded him for a second, and he collided with a solid chest as hands took hold of his arms to steady him. For a brief second, he thought it was Rue, but the smell was all wrong.

"Hold up there, little fella," said Cranny, a large lion shifter on the ranch.

"Sorry," Monty murmured, taking a step back so Cranny could unhand him. He was nice enough and had openly flirted with Monty, but after last night, Monty had no delusions about what he wanted. "Were you looking for me or Rue?"

"Rue." A wide grin stretched over his tanned face. "But I'm happy to find you instead."

"You've found me," Rue snapped behind Cranny, who had blocked Monty's view with his wide shoulders.

He didn't need to see Rue's expression to know he was pissed, his tone said it all. His voice had practically snapped like a whip on the ground.

Cranny's smile disappeared, and a frown appeared before he twisted around to look at Rue. The anger that had not dissipated at the cold shoulder drove Monty down the steps, stalking off in the direction of where he could see men, not once looking at Rue.

He heard a muttered curse, but he didn't know who it was directed at, and he wasn't in the mood to stop and find out. He stomped to the busy paddock, seeing Isley and Hollis helping Ethan feed and groom horses.

"Sorry I'm late," Monty said to the group, recalling he'd not said it to Ethan earlier. Rue's hot and cold routine had completely turned his head to mashed potato.

"Better late than never, suppose," Ethan muttered, stroking a hand down the chocolate mane of a horse called Bounty.

Hollis continued with what he was doing, barely giving him a look, which made Monty wince. Isley took the pressure off when he offered him a brush. "We still have four horses to groom." He indicated with his head in the direction of Blaze, a palomino. "I was going to do him next."

Brush in hand, Monty nodded his thanks. Manual labor was what he needed to clear his head.

Time slipped by and Monty kept his thoughts on the task at hand. The sun beat down on his back as he followed the instructions Ethan gave them. Dust got everywhere, sticking to his exposed skin as the heat built and the flies buzzed incessantly. Yet Monty found a kind of peace in the rhythmic nature of the strokes and how the horse's tail flicked out. He giggled at the horse's nuzzles when the brush occasionally hit just the right spot.

When they finished, Monty found himself feeling relaxed, the dark cloud of the morning having evaporated.

They tidied everything away, then Ethan suggested they find the others and head up to the bunkhouse for food. Monty suddenly realized he was starving.

Ethan headed off in the direction of the big house, leaving him with Hollis and Isley.

"Want to explain where you were this morning?" Hollis locked eyes with Monty, and he could tell he would not be fobbed off when they'd all been in the bar last night.

"I stayed in town."

Isley hid his grin a second too late for Monty to notice.

"You could have messaged me to let me know you were going to be late. This is a *working* week and not a holiday."

The reprimand was deserved. Hollis was a fair boss. "I should have done, and I meant it earlier, I'm sorry."

He was sorry for much more than being late!

Hollis lost the pinched look. "I know, I was worried."

"You knew I was with... Rue."

"That's why I was worried," Hollis confessed, looking far from comfortable to be having this conversation. "He's going to be my brother-in-law—"

"I know,"—Monty held up his hand—"and I didn't plan for things to go down the way they did." It was all he was willing to say when Rue was being evasive once more. And Monty had no clue what would happen later when Kendrick expected them *both* to go to his house tonight.

"*Rue*?" Isley questioned, scratching just under the brim of his hat, tilting it back revealing how wet his hair was.

"Yeah." There was no way he was mentioning Kendrick.

"I thought you were planning to..." Isley blushed beetroot red, eyes dropping to the ground where he kicked at the dirt, "sleep with Kendrick?"

Bollocks! How the heck had he forgotten that?

Rue. Rue was to blame for this!

He resisted looking away, barely. "It's complex."

Complex! Complex was a Rubik's Cube when taken apart and attempts made to put it back together. Monty knew how complex that was. Fuck, that was so inadequate to describe what the heck was going on. Kendrick gave Monty the chance to get close to Rue. To witness how much Rue loved to be pinned down and fucked, while buried balls deep in another man!

Kendrick loved all the kinky shit.

Monty discovered he had a kinky side that he didn't know he possessed. Three in a bed was most definitely something he wanted with Rue—again. Did the sensuality among all three happen because of Kendrick? How did he come to terms with his new reality? Until last night, he'd thought his feelings for Rue were the monogamous type—until Kendrick.

It was a whole heap of tangled problems, that's what it was with no way to unravel it all when Rue wouldn't even talk to him. He eyed Isley and Hollis speculatively.

"No..." Hollis held up his hands in a defensive move, the color draining from his face, "I mean it. I don't want to know what... what you got up to with whoever, right?"

"Hollis, stop being a prude." Isley smiled shyly at Monty. "It's okay to like different things."

Monty giggle-snorted, then burst into full-blown laughter. It was either that or cry. Laughing was better than tears. In the shower, he had shed enough and made a promise—no more.

Isley joined in, and not a second later Hollis giggled.

"What am I to do with you guys?"

"Hollis, you love us all," Isley pointed out, amid the laughter.

"Hey, what's going on here?" Frey said, motioning to them all as he came to a standstill, eyeing each of them with suspicion. "What's the joke?"

"My love life," Monty said without thinking.

"I knew it," Frey grinned so wide he looked manic. "You and Rue not showing up this morning. And Rue not answering in the alphahole group chat could only mean one thing."

"Wait up, alphahole? What is that?" Isley was the first to ask.

"Like our PA group chat. The brothers have one, too. It seems Jupiter named it alphaholes, and it stuck," Frey supplied, his shoulders shaking with laughter. "It suits them."

Monty agreed. It certainly suited Rue; he was an alphahole!

"I think ours is much classier, thanks to Ziggy."

"Do I hear my name?" Ziggy wore a smile that didn't quite reach his eyes as he strolled towards them, his gaze shifting to the paddock with horses in it. After he had fainted the other day, Monty understood why he was cautious when horses freaked him out.

"I was saying that our group chat has a much nicer name than the one the brothers' have."

"The brothers have a group chat?"

Frey nodded at Ziggy. "They do, alphaholes. Booker left his phone open on the side the other morning and I noticed it, so asked what it was."

"Did you snoop?" Hollis looked horrified.

Pink-cheeked Frey bit his bottom lip.

"Oh my God, you did," Ziggy accused.

"It was right there, and I didn't scroll back *too* far—"

"I bet it was all full of complaints about us!" Isley muttered, sounding utterly miffed.

Frey frowned at Isley. "They rag on each other, like brothers do."

Monty suspected Frey was being vague on purpose, but as the conversation was directed away from him, for now, he kept quiet.

"Where is everyone else?" Hollis asked Ziggy.

"Coming with Taylin. I think he mentioned going to find the others."

Monty kept the groan all in his head at who the others were and the sight of Taylin with Bowie, Lennon, Wilder heading their way.

As a group, they headed towards the stables, where Bowie informed them, the brothers were.

The sound of raised voices traveled from inside as they approached the main barn.

"Move sideways, this fucking thing is awkward to carry?" Kodi complained.

"I carried in two on my fucking own, so shut up with the whining," Rue groused. "Why y'all stood around the pile of shit? Am I missing something?"

"Silas is engaged," Laken announced with what sounded like glee to Monty, who tripped over his booted feet just as Jupiter spoke.

"Our brother has joined the insanity club."

"Engaged?" That sounded like Kodi.

They all picked up the pace, Taylin leading the charge with Ziggy right behind him, giving Monty a clue who they might be referring to by the confused looks everyone else was sporting.

"What? They love me the same as everyone does," Jupiter said, making no sense.

"I think Ethan is rubbing off on you," came Silas's response.

There was a pause before laughter spilled out of the doors in front of them.

"So have you told Popi yet?"

To Kodi's question, Silas answered, "No."

"Told Popi what?" Taylin asked with amusement as he came to a halt in the open doorway, just a little breathless.

"That I'm engaged to Ziggy," Silas announced proudly, staring at Ziggy in a way that made Monty wonder how the heck they'd all missed it.

The barn erupted, and Monty was glad of the distraction with how Rue was staring right at him with the same look he'd worn when he'd kissed Monty senseless. It made no fucking sense. What the hell was with the hot and cold routine?

Monty had whiplash.

Why couldn't he just be one thing and stick with it!

Chapter Thirteen

Kendrick

Kendrick ran a critical eye over the living room, ignoring the nervous ball making its presence known in the base of his stomach. He fluffed the cushions once more and switched on a lamp next to the massive sofa. His eyes narrowed before he lit the candles sitting around on ceramic plates in the corners of the room. He noted several needed replacing, as he used them often when he came to read or watch TV. The scent of citrus tickled his nose as he stepped back to view the room once more.

Nodding his approval, he walked through to the kitchen, placing beer glasses on a tray along with several bottles of beer. He'd picked up some of the IPA, but he'd chosen others too when Monty had no actual preference, from what he could recall.

Adding bowls with snacks in them, he took the tray through to the living room and laid it on the large oak coffee table that sat in front of the couch.

Was he trying too hard?

Possibly. He hadn't been this fussy in a long time, and it was disconcerting when he understood it was because he wanted to give a good impression and get to know Rue and Monty—with their clothes on. Doubt crept in to mix it up with the nerves. Then came the second-guessing as he eyed the tray, then the flickering candles. It all screamed romance.

Christ, he was romancing them.

There is nothing wrong with that.

Please don't fucking start. We don't know whether they'll show.

It was that which created the nerves. Kendrick had messaged both men earlier, just to confirm times, and had only received a response from Monty. Did that mean anything? He didn't know Rue well enough to make an assumption.

The sound of an engine cutting out got him moving to the window and poking at the blinds to look out. His lips tugged into a warm smile as Monty got out of the truck, staring up at the house. Kendrick felt anticipation hum inside him at Rue's appearance out of the other side of the vehicle. Except, all that was missing was a big 'back the fuck off' sign on his chest, his stormy expression never so much as flicking in Monty's direction.

This did not bode well, but Kendrick had faced worse situations, so he wasn't overly worried. Rue had shown up, which had to mean something.

Through the doorway, he had the front door open before either man was at the top porch stair. He stepped aside wordlessly, smirking at Monty, who paused as he passed and puckered up for a kiss.

"Cheeky, I like it." Kendrick didn't disappoint and kissed him with an unrestrained passion that hadn't dissipated fully since he'd left them.

Monty clung to him, whimpers sending thrills of torture, the good kind, through him. Rue's presence right there, watching, added to the level of lust building between them.

Kendrick had to remind himself that getting naked straight away wasn't on the cards. Reluctantly releasing the slick-lipped, lust glazed Monty, he turned his attention to Rue.

Rue was visibly vibrating with energy; Kendrick could sense it with how close they were to each other. A pained expression went with the large bulge he sported in his jeans. Yet, Kendrick picked up on the reticence.

"Come inside, I've got beer and snacks." Kendrick witnessed the startled look Rue got before he shuttered his expression.

Did he think they'd all just strip and dive into bed? Kendrick believed that's exactly what Rue thought when his lips thinned in disapproval.

Monty fired a look at Rue, one Kendrick didn't understand. He walked inside, leaving Rue still standing on the porch making no move to enter.

Kendrick gave him a measuring look, concluding Rue might want what Monty had freely asked for. "Do you want a kiss?"

Silence. It was electric as he held Rue's stormy gaze, seeing indecision along with desire. Whatever was going on inside his head, Kendrick had to wonder if the battle was with himself or his animal side.

He took a step towards Rue, assessing the other man and hoping he was picking what he wanted correctly. Slowly, so as not to spook him, Kendrick slid his fingers around the base of Rue's tense neck, stroking softly, waiting for the moment Rue relaxed into the touch. Rue's eyelids fluttered as his body swayed towards him, then Kendrick dipped his head. Rue's breath was sweet as he breathed him in, running his tongue over the lower lip, before nibbling at the corner of his mouth. "Honey, do you want a kiss?"

The moan and head moving a fraction got Kendrick slowly claiming the kiss he desperately wanted. Where he'd unleashed his passion on Monty, he treated Rue's lips to a gentle, sensual assault. Drugging him, holding

Rue captive with his hand, their bodies not touching. The kisses were so different, yet equally potent. They were a drug; they clouded his mind, took him to a place that was beyond reality. He wanted more, because one, two, even three hits would never be enough to satisfy him.

It was that knowledge that got him easing out of the kiss, breathless and shaky.

Rue's eyes were closed, but he looked no less affected than Monty had. Kendrick didn't need a mirror to know he looked stupefied by the kisses when he could still taste both men, wanting them with a need that crawled under his skin.

He took a deep inhale, working to get himself under control. "As my neighbors are nosy, shall we take this inside?"

Rue's eyelids fluttered open, and the dazed look didn't harm Kendrick's ego or the two seconds it took for Rue to register what he had said. Rue glanced over his shoulder, looking at the street.

With his lips pursed, Rue walked past Kendrick, and he resisted sighing at witnessing the tension returning. Kissing to keep Rue out of his head could easily become a full-time job. How much he wanted that shocked Kendrick into a statue, staring at the retreating man.

Double fucks. I'm double-fucked.

He rubbed at the center of his chest and shook off the stupid notion. He didn't know these men well enough to have thoughts like that. It was a fling. A few nights of sex. With that anchored inside him, and the door locked, he followed at a slower pace, putting barriers in place—because he needed them.

In the doorway, he took in the scene. Rue stood by the coffee table, looking anything but comfortable. Monty, however, lounged on the couch holding a glass of beer, nibbling on a corn chip. Despite his seemingly relaxed position, he was as equally wound up as Rue.

"Rue, do you want a beer?" Kendrick walked over, picked up the IPA and offered it to Rue. At his nod, Kendrick opened it and poured it into a glass, considering how best to play it. He could have cut the tension in the air with a blunt knife.

When Rue took the beer, Kendrick poured himself one and went to sit on the couch next to Monty.

Monty's openness was more obvious as he snuggled against Kendrick's arm without waiting for an invitation.

Rue never took his eyes off them, but he revealed nothing of his thoughts. His body, however, did. Tension coiled in muscles that twitched.

"Last night, we didn't talk about expectations—"

"What expectations?" Rue demanded, the glass halfway to his lips, a look of suspicion in the depths of those beautifully expressive eyes. "There are none. I thought this was just fucking."

Monty stiffened against Kendrick but remained silent.

Kendrick slipped an arm over the back of the couch and laid his hand on Monty's shoulder, giving it a gentle squeeze of reassurance.

"As I was saying," Kendrick deepened his voice, adding a bite of authority. "We didn't talk about expectations. Sex comes with them regardless of whether it's just that. You two have had sex before last night." It wasn't a question.

"How do you know that?" Rue blustered, aiming an angry stare at Monty.

Kendrick squeezed his shoulder again when he went to move, just enough pressure to assure Monty he would handle this. "The ease with which you wrapped your body around Monty's while you were sleeping. It reveals a level of intimacy that speaks of a shared past."

A strangled, choking sound came from Rue, whose lips parted, yet he looked at a loss at how to respond with color riding across his cheekbones.

"I bridged a gap between you. Offering something you need, Rue, to allow you to feel able to connect with Monty." He held up one finger and shook his head when he could see Rue was going to deny it. "No lies. They aren't needed here. We are consenting adults who are old enough to admit what we want. *What we need.*"

This wasn't quite the conversation he had considered they'd have, but Kendrick went with it when Monty relaxed against him once more and Rue moved to pace.

"I don't... it isn't..." Rue paused and flung his empty hand up. "What do you want from me?" he growled, teeth snapping.

"For you to be honest," Monty answered when Kendrick waited.

"Honest about what?"

Monty shifted against Kendrick. "Why did you put distance between us after you came to my apartment?"

Kendrick, watching Rue closely, saw a flash of distress before it was gone. "I... you wanted to know about Drinkwater. I... comforted you after."

Monty shot off the couch, his beer sloshing over the rim of the glass—not that he noticed as he slammed it down on the wood. "There was no talking first. You fucked me against the door fully dressed. Is that what you call comforting? I call that unrestrained passion. The seven rounds we went after that—what were those? You couldn't keep your damn hands off me, so I call bullshit when Drinkwater wasn't why you came to my place at fucking one-thirty in the morning."

Kendrick lounged back and sipped his beer, letting it play out.

Rue's glass joined Monty's, and he towered over Monty, posturing aggressively. "Bullshit is thinking it was more than what it was."

"And what was that?" Monty asked with a calmness that didn't fool Kendrick one bit. The man was furious.

"Sex. A release of tension we both needed *at the time*."

Monty's chin poked out. "*At the time*. What the fuck was last night? Tell me that? If it was just sex, then why the hell are you hiding from what we did? Why won't you talk to me like a normal human being, to clear the air? You've acted like I have the plague since that night, which suggests you have an issue!"

The challenge thrown down between them was for Rue to pick up. Kendrick wasn't so sure he was ready to admit his reasons, which Kendrick suspected had a lot to do with how much Rue needed a third in his bed.

"What do you want?" he scowled darkly. "We fucked, we fucked again, that is it. It was nothing more than that."

Didn't Rue hear how unconvincing he was?

"You're lying." Monty unbuttoned his shirt, dragging it off, exposing his chest, the skin glowing like warm honey. He threw it on the floor, his hands going to the fly of his jeans.

"What... what are you doing!"

"What does it look like!" Monty sneered sexily at Rue. "I'm getting naked to ride Kendrick's monster cock. It shouldn't bother you. You aren't interested in more. I am. I've tried to talk about it. Before and today, but you just keep shutting me down. Last night I thought with... what happened between the three of us... things could be different. If you can't be honest, then I'm done."

Jeans shoved down with his underwear, Monty's dick was on display, hard and slick. His body was all smooth lines. Kendrick couldn't breathe as he waited for Rue to make the next move.

The growl was threatening, as was the glint in the darkening eyes staring at Monty, drilling into him. Kendrick prepared to step between them.

"How the fuck do you tell someone that they aren't fucking enough without hurting them? How? Tell me?" he rasped painfully, throwing a deadly look at Kendrick, holding him still. "He gives me something you can't, that I need too. How many folks do you know that would be happy realizing that they *aren't enough*," he snapped angrily, their noses nearly touching.

"Did I look upset last night? Did you even consider that I would be willing to try something unorthodox? To see if we could find a middle ground because *you are worth the effort*?" Monty spoke so quietly, yet the impact of his confession had Rue blanch and pale.

"What..." he licked his lips. "What are you saying?" He sounded strained.

Monty shook his head, pointing a finger at Kendrick and then at Rue. "This. I want to try. *I'm attracted to both of you.* I know it will be difficult because we are here temporarily, but I want to try, however it works out."

Kendrick's heart beat faster at what he hadn't considered, a possibility of more between them, when Rue's expression turned... *hopeful*?

Rue was on the other man without hesitation. The noises both men made, as their lips clashed in a heated kiss, scorched Kendrick. His desire was forceful enough to make him place his own glass down when his hand shook.

He stood, undoing the buttons on his jeans before his cock broke at the speed of blood filling it. Around the coffee table, he placed his hands on the necks of both men feeling them shudder under his touch.

"As it seems we've cleared the air, it's time to rid you both of those remaining clothes," he murmured next to their ears.

Both men turned to stare at him with unbridled lust. Breathing unevenly while working to gain some semblance of control the two men tugged at viciously, he let go. He lowered to his knees and tapped at Monty's trapped leg. "Lift." His voice was unrecognizable, filled with passion.

He removed both of Monty's boots and socks before ridding him of the remaining clothes. Once naked, Kendrick rose, stroking his hands over both men's backsides.

The jean-clad one clenched and pushed into the touch. "Have you ever been tied to a bed before and kissed from head to toe by two men?" He aimed his question at Rue.

A jerky head shake was the reply.

Kendrick's devilish smirk appeared when Monty whimpered. "Monty, shall we show Rue how much fun that can be?"

Monty took hold of Kendrick's hand and Rue's, dragging them to the doorway.

Kendrick met Rue's wide-eyed look, chuckling when Rue went willingly. "I think we have our answer, Monty."

Chapter Fourteen
Rue

Naked, aroused to the point of pain, tied to the bed-posts, and spread-eagle, Rue had very little ability to distance himself from the two men crowding over him. Did he want to move away?

Goddesses, no.

It was a hell made of pleasure. His past experiences were no comparison. Not even the night before could compare. Kendrick was a master of sensual torment. He took what Rue thought wasn't conceivable and made it so.

He shuddered at the next open-mouth kiss to the side of his neck, teeth dragged over the pulse leaping against the skin. A moan tore from him as another hot, wet mouth latched onto the hard bud of his nipple. Monty bit hard enough for a shard of pain to lodge in the base of his spine, curl under his balls and up his throbbing cock.

His untouched cock leaked onto his rippling abdomen, pooling and having no time to cool with what both men were doing to torment him. There was nothing but blissed-out pleasure circulating like the elixir of life through his body, replacing the need for blood. For oxygen. Rue was long past needing them, unsure how long they had tormented him, never wanting them to stop. His body was a mass of tingling flesh from every caress, stroke of fingers, tongues, cocks against him. They had touched him everywhere.

He cried out when a finger pressed on the base of the butt plug vibrating in his ass. A butt plug Kendrick had directed Monty to slip into his ass after using lubed fingers to prepare him. The low-level vibration was maddening, now it made him utter senseless, nonsensical words. "Urgh… wha… noooo… yessss… chri-ist…"

His muscles tensed and clenched at the maddening need to come, for someone to touch his cock, which bucked in time with his heartbeat. The brush of warm air over the head made him shout before a tongue jabbed into the slit. Nothing more than the tip delved in. Once, twice, three times and he howled, cum forcibly leaving his body to spurt like a geyser. Pain gripped him by the balls. Neck arching, his muscles strained, all the while he couldn't breathe, couldn't figure how to when his world became white pleasure. His brain shut off as it flooded through him faster than a dam being blown apart.

Rue groaned, rolling onto his back when his shoulder joint protested from his current position, only to find he couldn't. His eyes flew open, the sleepiness disappearing at registering where he was. His arm was trapped under a warm body—Monty—and there was a solid wall of muscle pressed against his back—Kendrick.

He shut his eyes, breathing in their combined fragrance of sex, and attempted to recall exactly what had happened after he'd... blacked out after coming so hard he wasn't sure his balls would ever forgive him. A pleasant ache remained as a reminder.

A wave of embarrassment heated his cheeks, making him glad of the surrounding darkness. He had no recollection of them untying him, in fact, he had no idea how he ended up cocooned in the middle of Monty and Kendrick.

For reasons he didn't want to consider too hard, he was grateful there'd been no more talking. Talking in general, actually. What Kendrick had purposely started got Rue angry enough to rip off the festering plaster that held onto his feelings. Maybe not all of it, but enough to say why he hadn't allowed Monty to get closer to him.

He ran a hand over his unshaven cheeks, rubbing and releasing a shuddery breath, unsure if they'd really fixed anything when, in two days, they would head back to Hazardville, leaving Kendrick behind.

Was it cowardice to use Kendrick as a shield?

He didn't need to answer when he already felt the tug, low in his gut. He sighed quietly.

The mattress shifted and Rue felt the weight of a heavy arm on his chest before lips pressed to the pulse at the side of his throat.

"It's gonna be alright," Kendrick murmured sleepily, reading Rue better than most. "You'll see, it'll all work out."

"How?" he whispered back, the fact nobody could see him allowed the fear to seep out.

"We can try long distance. Set up a group chat for the three of us. Video calls could work. Something that gives us the opportunity to see where this might lead."

Monty, as if sensing his agitation, rolled to face him, tucking his head closer to his chest, a thigh slipping over Rue's. His lungs tightened, and he kept still, unwilling to have this conversation with Monty when he felt vulnerable and exposed, despite the darkness.

"What happened to you?" Kendrick asked instead, sounding much more alert, even while he kept his voice low. "In your past, that makes it hard to trust your feelings?"

Rue shuddered at how Kendrick had surmised so easily that there was something he hid from.

Monty murmured in his sleep, his lips pressing against his hot skin, a hand clutching him tighter. Yet Rue didn't think it was a conscious move, and that made an ache form at the back of his eyes.

"I..." Can't or won't talk about it? He couldn't decide, when both fit. "It's not the time. But the rest, the long distance stuff, maybe we could try?" he murmured.

"I'll be here when it's the right time." Kendrick increased his hold until Rue became sandwiched so tightly between the two men, he didn't know where he started, and they ended.

It wasn't that which drew a sob unwillingly from Rue; it was the depth of sincerity, something he'd rarely experienced outside of his family.

Because really, how could Kendrick say that?

How?

They didn't know what Rue had done—not done—to save his family. It would change everything if they discovered his secret, of that he was sure. Blood tainted his soul, and nothing and no one could change that.

A loud pinging gave him the excuse to move, to escape.

Alphaholes

Jupiter: Why am I only hearing about the shit that's gone down at Drinkwater since we've been on the ranch secondhand? You gotta stop fucking sugar coating it for me, Silas!

Silas: What are you talking about? The only people who know are Dad, Popi and Oakland and those in Drinkwater.

Booker: What happened in Drinkwater?

Silas: The shit hit the fan epically. I wasn't going to say anything until we got back to Hazardville. Four of the omegas went into heat, and it was a catastrophe. One is okay. The other three are those who have chosen not to go back to the factory and didn't want to talk about their heats. Y'all know we decided not to pressure them or force them to do anything against their will. It backfired. Oakland warned it would, and he was right to worry. One poor bastard trapped himself in the heating vent in the ceiling, terrified someone would touch him. The other two fared little better when they couldn't put the hotel in lockdown to prevent alphas from registering as guests on the floors below.

Taylin: *Dear gods!*

Silas: *Yeah, that and a whole fucking heap of fucks. I spoke to Dad. We are going to bring the omegas up to the ranch. It's going to take a bit of sorting, and Oakland needs to agree, but it is the safest place I could think of for them while they figure out what they want.*

Booker: *Makes sense. But won't one of us need to be here too? It's gonna take a lot of negotiations, isn't it?*

Silas: *I haven't gotten that far yet. As I said, I hadn't mentioned it to anyone as we don't know the full extent of the fallout. If Jupiter has heard, that means it's leaked out, unless Popi or Dad told you? Which if not, then that is another fucking minefield to work through.*

Jupiter: *It doesn't matter who told me.*

Silas: *Yes, it bloody does when we might have someone speaking out of turn to fuck knows who besides you.*

Jupiter: *Oakland told me.*

Laken: *What? Why would you have contact with Oakland? You barely know him.*

Dad: *Leave it, Laken. We will talk about this when y'all are home.*

Rue rubbed at his bleary eyes, reading as Kendrick moved quietly around the coffee-scented kitchen, having gotten up with him. Rue had been surprised at such a move, but he kept it to himself.

Kendrick placed bowls and boxes of cereal on the counter, looking all kinds of charming. "I can fry up some bacon, eggs and mushrooms, if you've time?"

Rue shook his head, offering a smile that he couldn't do justice to when ice had formed in his gut at what he'd read.

"Coffee is fine, I'll grab something in the bunkhouse later," he muttered distractedly, his thoughts on how much of a mess everything was.

He had no idea how bad things were in Drinkwater with the abused omegas, but he suspected it was far worse than even he could fathom. The smells and the images of the factory basement had taken them all by surprise when they'd discovered the fuckers had taken advantage of the omegas. Taken advantage. If it were only that.

Those bastards held them hostage, raped and abused them until they were terrified of their own shadows. He wasn't at all surprised that during their heat, they wanted no one near them.

Unable to shake off the effect it had on him, it was in that moment he'd given in to the attraction for Monty. Until then, he'd had no intention of acting upon it.

He shut off his train of thought, not ready to have more recriminations, when he felt Kendrick's presence at his back. The big man ran his nose along the line of his neck, placing a kiss next to his ear. Although brief, it was no less impactful because of the intimacy that came with it. A silent offer of support, even when Rue hadn't asked or explained what was wrong, that made him struggle to catch his breath. Of all the things they'd done, this he didn't know how to react. Before he was forced to make that decision, Kendrick stepped away, picked up his mug of coffee and took a sip, unaware of how off-kilter Rue was.

Monty's appearance broke the tension building inside him.

"Coffee, I could kiss you." Monty came in smelling like sunshine and looking equally refreshing. Rue had no idea how, at the ungodly hour, when they'd all had very little sleep.

Monty took the offered mug and inhaled the smell before sipping and groaning in approval. "How folks survive without caffeine, I'll never know."

Rue didn't answer, mulling over how to explain the news about the omegas when it would wipe away the sunny smile. Fuck, it would affect all the PAs, not just Monty.

"What?" Monty rubbed at his nose, going slightly cross-eyed, looking utterly adorable. "Have I got something on my nose?"

"No... we're gonna have to head out."

Monty gave the expected grumble of complaint. But Rue was looking at Kendrick, assessing, before going with his gut and the desire. "Last night, you mentioned setting up a group chat... trying something long distance." Rue glanced at Monty and could see surprise but, more than that, excitement. "How would you feel about that, Monty?

"If I get to keep you both, then I'll try anything."

Kendrick slung an arm around Monty's shoulders, looking so damn pleased Rue released a shuddery breath. Fuck, they were doing this. All he could think about was taking advantage of the remaining time they had in Bayfield.

"So, what time do you get off work later?"

Chapter Fifteen

Monty

They were leaving. Where had the time gone?

Monty could only cling to the knowledge it wasn't over—hopefully.

Kendrick won't be in the same place with us.

Honestly, can't you see I don't need the fucking reminder.

He didn't when it was difficult to breathe, to get the air where he needed it to be able to speak as Kendrick walked down the stairs towards the front door wearing just a pair of sleep pants. He radiated sex appeal that left Monty wanting to turn tail and head right back up to the warm bed he'd left minutes before, when Kendrick's alarm had gone off.

Kendrick ran a hand over his cropped hair as he reached the bottom and stood by the door wearing a tired smile. They'd slept an hour but, despite being physically ex-

hausted from ranch work and a little sore after their nocturnal antics, Monty chose not to complain. Why would he
when he was absolutely sure that whatever this was they'd
all been doing, was *changing into something else*?

Would Rue go back to behaving as if there was nothing
between them without Kendrick present? It was a sobering thought. It saddened Monty, hurt him to think it was
a real possibility. Past relationships had taught him that
allowing his emotions to tangle themselves around a person—or persons—never worked unless everyone wanted
more.

The two men stared at each other, tension rolling off
Rue, meaning Monty needed to be careful with his heart.
The bitter laugh was all in his head when he'd handed
that same heart over to Rue months ago, whether or not
the man knew it. Monty suspected that spending more
time with Kendrick this would put him in an even worse
situation because it would be easy to fall for both men.

Would long distance video calls protect his heart? He
doubted that very much, but Monty wanted more, making
him willing to try despite the risks.

Rue shoved his hands into his jean pockets, looking
down a moment later, shoulders drooping. Loving just
one person was hard enough. Monty wanted to kick Rue,
get him to say something, only there was little he could
do about it when Rue wasn't a brilliant conversationalist
about feelings.

After the heated conversation they'd had, which broke the ice, there was little more said beyond agreeing to try calls. It was as if they'd all come to a mutual agreement not to waste time on talking when they had so little of it. Just now, Monty wished they had laid things out about their expectations a little more.

"You've got my number stored in your phones. I've created a group chat on WhatsApp, I'll call y'all when you get back."

Rue jerked his head up, nodding eagerly, and Monty witnessed a flare of desire, the same one he felt at the prospect of more—of the vocal confirmation, once more that they were continuing to have Kendrick in their lives, despite the distance.

"A call, when?"

Hesitancy, Monty detected a ton of it, but he kept quiet. This was between them.

"Whenever suits you both. Unless you've changed your mind." Kendrick's naked shoulders moved in a casual shrug, yet his expression said differently as Monty watched. His jaw bunched and the lines around his eyes deepened as the time ticked by with Rue saying nothing. "It's up to you."

"Yeah... I mean, if you're serious, we could do that. I can do it any evening." Rue, for the first time, looked at Monty. "If you're still interested, we co-ordinate?"

Shit on a stick, the conversation made it hard to get Monty's voice box to produce a sound with his heart rate thundering through him. Rue being the one to initiate this, yeah it was epic. He nodded, trusting that was enough.

"Great, I'll send my work schedule," murmured Kendrick, coming forward to cup Rue's cheek and then reaching for Monty's, encouraging them both closer. The three-way kiss was a little messy, tongues, lips and angles still weird, but Monty didn't care. He moaned at the two tongues vying for entry into his mouth, sweeping over his lips, tasting, sucking, teasing until he was mindless, hanging on to both men, fighting to get closer as they lifted him to them to make the kissing easier.

He was floating in the air between them; it was fucking hot.

When Kendrick eventually let them go, Monty wasn't the only one to moan in complaint. They were all flushed and breathing hard when, wordlessly, Kendrick went and unlocked his front door.

Whatever he'd expected after the last few days, it wasn't this anticlimactic feeling lodged in his chest as he walked out of Kendrick's home, Rue at his side. Unfinished business. It was unfinished business.

"Later," murmured Kendrick, standing at the top of the steps, his gaze unreadable.

In the truck they'd borrowed once more, Monty looked out the window, and Kendrick gave them a salute, then stepped back inside as Rue gunned the engine.

Minutes ticked by, the radio playing softly as they made the return trip to the ranch—for the last time.

Blowing out a breath, Monty sighed heavily, his fingers fiddling with the button on his shirt.

"Do you want to continue... this? Really?"

Monty didn't pretend like he didn't know what Rue was referring to, despite how he never looked in Monty's direction.

"I wanted to continue it after you left my home," he replied honestly, deciding while Rue was willing to talk, that he'd use the opportunity when there might not be another once they returned to the real world. "I'm attracted to you. In fact, I'd go so far as to say that what's between us is mutual, always has been. Now I understand better that you have needs I could never meet alone, I get the distance you placed between us after we had sex. If I wish you'd mentioned it before, then that's something I have to deal with, not you. Now I realise why you didn't."

He twisted in his seat in the cab. With the sky still dark outside, Monty couldn't clearly determine what Rue thought. "What we've been doing these last few days with Kendrick"—he didn't say that he'd do it with a different third, he wasn't sure about that—"I don't want it to stop. Is that clear enough for you?"

"You aren't…"

Monty waited but when Rue didn't look to continue, he prompted, "Aren't I what?"

"Put off by…"

"You and another alpha getting it on with or without me being involved?" Monty went with, doing his best to contain his amusement.

"Yes," Rue replied, not sounding particularly happy.

Monty considered his answer, knowing it was important. "I'm gonna say it again, just to be clear. Rue, I'd have taken you any way I could after you paid me a visit. *Any way, if you had given me the chance. If you give me the chance now.*"

Did it leave him vulnerable, confessing? He supposed it did. Except Monty never shied away from the truth, not when it came with the potential to give him something important.

"Having a third in my bed, *as part of a relationship*, wasn't something I'd given any thought to, I confess. However, I'm attracted to Kendrick and you… at the same time. It changes things. And I'm happy with that. Fuck, more than that…"

The truck slowed, and Monty noted they were back at the ranch. A sense of urgency came over him, and he placed a hand on Rue's sleeve as the truck came to a halt outside the main house.

When he glanced at Monty, out came the worry. "All I ask is that you don't shut me out like before. I know things will be different without Kendrick to be a buffer for you. Just don't lock me out, okay?"

The door opened and Ethan stood there in the glow of interior light, and Monty cursed under his breath.

Ethan's assessing gaze moved between them, his lips tugging into a smile. "I see we've been playing hide the sausage in town."

"Mind your own damn business."

Monty got out, seeing the conversation was over for now, when Rue continued to have words with Ethan.

Monty walked off in the cabin's direction, needing a little space to figure out how to act and not alert his friends to what was going on with him. Inside the cabin, he stared at their packed bags lying on the beds they'd not used for days. A sense of dread he'd done his best to ignore for the last twenty-four hours crashed down on him. Did his budding relationship with Rue stand a chance?

Was it just sex?

Could the distance between Kendrick and them really work for them all?

In the middle of the night, when Rue gravitated towards him, wrapped himself around Monty, the answer was less ambiguous. Feelings were tricky, more so when he was the one carrying the burden of them alone.

You aren't. His animal side was so much more confident.

Then why does it feel like it?

Give it time. You're always in too much of a hurry.

If you say so.

Boots hitting wood got Monty heading to the bathroom to shower. Up to now, bar the first night they'd stayed at Kendrick's, they'd kept the trips to town under the radar. Stinking up the plane would give his friends the opportunity to interrogate him that busy ranch life had prevented. Monty could thank Ziggy and Silas's engagement for deflecting attention from him and Rue, only it wouldn't last long.

He knew his friends. Monty had spent three years with most of the PAs. Ziggy, being the newest recruit, was the one Monty knew the least about. That being said, Ziggy was the one everyone talked to about their problems. He was a good listener, Monty could see that. But he'd never had cause to talk to anyone about Rue. It would have felt like a betrayal, especially when Rue was such a private person.

Would it matter now, talking it out with a friend?

Monty chewed this over and still had no answer by the time they boarded the company jet to leave the ranch.

"I miss the ranch already," Bowie murmured, looking down at the little stuffed chicken that Cassidy had given him, or so Monty believed, as he took the seat next to him.

"I won't miss the early starts," Monty pointed out, yawning genuinely, just not because of work.

"You might have gotten a bit more sleep if you'd been in your own bed," Isley whispered into his ear.

Flustered at being caught when Monty thought he'd been good at acting like he'd been in the cabin when everyone rose, he blushed hard enough to feel it creep up his neck as he met Isley's knowing stare.

"My comfy king-sized bed is in Hazardville. A two-foot six wide bed just isn't the same," he lied through his teeth, the continuing heat flooding his face making it impossible to maintain eye contact when Rue's brothers were right there.

"Whatever you say," replied Isley, giving him stink eye, which Monty caught before looking at his hands, thinking he'd need to apologize once they were off the plane.

Monty tugged at the collar of his shirt, not quite meeting anyone's gaze. "Do you think we will have to go into the office today?" he asked to change the subject. It was Friday, and Monty had refrained from asking why they needed to return when they had the weekend in front of them.

A lonely weekend to look forward to.

Far enough away from the brothers not to hear, Frey answered, "'Cause we did all those extra hours, Booker said we get the afternoon free. I'm ready for some Emmy cuddles."

"Do you think she missed you?" Bowie's question got a head shake.

"She's had the best time with Lane and Derick. I can tell with all the giggling in the mini videos Lane sent me." He tugged out his phone, and they all gathered closer to watch the small screen as Frey hit play.

Baby laughter—was there any greater, more joyful sound? Monty didn't believe so. He'd admit he'd missed the little girl too. And from the conversations with the others, he wasn't alone. The hour every day they got to have her was something they all enjoyed. Lane had organized a rota to allow Frey to continue to work and keep Emmy close by. There was no hard sell when it came to Monty, or indeed any of the others. He'd discovered that his favorite time was the third hour of the day when Emmy liked to snuggle and nap in his arms. Monty had found a big comfy chair on the fourth floor in a coffee lounge that got little use. He liked to go there and sit in the quiet with Emmy in his arms. If he pretended she was his, it hurt no one.

The kit he'd come from gave him three siblings that were much older than him. They had all left home by the time Monty was old enough to play with. His parents were busy in the grocery shop they owned, meaning Monty spent a lot of time in the shop. By the time he was old enough to go to school, he'd learned to occupy himself. His parents had done their best. They loved him, but didn't seem to notice how lonely he was. After school, he headed straight to the shop to help, unlike everyone else, who got to go out and play with friends. For this reason, Monty had very few friends as he grew up.

University hadn't changed that when Monty didn't seem to fit in any group. All that changed when he'd come for the interview at Starling Enterprises. After already receiving two other job offers, one he planned on taking, he'd gone for the interview more out of curiosity after the phone call with Lane. Lane's ability to foster friendships with those who worked with him got Monty turning down the other jobs. It was the best decision he'd ever made, moving to Hazardville. Even with the turbulent relationship with Rue, Monty wouldn't want to work for anyone else. They were friends, only more like family the way they all stuck together and supported each other.

The guilt of keeping secrets left him shifting uncomfortably on his seat. He glanced down the plane to where Rue sat with Booker. They both wore grim expressions. Rue met his stare. For a brief moment, the grimness faded. He did no more than incline his head a fraction to acknowledge Monty, and it was enough to set his heart fluttering like a bird trapped in a cage.

"What do you think, Monty?" He turned his attention to Isley, frowning. What had they been talking about?

"Catch me up, I was thinking about what I could do with my free time." It wasn't exactly the truth, but he had wondered how he was going to fill his time.

Isley frowned at him. "That's what we were talking about. Do you want to go to Frey's to see Emmy? Maybe head to the park and try out the place Frey raves about that makes brownies?"

Monty nodded eagerly, and not just because of Emmy cuddles and brownies—both were reasons to be eager—when Frey lived in Lane and Derick's home, with the brothers. With Rue. Could he get a few minutes alone to finish the conversation he'd started in the truck?

"As long as I get to taste the brownie you raved about last time!" Ziggy stated dramatically, making them all laugh. Last time he'd gone, Ziggy had gone all snake because of an incident that involved Frey, which resulted in him missing out. "Then I'm in."

Frey grinned sassily. "Good, because then we can talk about your... *engagement!*" Relief at how Ziggy was the focus died a second later when Frey glanced in Monty's direction. "And we can talk about you and—"

"Frey!" he hissed, giving Frey a warning look. Out of the corner of his eye, he witnessed Rue grow still.

Please don't mention it. His eyes begged his friend. *Please don't mention it.*

Chapter Sixteen

Kendrick

Friday night had been brutal. Kendrick could admit it. His bed felt far too big, and he couldn't settle, regardless of how tired he was. The bar had been slammed with customers, and that gave him a distraction, right until he'd walked through his front door.

The quiet was off-putting. Where he usually took comfort in his space, he found none. He wasn't fooling himself that it would get better, when the dull ache in his chest didn't let up as the weekend had passed. Fuck, if anything, it had increased after the call he'd arranged for Sunday night, thinking that would work.

Big fucking mistake.

The counter he'd placed the unopened bottles on was not where his thoughts were when all he could think about was how he'd wanted to be in Monty's apartment, be present while he... vivid images of the couple flooded his mind.

"You have too many clothes on." Kendrick witnessed how Rue's cock pressed against the sweats he wore, in lieu of the denim he'd worn in Kendrick's home.

"Want me to strip Rue?" Monty offered eagerly, already getting up off the forest green couch they sat on. The iPad they were using for the call sat on something high enough to give Kendrick a view of the room beyond the couch. Stylish and comfortable sprang to mind, with lots of personal items scattered over any available surface. Muted colors complimented each other and provided an aura of peacefulness.

Nice.

"Absolutely, but first, do you have any toys in your apartment?"

Monty met his stare with a playful one. "One or two."

"Go get them."

A strangled moan came from Rue, who buried his head in his hands.

Kendrick chuckled, his blood warming at how the screen didn't prevent him from having the same effect on Rue as in person. "You want to play."

Rue didn't deny it as he twisted when Monty came back into the room carrying a shoe-sized box. He placed it on the couch facing Kendrick and took the lid off.

"Angle it so I can get a better look."

Monty obliged, and Kendrick, who'd been semi-hard since the call started, became fully hard at what was inside. "All the right toys to have fun alone, I see."

Unabashed, Monty beamed at Kendrick. "There isn't always a willing alpha to tell me what to do, so I improvise."

"You like the feel of your balls being stretched." It wasn't a question, but Monty nodded. "You have two different rubber cock rings, do you use both at the same time?"

Any thoughts that this wouldn't succeed fled when he could make out Rue quivering with need, and they'd barely started. Rue's hand went to his lap, and Kendrick shook his head. "No, honey, you don't get to touch until I say so."

The hand moved to the side of Rue's leg without question, but he heard the frustrated noise through the speaker. Rue aimed a heated stare at the iPad when Kendrick grinned sexily.

"The anal beads—I see something attached—do they vibrate?"

"It's got a ton of different settings." He lifted it out and revealed a small remote. "See, you can have the beads on all together, one at a time, different ones going at differing speeds," he explained excitedly, as he demonstrated.

"Nice." Kendrick shifted to adjust himself. "Strip Rue for me, then we can position him so his ass is hanging off the couch and we can both watch the fun."

The groan that escaped Rue sounded painful, and Kendrick's chuckle was pure menace. "Don't worry, honey, once we've got you nice and relaxed, I'll let Monty fuck himself on your cock while those beads are buzzing in your ass."

Monty switched off the toy and dropped it back in the box to skip to Rue and impatiently tugged off his T-shirt, dropping it carelessly on the floor. Then got on his knees to remove the sneakers before getting Rue to lift his hips to get the sweats and underwear off. They got shoved aside when Monty divested himself of his own clothes.

Kendrick pulled his throbbing shaft out of his pants, grabbing a tube of lube and slicking up his hand. "Put the cock rings over his balls first," he rasped huskily.

Fuck, he wasn't sure he would last long at this rate, with how eager both men were.

Monty sat off to the side, not obstructing Kendrick's view, and he witnessed Rue's full body shudder when Monty stretched the second cock ring over the first, tugging his balls down.

"Feels so good, that tight squeeze, like my fingers wrapped around your balls, tugging and stretching them."

Rue's eyelids dropped and his cheeks bore splashes of dark red as his labored breathing came through the speaker. His fingers curled around the edge of the cushions next to his spread thighs.

The snug fit of the two rings would be intense, and with Rue's arousal already bobbing at Kendrick's comment, he considered playing for a prolonged time might have to be

*forfeited to prevent Monty missing out on what Kendrick had
promised him.*

Kendrick heard a curse and jerked guiltily, glancing
down quickly to check he'd not embarrassed himself. Jesus, he'd nearly come in his boxers not two feet from Trey.

"If you keep wipin' at that like it's pissed ya off, the thing
is gonna need replacin'." Kendrick needed an interruption to get his thoughts away from the kinky fuckery that
was messing with his head. He'd already come twice that
morning, once in bed and then again in the shower. At this
rate, he could become a sex addict—fucking alone!

Trey's brooding eyes landed on Kendrick, and he suspected his expression wasn't any better than his friends.

"Whatever ya got goin' on in that head of yours, forget
it. I ain't in the mood for a boxin' match when we gotta
open up in half-an-hour," said Kendrick, in no mood for
whatever Trey was thinking of doing to alleviate his own
bad mood.

"You sure? I ain't the only one in a fuckin' mood."

He wasn't. Kendrick could not shake off the sense of
lack in his own life as the days apart from Rue and Monty
grew. It wasn't like him, and he wasn't sure how to change
it unless he *changed* location. Was it too wild a move to
consider after a few days of fucking?

"Your new fuck buddy leave town?"

Trey, he suspected, was hazarding a guess because he'd
been way too busy with Cassidy to pay much attention to

Kendrick. That didn't mean someone hadn't said something up at the ranch. "What you know 'bout that?"

"I ain't heard anythin'. Just putting the numbers together, is all."

Kendrick eyed him for several seconds before he cursed and decided to spill. He realized he really wanted to talk about what was on his mind. "That guy Rue, him and one of the others in the group he came with. We got a thing goin'. It was... interestin'." Fucking understatement of the century, but it was all he had right then.

Trey arched his brow. "Interestin' how? And I didn't notice anyone hangin' with the rhino shifter."

Kendrick became amused despite what they were talking about, recalling Trey's impressive leap over the bar and what came after. "Did you notice anything other than Cass sitting at the bar eye fuckin' ya?"

Trey grinned. "Why would I want to notice anythin' else?"

"Fuck you!"

"Only person doin' that with me is Cass," Trey pointed out, the grin widening. "So Rue, he gone back to Hazardville with Silas and his brothers?"

Kendrick gave a disheartened sigh, and Trey narrowed his gaze on him. "You're interested in more than fuckin'," he exclaimed, not giving Kendrick a chance to answer.

"It seems this"—he lifted his hands, air quoting—"wantin' more, seems to be catchin'." It was the truth, and wasn't that a bummer. He was the one who desired more, who wanted to see where things would go. Wanted time in the same place for more than a few days.

Trey slapped at the bar. "Holy fuck, man, I never thought I'd see the day—"

"Don't go fuckin' gloatin'. You were the one pissed off 'bout Cass not comin' in tonight."

"What a fuckin' pair we are."

"At least you have Cass. He's your mate." Pointing out the obvious made the reality even more hard-hitting.

"You wanna mate with Rue and this other dude?"

Kendrick wasn't going to answer, his attention turning to the dishwasher when it signalled the cycle had finished. He lifted out the steaming tray of clean glasses and finally muttered,

"Thinkin' 'bout possibilities." But mating...

"Would they be interested?"

Trey's question was one he'd asked himself in the middle of the night in his lonely bed. He shrugged while emptying the tray of glasses. "Don't know."

And he didn't know because how could someone want that after just a few days?

"If there's anything I can do to help, ya know I will."

"I know, thanks." He glanced back at Trey. "Did you know ole man Granger? He's selling his small holding out on the Hudson?" Kendrick needed something else to think about, and knowing Trey's struggle with balancing his new mating, he thought this might be a solution.

"I didn't hear that."

"Yep, he's movin' in with his daughter after a fall left him with a dodgy hip. Think it's just gone on the market. You're acquainted with Granger, maybe there's a deal to be struck there. Ya know, if someone was looking to set up a home that had land for their little chick. Also, maybe it's time to get someone to do some of the bar work to free up your time in the evenin's." Only it would benefit Kendrick too because it would allow him the chance to find someone to help Trey if he should decide to take a trip—leave—and try something different.

"Is that right?"

Kendrick chuckled at Trey trying to play it cool and failing. "It is. Way I see it, you could take a trip out there and have a look for yourself before it gets busy. And say I put out some feelers to see if anyone is lookin' for some bar work?"

"Don't suppose it would hurt."

Alone some ten minutes later, Kendrick pulled out his phone and opened the group chat.

Kendrick: *Gonna be home this evening, you both free for a call?*

Kendrick waited, watching as dots appeared.

Rue: *Yep. Monty has Emmy right now, but I'll answer yes for him too.*

Kendrick whistled through his teeth as he slipped the phone into the back of his jeans and continued to set up the bar. Anticipation gave a pep to his stride as he finished what he was doing, already thinking about what else was in Monty's box that maybe he could add to.

Chapter Seventeen

Rue

Rue blinked the sleep out of his eyes and the room came into focus. It was still early, the sun barely up. The blinds were open, and he could see pinks creating patterns in the white wispy clouds. Then the nose pressing into his armpit got all his attention. The man plastered against him breathed out and worked to get closer.

The sense of strangeness came and stayed when there was no large body crammed in behind him. It made him a little uneasy to realize how much he missed it. How was it that someone could get addicted to something so fast?

They had been doing this—whatever this was—since they'd got back, and Rue admitted it sort of worked. If he didn't think too hard on what was missing, Kendrick's presence with them, in person.

Two weeks in, and last night was the first time Rue had stayed over after the call with Kendrick. It wasn't like they talked about it, it just kind of happened.

Just happened! his rhino snorted. *You curled around Monty and didn't let go!*

Both of us were in a post-orgasmic haze.

Are you saying that's the only reason we stayed?

I don't want to send out the wrong message. Rue didn't want that. Getting his kinky needs met was one thing, but having a relationship while Kendrick was absent from the bed felt *wrong*. His uneasiness grew when the problem was his needs was growing so fast that it made it harder to leave after the calls.

They'd settled into a routine where he would go to Monty's when Kendrick planned to call. There were no dinner plans. No dating. No misunderstandings about what they were doing. Had last night shifted a boundary?

It sure as hell felt like it.

"Whatsup?" Monty murmured, his hot breath tickling Rue's underarm.

Rue chuckled, shifting back to hear a complaint. "Where ya going?"

"You're tickling me," he grumbled playfully at the sleepy man.

Monty's hair was a mess, one side stuck up. He had sheet creases on one cheek, yet he was too cute for words with the sulky pout. "I wasn't."

Monty rolled off the bed, scratching his tiny ass. One that bounced when he walked into the bathroom, distracting Rue.

His morning wood took notice, and Rue found himself in a predicament. Should he go after Monty? They hadn't had sex without Kendrick's presence in one form or another since the first time he'd come here in the middle of the night. It was like an unwritten rule that sat between all three of them. That's what it felt like to Rue.

"I was just breathin'," Monty called from the bathroom before the sound of the shower starting.

It struck Rue that he was laughing when Monty's head popped out of the bathroom and he gave him a mock glare before disappearing once more.

Rue blushed self-consciously as he eyed the open door. It was all so normal. Relationship normal.

His unease turned to panic, and he shot out of the bed like his ass was on fire, hunting up his clothes to dress and head home.

What the ever-loving fuck was he doing? "I'll catch you at work," he called into the bathroom, keys in hand. He was heading out the door before Monty even replied.

All the way home, he kicked himself for acting like a dick. Like that asshole who was a commitment phobic and didn't have the decency to hang around. Seeing it was early, he thought he'd be able to slip into the house undetected and shower before anyone noticed he'd not been home. Only the universe had other ideas as he came through the front door, face to face with Jupiter.

His nose wrinkled, and he laughed so hard his body shook. "And another bites the dust!"

The panic he'd felt at Monty's reared right back up.

"What are you talkin' 'bout!" he asked stupidly. Clearly, he had lost all sensibility, engaging in this conversation with Jupiter when he'd not even had a coffee to get his brain firing.

"First Taylin, then Booker, followed by Silas. Now, the mighty Rue has joined the PA shagfest." A light shone in Jupiter's eyes that made Rue wary, and with good cause when Jupiter continued, "Only little brother likes to crowd his bed with extra meat. How's that workin' for you with Kendrick back in Bayfield?"

Rue was at a loss on how to answer. Fright quickly drove him to glance around, making sure no one else was within earshot. "None of your damn business," he spluttered indignantly.

Jupiter's slim shoulders shrugged as he came forward and patted Rue's arm. "If you ever want any pointers, then you know where I am. But I suggest you pack a bag to avoid the creeping in and acting shady."

"Pointers from you, how would that work when you're all about fucking and pissing off before anyone gets attached cause you're too fucking scared of relationships?" It was temper that had him saying what was in his head.

Jupiter blanched and Rue regretted it immediately, knowing he was just deflecting from his own lack.

"Touché, little brother. But I'm not the only one scared of relationships. You, at least, have a chance of getting what you want. Don't squander it."

The distress coming from Jupiter made it hard to know how to answer. Sadness dripped from the words, like someone had turned on the tap and drenched them both, leaving an icy chill in its wake. Then he was gone, out the door, closing it quietly behind him.

"Fuck it all!" Rue ground out, feeling like shit.

"He's more sensitive than all of you." Popi's quiet voice made Rue jerk around to the stairs and groan under his breath, wondering how much of the conversation he'd overheard.

His expression wasn't one of disgust, but that didn't mean Popi hadn't heard what they were talking about.

"He's…" Words failed Rue because, like all the adopted brothers, they all had secrets. Secrets they didn't share. Jupiter never spoke about his past.

Popi came towards him, wrapping his arms around his waist, hugging hard. The effortless affection, Rue had learned, could still make him tremble. Popi was so small next to Rue, so he was careful when he hugged him back, needing it like oxygen to soothe the pain in his chest. This man was his savior, and Rue never forgot that.

It took several seconds for two things to sink in past the morning chaos: he smelled of Monty, and sex.

Why me!

He dropped his arms, hinting that it was time to let go, so he could escape.

Only, Popi didn't let go. Instead, he looked up at him and smiled in a way that said the questions were coming. "So, what time do you call this getting home?"

"Popi!" he groaned, unable to look away from the inquisitive stare. It had always been this way. The man was the best inquisitor Rue had ever met, and professionals had trained him not to spill secrets. It was all in those love-filled eyes, they slayed Rue's heart.

"What? Shouldn't you take some clothes to Monty's, so you don't have to sneak back in the house in the morning to shower for work?"

The comment revealed Popi had heard the entire conversation, and it took effort not to hunch. *Popi knows what I like... dear Gods!*

"My love, stop teasing Rue." Dad's appearance from the direction of the kitchen was a welcome relief.

Except Popi didn't let go, and Rue could hear voices upstairs. He didn't want to have to face his other brothers, too. Not when he'd already proven his brain wasn't in working order.

He gave Dad a begging look, and the traitor's lips twitched. Eventually, he came and kissed Popi on the forehead. "Let Rue go, love. He needs a shower, it smells like he visited a brothel."

Rue sent Dad a horror-filled look at being so blatantly called out, except it worked and Popi let go to swing to face Dad, hands going to his slim hips, his chin jutting forward. "And how would you know what a brothel smells like?"

"Brothel, who's been to a brothel?" Laken's voice carried to them from above, and Rue rolled his eyes at his misfortune.

"Ask your dad," Popi said, so sickly sweet.

Rue sent Dad an apologetic look, grateful despite how he'd achieved the deflection. He took that as his cue to leave and made his escape, dashing for the stairs. Laken eyed his suit with raised brows as Rue skipped past.

"It was just an analogy, my love," he heard Dad say.

"Is that so?"

Shutting his bedroom door a minute later, Rue breathed out a sigh of relief that Laken hadn't followed. He stripped off his suit jacket, wondering how a man of twenty-seven years old could act like a teenage boy caught coming home after the first time they'd had sex? He'd got caught out that time too, Popi really was like a ninja!

∞

Ten hours later, Rue had given the question from the morning way more attention than he should. It infuriated him when the answer was doing what Jupiter and Popi suggested and packing a bag. Yet, wasn't that sending the wrong message?

Monty hadn't been off with him when he'd arrived at work, except there was something about his eyes that Rue hadn't been able to pinpoint. Monty had acted the same way he always did... just those damn eyes gave Rue the guilts. Was he casting his own feelings onto Monty? That, he couldn't say.

"Do you know why we've been summoned?" Laken sidled up, matching Rue's pace as he headed to the boardroom down the empty corridor, bringing his thoughts back to where he was headed.

It was late, and Rue's plans for the evening had gotten scuppered by the call from Silas asking him to stay for an urgent meeting with his brothers. "Not rightly sure, but I saw the press dude in the corridor earlier. Last time he was here it was to do with Drinkwater."

When Rue glanced sideways, he tripped over his shoes, frowning. "What the fuck happened to you?" he asked, flabbergasted, his lips twitching before he burst out laughing.

Laken's hair resembled a bird's nest, and his shirt buttons were mismatched. Rue blinked several times, sweeping his gaze over his normally impeccable brother.

Laken raised a self-conscious hand to his hair, stiffening at Rue's laughter. "I don't know what you mean!" he replied indignantly, sniffing loudly, nose going up in the air like he'd smelled something bad.

Rue knew that look all too well, Laken was putting on his Mr Frosty Pants front. It was too much, and Rue shook with the force of his laughter. "Man, you need to go to the restroom before you enter the boardroom. Jupiter will make mincemeat of you."

His brother stomped off, muttering something Rue didn't quite catch. Rue wasn't gonna poke his nose in Laken's business when he didn't want anyone doing that to him after this morning. He'd gone to apologize to Jupiter, only to find he wasn't in his office and hadn't been all day.

In the boardroom, he took a seat, his gaze sweeping the table, landing on Jupiter. The man didn't so much as acknowledge him, and Rue sighed, disheartened. He hadn't really expected anything else.

His phone vibrated, and he tugged it out of his pocket. Seeing Monty's name on the screen, he winced. With one glance at the others to check no one was close enough to read the message, he opened it.

> **Monty:** *Does that mean you aren't coming at all tonight?*

> **Rue:** *Silas has called an urgent meeting, like I said, not sure how long I'll be here. Didn't want to put you or Kendrick out. I messaged him too.*

The dots danced to say Monty was answering, so he waited.

> **Monty:** *Kendrick said he's still going to call. Can you come after the meeting… if you want to, that is? We won't mind the lateness of the hour.*

How much he wanted it should have him saying no.

> **Rue:** *Alright, I'll message when I leave here so you know when to expect me.*

The dots appeared again.

> **Monty:** *I have some leftovers if you're interested.*

> **Rue:** *Don't go to any trouble.*

> **Monty:** It's leftovers, no trouble. See you soon. X

Rue felt a blast of emotions wash over him at how considerate Monty was being, but he wasn't sure how he felt about it.

"Great, now that Laken has arrived, we'll get started. Unless Rue has something urgent to do on his phone?"

Silas sounded tired, and Rue noticed the dark circles, so kept his sarcastic comment to himself. Nodding curtly instead, he pocketed his phone.

The tension in the room was palpable.

Silas lifted a newspaper and slammed it down on the boardroom table. "This shit hit the fan in the evening press."

"What now?" Kari was the first to ask.

"Some fucker down in Drinkwater has sold their story to the press about what happened when we were at the ranch. The press is all over the hotel like a bad fucking rash. Oakland has his hands full after the original fallout. He's mightily pissed and feels it's too risky to leave the vulnerable omegas in the hotel." He rubbed his temples, eyes flashing with temper. "Not that they aren't all vulnerable, but we need to move those who are struggling the most out of harm's way, as soon as possible. And what I mentioned before, I wanted to plan more thoroughly before we moved the four from the hotel to the ranch in Bayfield, it needs to happen faster."

At the collective nods, Silas grunted, a hand running over the back of his neck as his gaze swept the table. "Oakland is interrogating the staff to prevent further leaks, because we can't have anyone following them to the ranch. It would defeat the whole purpose of sending them there." Silas drummed his fingers on the table, looking pale and somewhat older than he had.

Rue felt the beginnings of a headache at his temples, at what the press could cause if left to run amok. The alphas who were fighting the case against them over the treatment of the omegas had their dirty hands all over this, Rue just wasn't sure how.

"How is this going to work, then?" Jupiter questioned, a finger rubbing at his eyebrow in a continuous movement, one that revealed the distress his expression didn't.

Silas pinched the bridge of his nose, his eyes sweeping the boardroom table. "There's a lot to consider."

Silas had laid out the priority: re-home those who were struggling, safely and quickly, which meant one of them needed to assist. When Rue had originally read the group chat in Bayfield, he'd had an idea, though he cast it aside for many reasons. The main being that doing whatever he was doing with Kendrick and Monty would never be a long term thing. But could going back to Bayfield give him a chance to fuck this infatuation with the pair out of his system? Neither man would want him long term, he accepted that. But short term? That was more plausible, wasn't it?

Take the chance.

Leave me be. Rue made sure his animal side got he wasn't messing.

"Oakland is going to pay a visit to the ranch. He's leaving in the morning to assess the risks and work to mitigate whatever he finds. I've had some ideas about this. I'm stopping all the team-building packages at the ranch. This prevents any newbies, or press, from showing up and pretending so they can get information. I called Ethan before I came here, and he's working on cancelling and refunding folks. Once that's done, we'll be able to think about potentially transporting the omegas beginning of next week. I can't do it this week as we have paid visitors for the entire week."

"How's that going to happen? Can Oakland manage all the logistics and settle the omegas at the ranch? From what I've seen, Ethan can't help. He's got his own workload and yours on his plate." Rue laid out the issues as he saw them, his mind considering how to get what he wanted without raising suspicion.

"That's part of why we are here. I need to discuss how we help Oakland. He is going to take Brier along with him and leave his remaining team with the others."

"If Oakland is dealing with just those few, who will be in charge of keeping the other situation confined? It feels a bit like overkill to send Oakland to the ranch when so many are staying behind. And how long is he planning on staying there?" Laken questioned, his lips thinning, looking more like himself after his visit to the restroom.

"Oakland is considering who will replace him long term. He's the best placed to keep the most vulnerable safe, and he won't consider anyone else doing it."

"Isn't that strange?" Kodi looked at everyone in confusion. "Surely, he should stay where the majority are, as Laken said? Isn't he needed at the hotel to aid in planning what comes next? I mean, I'm sure there are others out there who could do what Oakland does, but that's gonna take time to find that we don't have, no? I'm seeing more problems than solutions in this option."

Silas shrugged off the concern. "It's his decision, and I agree with him after he explained the carnage after the heats. They trust him, and that is fucking vital. What we need now—"

"I'll help." Rue interrupted, doing his level best to contain his embarrassment at rushing to speak before anyone else could even consider offering. "I can go and stay in Bayfield."

Rue made a point not to say he'd stay at the ranch because he hoped it wouldn't be long term anyway. "Until such time as things calm down. My military training could be useful." He looked at Jupiter. "And not everyone enjoyed being on the ranch. I can manage my workload via email right now."

He would check, or get Monty to, once they'd discussed it. He was flying by the seat of his pants, and hoped the fuckers didn't catch fire, burning his ass for making assumptions on Monty and Kendrick's behalf. Burning his ass could be the least of his problems if he was reading both men wrong!

Jupiter laughed, rolling his eyes. "Some of us definitely got *more* out of the ranch experience than others. *Right, Rue?*"

"What's he referring to?" Kodi questioned, looking between the two.

"Shouldn't we all take a turn? Do a few weeks each?" Laken offered, and Rue resisted telling him to shut up when it was clear he was deflecting for Rue.

Rue offered a pinched smile. "Do you have the skills I have?"

"What, stomping shit?" Laken fired at Rue, getting chuckles from Kodi and Taylin.

"Would you take Monty?" Booker's lips were twitching.

No one had said anything aloud about his visits to town. He knew well that some, if not all, of his brothers had an idea about his nocturnal trips. They were all far too observant, as the conversation with Jupiter made glaringly obvious.

"Yep." It was getting harder to hold on to his embarrassment, while starting Booker down, hoping like heck he revealed none of his internal conflict.

"What if Monty doesn't want to stay at the ranch for weeks—months without knowing when he could come home?" Always the voice of reason, Kari had a valid point.

It was something they would talk about later tonight, after they confirmed he was going. "It's in his contract. He goes where I go."

"You can't fucking force him," Silas muttered angrily. "Popi would have a fit if you tried to do that!"

He blew out a frustrated breath. "Leave it out, I'm not fucking forcing anyone. Monty knows the score. Hollis pointed it out to all the PAs in the e-mail he sent us all when he allocated them. Or have you lot forgotten that? If I remember right, you all had a bitch about it."

"We're getting off track." Kodi drummed his fingers on the table much like Silas, looking most uncomfortable. "If Rue can wangle it to work being based up on the ranch, then why are we looking for another solution when we have one?"

"Are you sure, Rue? I could go."

Silas was the obvious choice as it was his ranch, but Monty had shared that Ziggy had a major fear of horses, explaining the fainting episode at the ranch when they were there.

"Would Ziggy want that?" It was a low blow, but he was desperate for them to agree, despite how unsure he was whether this was in his best interest.

"No," Silas replied, after only a minor hesitation. "If you're sure, Rue?"

He nodded before Silas had finished speaking.

"As that's decided, are we done?" Jupiter rose before anyone answered.

"Sit, we aren't done. If Monty goes, that leaves a gap in Emmy's childcare—"

"I'll do it." Jupiter might as well have said he'd run naked through the building after he'd set fire to it. He didn't sit down, just stood with raised brows challenging them all. "What?" he finally asked when the deafening silence continued.

It wasn't really a surprise, Jupiter loved Emmy and spent most of his time, if allowed, when he was home with her. What surprised Rue was how many nights Jupiter stayed home for the privilege when others were out. He was a man whore, yet with Emmy, he was something different.

"It seems we're done," Kodi motioned at Jupiter, also getting up.

Rue rose too, ready to leave, eager to get to Monty's to discover whether what he was proposing fit with Monty and Kendrick.

Preoccupied, he didn't notice Silas following him to his office until he spoke. "Are you sure about this?"

Rue paused in tidying up his desk to look at his big brother. A brother with whom it had taken a year to really feel like they were family. Silas had persisted, despite Rue's obstructive behavior, in making him feel he belonged. He'd always be grateful for that, loved him for it.

He witnessed concern and gratitude. "I am. Don't stress 'bout it. I went through my workload,"—or he would later—"and there isn't anything I can't do from Bayfield for the next six months, at least." He grinned deliberately. "As long as you don't let the others pull any shit on me."

His office filled with Silas's booming laughter. "Like I can stop them?" Silas spluttered. "But I'll get Dad on the case if they don't play fair. He'll sort them out."

Rue rolled his eyes. "Good luck with that."

Chapter Eighteen

Monty

Last night differed from the others, and Monty had got—hypothetically—why Rue had rushed out while he was in the shower. Not even a goodbye kiss—was that too much to ask for?

It seemed it was, and it nagged like a broken tooth, except Monty didn't want to rock the boat when Rue wasn't a sure swimmer in the sea of relationships. It was becoming more and more obvious when he didn't appear to know how to react when he came to Monty's if sex wasn't immediately on the cards. It had taken a full week before Rue came into his apartment and didn't just stand around like a spare part.

Progress was progress.

If he kept telling himself that, maybe Monty would believe it. Except last night felt like a giant leap forward, only for Rue to take more steps back by leaving the way he did. *Without talking.*

He couldn't deny it, this was Monty's issue. He planned to talk about it tonight during the call with Kendrick, who he was clearly a conduit to openness. But something was amiss at work with the urgent meeting Rue messaged about. As the PAs weren't invited, it came with a feeling it wasn't good news. Monty could try to guess but the list could be endless, so why bother?

He checked the time before plating the leftover chicken parmigiana and placing it in the oven to warm. He'd washed up, had a shower, tidied the living room, changed the bedroom sheets, and now was at a loose end.

Chimes coming from the living room got him eagerly rushing to answer the iPad call. The thrumming of excitement increased as he pressed the green button to accept the call and Kendrick's grinning face filled the screen.

"Hey honey, don't you look sexy."

Monty gave a twirl in his new black lounge pants. They fit perfectly, to show off his backside to its full potential. Monty was well aware of how much both men loved his ass. He'd paired the pants with a dark gray, loose-fit T-shirt with a wide neck that slipped off one shoulder. He felt it added a sexiness to the casual wear, and by Kendrick's comment he'd say he was right on the money. Now he hoped Rue thought the same, and it encouraged him to stay again.

"Why, thank you." He fluttered his eyelashes as he sat cross-legged on the couch in front of the iPad.

"Where's Rue?"

"Running late. Silas called an urgent meeting," Monty explained.

Kendrick had pulled quite a few double shifts with Trey needing time to organise house renovations on the place he'd bought for him and Cassidy. Monty could see Kendrick's exhaustion despite only seeing him on the small screen.

"Bugger. I hope it ain't anything serious."

"Me too." Monty perched his elbows on his knees and rested his chin on his fists. "Are you gonna get some time off after all these extra shifts you're putting in? You look tired." Monty didn't have the same worries about talking freely with Kendrick as Rue did.

"I've interviewed several guys this afternoon. A couple looks like they may be a good fit. They're coming in to do a couple of shifts, and if they pan out, then I can take a few days off." He sat forward, holding Monty's gaze. "Maybe take a flight up to Hazardville? You up for a visitor and putting me up at your place for a few days?"

Monty wiggled his butt and giggled outrageously loud at the excitement bubbling inside him. He didn't care if he was being very obvious. "Yes. Yes. One hundred percent yes."

Kendrick's laughter came through the speaker, filling the room. "So that's a yes then?"

"Silly," Monty snickered.

A message popped up on the screen. He caught the "I'm on my way," before it disappeared, and the wiggles were back.

"Rue's on his way, should be about ten minutes."

"We can hope he's as happy as you." Kendrick didn't sound as confident, despite the jokey tone.

Then Monty recalled the disappearing act this morning, and his bubble burst. "He stayed last night."

Kendrick's only reaction was a brow arch. "You sound conflicted."

The man was good at picking up on things Rue tended to miss. "Not about him staying, more the fact he did a cut and run while I was in the shower. Weirdest thing. It was all chill, heck, he laughed at something I said, then he was hightailing out the door shouting goodbye without the decency of saying it to my face." He hated how it came out as a whine, but there it was.

"He's still adjusting, honey. Rue's a man who sees things in black and white. He has his reasons for this, I'm sure. We just need to be patient with him. He's worth it, isn't he?"

"You both are," Monty confessed, releasing a shuddering breath. Two weeks in and he was making room in his life and heart for Kendrick, the same as he'd done for Rue, whether or not the other man got that.

"Honey, I wish I could kiss you right now." The need shone out at Monty and brought with it a splash of cold-water reality. Making room wasn't going to be enough with the distance between them. A holiday wouldn't always be enough when Monty wanted... more.

Stop being greedy.

It's not greedy to want more. His animal was adamant about that, making Monty struggle to contain a discontented sigh.

The sound of an engine idling got Monty shifting to get up. "I think Rue's here!" He went to the window and saw Rue parking in the empty space in front of his apartment block. His pulse gave a mighty leap as he considered how Rue would react to the news of Kendrick coming for a visit. "It's him," he said aloud, and *please let him be happy,* though he kept that part inside his head.

Monty buzzed Rue in and was at the door of his apartment when he crested the top step. "Come on, Kendrick's waiting for you."

Something about the wariness in his expression set Monty's nerves aflutter. Shit.

He came in behind Monty, shutting and locking the door wordlessly.

The hope of Rue accepting what they were about to talk about left Monty dry-mouthed.

In the living room, Rue's gaze went straight to the iPad, and a sense of trepidation grew inside Monty.

"I've heated some chicken parmigiana, I'll go grab it." He darted out of the room, hands shaking. He ran them down the sides of his legs, halting in the kitchen and taking a deep inhale, then another after slowly releasing the first. It did fuck all to help, so Monty grabbed a cloth to lift the plate out of the oven, placing it with some cutlery on a tray.

He paused in the kitchen doorway to see Rue standing, his laptop bag still in his hand. Wasn't he planning on staying?

"Here we go. You can give me your laptop, I'll store it with mine while you eat." Monty swapped the tray for the laptop bag before Rue could say differently. "Sit. Keep Kendrick company, he's got something to talk to you about."

Rue, who bent at the knee to take a seat, looked like his back had seized up on him and he'd got stuck the way he froze. His unreadable gaze went to the iPad.

"It's all good, honey, sit. I can explain what I was planning while you eat."

The pace at which Rue moved showed his reluctance and Monty's nerves were now climbing the walls like a professional rock climber. What was wrong?

He chanced a glance at Kendrick, seeing signs that he had also noticed something was off.

Alone in his bedroom to get some perspective before he had a freak out, Monty told himself off. "You're over-reacting because of this morning. Rue has not come to tell you that whatever this is, is over. Now stop catastro-phizing and get your butt in the living room."

He used the bathroom, having a nervous pee. When done, he plastered a smile on his face and went to sit cross-legged next to Rue. His plate was nearly empty, and Kendrick was regaling a funny incident about Trey and coping with Cassidy's pregnancy.

Had he mentioned the trip to Hazardville?

He looked between the iPad and Rue, unable to tell.

When Kendrick's laughter died down, Monty was bouncing with anxiety. "Did you tell him?" he blurted out.

Kendrick's chuckle said not.

"Told me what?" Rue placed the tray on the coffee table, away from the iPad, shrugging out of his suit jacket. His moves were jerky as he slung it over the back of the couch, next tugging at his tie like it could be strangling him as both Monty and Kendrick eyed him with appre-hension.

"You know all the double shifts I've copped recently?" Rue had the tie sliding from his neck as he nodded. "I've got some time owed to me, and after interviewing today, I could potentially have two guys who could fill in when I take time off." The shrug he gave suggested it was nothing big, but the way his lips pinched said otherwise. "So, I was thinking of flying up to see you both. Staying at Monty's for a few vacation days."

With the air hissing through Rue's teeth, Monty couldn't assess whether the reaction was good or bad. His expression remained unreadable. The man had a great poker face.

"How'd you feel 'bout that?" Kendrick asked, when Rue didn't reply.

"I… you wanna see me—us?"

It was a damn odd question when that was clearly what Kendrick was suggesting? What were they missing?

"Isn't that what I just said?" Kendrick's amused tone sounded forced to Monty.

"I had an interesting meeting this evening… *very interesting.*"

"Good or bad, interesting?" Kendrick asked, a furrow appearing between his brows, revealing his unease.

"You two can tell me." For the first time, Rue looked directly at Monty. "How do you feel about moving to Bayfield for a few months, possibly six?"

"What!" Monty exclaimed, swamped by a wave of want that left him drowning.

"You serious?" Kendrick growled.

Rue looked between the two of them, nodding. "Very. Someone needs to facilitate the move of the omegas from Drinkwater to Darling Ranch… and I offered."

At Kendrick's confused look, Monty explained, "Drinkwater is a place where we visited a factory. The conditions the workers were forced to endure got Starling Enterprises buying the factory. It was in the press—"

"It's not the only thing in the fucking press," Rue muttered angrily, and Monty got a sinking feeling.

"What this time?" he asked with trepidation, already aware of how the omegas had suffered.

"Someone in the hotel sold their story about what happened with the omegas three weeks ago."

Kendrick held up his hand. "Sorry, what happened three weeks ago? I don't read newspapers, they're full of shit."

Rue ran through everything, giving brief highlights, then explained how four of the omegas were moving to the ranch.

"You've offered to be the one to facilitate the move here?" Kendrick clarified deliberately.

Rue nodded slowly. "I have skills from my army days that could help. Only two of the security team are due to be coming with them."

"What am I missing? Are they in danger from more than just the press?"

Monty witnessed Rue's hesitation at answering Kendrick, his stomach twisting into knots. "There have been threats, I won't lie. The alphas involved in the abuse aren't happy that this is all going to court and they could get prison time."

"Fuck, so you're putting yourself in the firing line."

Those words rang through Monty, but not because of the threat. Hell, no. For Rue to consider this... then surely, he must have feelings for them? Want to see where this thing was going? Was he reading too much into this?

"I can handle myself, Kendrick." Rue smirked sexily. "I might like you to pin me down and fuck me, but if I wanted to do the same to you, I could, *easily.*"

Monty groaned aloud, his body responding to the visual of something that hadn't—as far as he knew—been on the cards.

Kendrick looked ready to burst through the screen. "That can be arranged." He was so close to the screen his face filled it. "I'm going to assume that you'll both need a place to stay—*with me.*"

It really wasn't a question, and Monty giggled, although Rue's laughter surprised him.

"Bossy much?" Rue ran a hand through his hair, his expression turning serious. "Is that ideal? We... what... shit I don't even know what we're doing here."

"Figuring our shit out is what we're doing. *I miss you both.*"

Raw honesty gave Monty a hard knock to his chest, his hand trembling as it pressed against his racing heart.

Rue's throat clicked when he swallowed. "We could try—"

"I'm in." Monty had no issues in wanting to see how this could work. Life was a gamble, and sometimes folks lost, but then some won big. Hollis, Frey, and Ziggy had, so why couldn't he? Kendrick's home was gorgeous and big enough for them not to be up in each other's space all the time. A definite bonus.

Rue's groan was long and pained. "Is that right?"

Monty leapt into Rue's lap, not overthinking it, and slung his arm around his neck. Grinning cheekily at Rue, and then Kendrick, he said, "He offered, I don't want to offend him, but staying in a tiny cabin versus Kendrick's big house is a no brainer."

"Thanks, I think," Kendrick spluttered through his laughter. "What about you, Rue?"

His smile was hesitant. "It could be too much, having us there—*all the time?*"

"I'm a big boy. I can express myself if I've a need to. You don't need to add that to any pile of worry you've got going on in that head of yours."

"If you want us to leave, feel it's not right, then just say and we'll head to the ranch," Rue persisted.

Monty's stomach flip-flopped. Was that a yes? "Are we doing this?"

A saucy smile aimed at the iPad got Monty wiggling on Rue's lap. "A two-foot-four cradle for a bed versus your enormous bed? As my PA said, it's a no brainer."

Chapter Nineteen

Kendrick

"Will you stop the goddamn fussin', you're drivin' me nuts!" Trey grabbed the cloth out of Kendrick's meaty fist and shoved him towards the end of the bar. "Go home. It's where you should be, and it'll get you out from under my damn feet."

"Don't even know if they've finished up at the ranch. They only got in a few hours ago." Kendrick was like a cat on a hot tin roof, and he knew it. If he wasn't thinking about how fast he offered to have both men stay in his space, something he'd never have considered he'd do, he was busy fussing over making his home look appealing so the men would feel relaxed and at home in his space.

Then there was the waiting for Rue and Monty to have a definitive date. It had changed twice, and because Rue and Monty were working extra hours to make it possible to remain in Bayfield, they'd only had one video call in the past couple of weeks. He acknowledged, late one night last week when Rue had moved the date of their arrival once more, that he missed them. It was as simple and complex as that. They'd messaged frequently, mostly late at night, but it wasn't the same as seeing them.

In six weeks, a lot had changed and Kendrick was too old to pretend to himself what was happening, at least for him, wasn't real. He wanted a relationship, a permanent one with both men. He could foresee a future with these men, which he'd not been able to do in any relationship for a very long time. It was expressed in the ease with which he offered them his home. It spoke to what his heart wanted to try, even when his head hadn't quite caught up. That was fine, he had used the wait these last few weeks to allow it to catch up.

Due to the setbacks, Kendrick was currently working on a 'see it to believe it' type situation. The desire to drive to the ranch to check they'd arrived, after the last two disappointments, had him decide, despite starting his vacation that morning, to go to the bar. That way, he could drive someone else nuts instead of himself.

"I don't care." It was clear, when Kendrick had told Trey he'd invited both men to move in with him, that he already thought he'd lost his mind. Kendrick wasn't sure Trey had recovered from the shock with how he kept looking at him weirdly, just like he was now.

"This weird shit you've got going on is freaking me out."

"What weird shit?" he asked, peeved at the implication he was acting differently because he wasn't. Was he?

"This mooning expression, man. It's like you've got possessed by a sappy looking alien. 'Cause you know you're wearing a sappy smile right now even when you sound pissed? It's fucking weirding me out!" accused Trey.

Kendrick didn't glance towards the mirror on the back wall of the bar; he did not need to clarify Trey's accusation when he could feel the tug of his smile at the corner of his lips. But mooning, that wasn't him.

"Give the fuck over," he said instead, snatching back the cloth to carry on what he was doing.

What had he been doing?

Trey belly laughed, pointing at him. "See? You don't even know what to do with yourself. Go, start your vacation for fucksake. I ain't giving you an extra day 'cause you chose to come in."

Kendrick felt a buzz at the prospect of the next two weeks' vacation time. He hadn't told Rue or Monty about his plan. He decided to surprise them with the news when they arrived.

Rue had mentioned the house sharing four times in messages, reiterating that they could stay at the ranch if Kendrick had a change of heart. He did not want to change his mind, and Rue didn't know him well enough to figure that out, so he didn't take offense.

Instead, he took vacation time to demonstrate how much he wanted to spend time with them. It was the plan of attack on Rue's doubt. Monty had no such qualms about sharing a house with Kendrick and gushed excitedly about the prospect. Once more, it reminded Kendrick of their differences.

With the new staff working out, and Trey's insistence he'd be fine even with Cassidy heavily pregnant and house renovations, Kendrick went with two weeks' vacation. He had assured Trey that if he needed him, then he'd be there to step in and help. Still, he sent out a wish that everything would pan out.

"What, are we playing statues now?"

Trey's laughing comment had Kendrick aim a narrowed eyed stare at his friend. "Remember, payback's a bitch," he smirked, throwing the cloth at Trey, who caught it, giving him a shit-eating grin.

"Are you two always like this?" asked Padrick, or Paddy to his friends. He was one of their new barmen, and he looked between them as he came around the bar counter, carrying his jacket. He was ten minutes early for his shift, something Kendrick gladly noted.

"Pretty much," Trey answered, nudging Kendrick, bringing his attention back to him. "Leave, or folks will think you don't trust me to be left unsupervised."

"I don't." He waited a beat then added, "All I'm gonna say is sex in the restroom when the bar is open."

Paddy made a choking noise.

Trey scowled at him, and Kendrick played along. "I feel like you can't get rid of me fast enough?" He threw up his arms in mock protest, walking in the direction of the office. "I'll take the damn hint then."

Trey grunted behind him. "Hint? I threw a fucking boulder at you."

Giving him the middle finger, Kendrick didn't look back, chuckling only when out of earshot.

In the office, he grabbed his truck keys and slipped on his jacket. Out the door, he hadn't even made it to the truck before he heard a shout behind him.

He spun around to see Monty, casually dressed, looking gorgeous as he sprinted towards him from the back entrance of the bar. Kendrick barely had time to open his arms to catch Monty when he launched himself at him. Monty's lips latched onto Kendrick's the second he was in his arms. His heart stuttered at the emotional depth of the kiss.

If there was ever a kiss that said, 'I missed you', it was the one. Monty didn't hold back as he wrapped himself around Kendrick. Legs wrapping around his middle, Kendrick dropped his truck keys without thought and boosted Monty up by his ass, even as one hand slid up the back of his head, fingers digging in possessively, holding him closer.

Kendrick groaned, lips parting as a large body pressed into his side. Rue's scent surrounded them as another set of lips touched the corner of his and Monty's mouths. Tongues and teeth clashed as they worked to connect all three mouths together in what felt like the hungriest kiss Kendrick had experienced in some time—if ever.

The difference was telling the longer it went on, and Kendrick acknowledged it, then set it aside, knowing one of these men wouldn't trust the depth of Kendrick's feelings... *yet.*

"Smell so good." Rue buried his nose in Kendrick's neck, who shuddered when, at the same time, he ran a proprietary hand over his ass.

"Are you done for the day?" rasped Monty, lips slick, eyes clouded with lust.

It took his brain a second to compute the question, getting a giggle from the sexy man who played with the hair at the nape of his neck.

"I wasn't really working, just hanging. But Trey got annoyed with me, so I was just heading home to wait for you two."

Rue took a step back at the sound of a door opening behind them, shoving his hands into his jeans pockets.

Kendrick glanced sideways in annoyance, witnessing Paddy's gawping mouth. Clearly Rue hadn't been quick enough.

"Paddy, meet Rue,"—he nodded towards Rue, who looked anything but comfortable—"and Monty." He brought Monty around onto his hip, not considering putting him down. He didn't care who knew about their relationship, regardless of the unorthodox nature of it. "Paddy's one of our new bar staff," he said, by way of introduction when Rue frowned at the very interested stare Paddy cast in their direction.

"Hey," Monty murmured, barely looking at Paddy. "Our bags are inside. Ethan dropped us out front when we went by your place and found it empty."

"Sorry, I was expectin' you to call when you were headin' my way." Kendrick turned his attention to Rue. "Things go okay?"

"They went," Rue replied cryptically, his troubled gaze remaining on Paddy, who watched them while holding onto a pair of bulging trash bags.

"Rue, you go grab the bags, and I'll bring the truck round front," said Kendrick, sensing Rue's unease, but not knowing why.

Kendrick inclined his head at Paddy, suggesting he get on what he'd come to do. When Paddy moved, giving an awkward grin, Kendrick bent to collect his truck keys. Monty clung to him, and he chuckled when he had to adjust his balance to grab the keys.

"Miss me?"

"Can't you tell?" An impish smile appeared before Monty kissed him softly. "We both did."

He acknowledged what Monty was doing. Rue might never be as expressive as Monty and Kendrick was alright with that. Not everyone was comfortable showing their emotions, it was a fact of life.

Seconds later, Monty now in the back of the truck, Kendrick pulled in front of the bar where Rue stood at the curbside with a mountain of bags. Kendrick's laughter boomed out. "What you got in there, the kitchen sink?"

What followed was a shy giggle and a sheepish look. "All my necessities for a long trip from home. The sink, I left behind," Monty replied cheekily, getting out of the truck to help store the bags.

When they were all back in the truck, Kendrick spilled his surprise. "I've taken a couple of weeks of vacation time." He glanced sideways, scrutinizing Rue to gauge his reaction. He was the only one that worried him. Seeing nothing that suggested Rue was uncomfortable, Kendrick continued. "Thought it would be nice to spend some time getting to know each other without my late evening shifts getting in the way."

"With everything we've done naked, I'd say we know each other pretty damn well."

Monty came through the gap, the seatbelt straining. "Stop being obtuse, Rue."

He kissed Kendrick on the shoulder when it seemed he couldn't get any closer, grunting when the seatbelt made a noise of complaint at the abuse. He then looked at Rue, whose lips formed into a scowl. "Do you think we could take a few days' vacation, too?" he asked, seeming unphased by Rue's reaction.

"We just got here," Rue replied with a snap in his voice.

If Kendrick had to guess at Rue's feelings in that moment, he would have said unimpressed, and possibly even unsure of his footing. Yet when he continued, there was enough sexual implication to his comment that they'd both have to be deaf and blind to miss it. "We'll have this weekend, and many more, along with evenings *and the nights.*"

Kendrick felt the tension that gathered in his neck and shoulders ease at Rue's promise. "We will."

If this was what kept Rue comfortable for now, then Kendrick would work with that. His gaze met Monty's in the rearview mirror, and he gave him an intrigued wink.

A light appeared in those pale eyes that Kendrick was glad Rue didn't see, suggesting they were going to war, and he had his battle plan already.

Bring it.

Chapter Twenty

Alphaholes

Silas: *Rue, why aren't you answering my calls? How did it go?*

Taylin: *I can ask Hollis to reach out to Monty, he'll respond.*

Jupiter: *Maybe Rue's busy…*

Laken: *Spit it out, Jup.*

Jupiter: How did you know I don't like to swallow?

Laken: I just threw up in my mouth. Did you have to go there? You need therapy for this sex addiction. I swear it's all you think about or talk about.

Booker: Jup, what do you know that we don't? And you're noticing Laken cause you haven't let little Laken out to play for a while.

Jupiter: Go back and read what I said!

Laken: Those damn dots you had trailing off says you're implying something. Implying you know more than the rest of us. Booker what the fuck, little Laken!

Jupiter: Baby brother couldn't wait to head back to Bayfield, could he.

Kari: I'm too tired to play a guessing game when there seem to be several *conversations going on at once. Rue offered. End of, as far as I'm concerned.*

Jupiter: Shows what you know... but then you are busy yourself.

Kari: Why are you keeping tabs on me?

Jupiter: I wasn't! Just noticed you haven't spent a night at home in over a week.

Kari: And? You should pay more attention to how your behavior is affecting those around you.

Kodi: What the fuck is that supposed to mean?

Booker: Boys, behave. No fighting!

Laken: Did you say that in Popi's voice? I bet you did.

Booker: Yep.

Rue: Silas, I know you spoke to Ethan, so what's the damn problem? I've worked my fucking ass off to make sure things go smoothly. They did, end of. Now if you don't mind, stop fucking ringing me, I got shit to do. Tay, Monty's tied up with something right now, so you don't need Hollis to be bothering him.

Taylin: Too late, oops.

Booker: That told you, Silas.

Silas: Booker... fuck off!

Booker: I'm so hurt.

Laken: If you are, then why can I hear your laughter coming down the stairs from your bedroom?

Booker: *Spoilsport.*

Laken: *Whatever.*

Kodi: *Don't complain about the laughing, remember Frey's heat?*

Laken: *As if we can forget.*

Dad: *I forgot just how mouthy you all were as teenagers, baiting each other. Did I slip back in time?*

Laken: *I fucking hope not, for Kodi's sake. Pimples were not a good look for him.*

Kodi: *Run!*

Chapter Twenty-One

Delicious & Vicious

Hollis: *Everything work out, Monty? Did the omegas cope with the travel? I haven't got a response to my emails, and Silas has rung Rue, but he's not answering.*

Frey: *I'm not sure Monty will answer, Booker said something about him being tied up??? But I caught the gist that Rue said everything was okay.*

Lennon: *Tied up... is that figuratively or literally? I bet you were looking* *over Booker's shoulder again, weren't you Frey?*

Frey: *Of course not. And why would you think Monty is 'tied up' literally???*

Bowie: *You've lost me. Tied up literally? Why would Rue do that when Monty wouldn't be able to do any work that way? Well, unless he left his hands free?*

Frey: *Bowie, it's after work hours.*

Bowie: *Ohh…*

Lennon: *You sure, Frey, that you're not spying… again?*

Isley: *At least he's got something interesting to look at, even if he's not supposed to spy over Booker's shoulder.*

Frey: *He's my mate so how is that spying? We aren't supposed to have any secrets.*

Ziggy: *Do you let him read through the delicious & vicious group chat?*

Frey: *As if!*

Ziggy: *I rest my case.*

Bowie: *Case? Why are we talking about cases?*

Ziggy: *It just means that Frey is doing something with Booker's group chat he wouldn't allow, so I was pointing out it is spying, Bowie.*

Bowie: *Right.*

Lennon: *Isley, if you're wanting something to do, wanna come over to mine? I'm having a baking fest. It's my turn to make cakes, and I'm trying out a new recipe for banana bread.*

Wilder: *Can I come too?*

Ziggy: *Me too. I need all the help I can get. And Silas, I'm assuming from what Frey said, is annoyed by something in their group chat as he's muttering and stomping.*

Frey: *You could do what I do when Booker is like that.*

Hollis: *Frey, no, I swear I'm running out of bleach the amount I'm using to rid my mind of everything you share.*

Frey: *Ziggy, you could share, too. That way I won't feel picked on by Hollis.*

Ziggy: *My snake…*

Hollis: *No. I mean it. I'll fire all of you.*

Isley: *I didn't do anything.*

Bowie: *Me either.*

Lennon: *Me too, why are we all getting tarred with the same brush?*

Bowie: *What tarred brush? Is there a shared one? I haven't seen it. Why is everyone talking in riddles tonight?*

Wilder: *It's all about someone thinking everything is the same, Bowie.*

Bowie: *Oh.*

Lennon: *Can someone bring more eggs, I'm gonna need them for you guys.*

Isley: *I got an extra dozen, I'll bring them. See you guys soon.*

Chapter Twenty-Two

Rue

Arriving on the ranch, Rue was riding the high of the last week spent with *his guys*. He wasn't giving too much thought to the emphasis he placed on that. Okay, he was, when it slid so effortlessly over his concerns about how living with Kendrick would work. Living with one man was hard enough—he'd never done that, but he suspected it was—so living with two should be very difficult. Yet somehow, it wasn't.

Kendrick was easy to be around, much the same as Monty. Rue found himself eager to get home—something else he'd noticed was how, after seven days, he thought of the house as home—at the end of the day. Whatever he'd anticipated, none of it matched his expectations. Rue worked hard not to think too hard on that. He wasn't always the easiest person to be around, finding peopling all day to be fucking hard work. Usually, he preferred to take himself off and be alone in the evening but he was realizing he didn't want to do that: shocker.

As he watched the two men striding towards him, filthy, exhausted and if he wasn't wrong, mightily pissed—Rue got the sense that his balloon was about to burst.

"What happened," he asked without preamble, nose wrinkling at the distinct smell of horseshit scenting the room.

Ethan took off his ball cap and slapped it against his palm. "The omegas. The cabins aren't gonna work for them. It seems they're too close to the other ranch hands. Last night, things came to a head."

"What's that supposed to mean? Explain that to me when things seemed to go okay, cause I was there when the omegas picked which cabins they wanted. How is that now an issue?" Rue glanced at the stoic Oakland. "You scouted out the area, did we miss something important?"

Ethan's ball cap slapped rhythmically against his thigh. "It's not the cabins themselves, but the alphas in the other cabins in the vicinity. *In the daylight*, it wasn't so much of an issue. One of the alphas brought home a playmate last night, and things got a little loud. The omegas freaked out big time. The quiet here makes any noise travel easily. They got spooked and thought—shit, who knows what they thought? What I do know is I spent half the night trying to find them and the other half reassuring them that none of my men would attack them. Which they don't really believe 'cause they don't fuckin' know the men well enough," Ethan grumbled in frustration.

"I didn't consider how much they've come to rely on my men to feel safe."

The weight of Oakland's confession pained Rue. "Then how do we fix it?"

On hearing the approach of someone else, Rue glanced and did a double take at the dirt covered man entering the room. There wasn't a part of Brier that wasn't covered in filth. His face bore streaks of something that looked like the shit stinking up Oakland and Ethan.

"What the hell happened to you?" Rue found himself amused, despite the situation. He'd never seen Brier looking so... out of sorts, and he wore his dejection like a jacket.

"Cace, he..." Brier blew out a breath, his nose wrinkling as he looked at his filthy hands. "Ventured in with horses, let's leave it at that."

"Is he okay now?" Cace was the jumpiest of the four that they'd brought to the ranch.

"Yep. He's sleeping upstairs next to Ivo. The four of them are all in the master bedroom. It was the only one with a bed big enough for them to share."

Rue nodded, his attention going back to Ethan. "Weren't you using the master suite? Is this going to be an issue, their staying in the house?"

Ethan shrugged nonchalantly, although the hat slapping never stopped. "Nah, I was already considering the main house as the best bet now, for everyone's sanity. The terrified crying frightened the fuck out of some of the ranch hands."

"Christ, what a clusterfuck!" Rue had only gotten Oakland's report on what happened during the chaos of the heat incident at the hotel. Ever since, things had been difficult for the four omegas.

"That about sums it up." Ethan put the ball cap back on, shielding his eyes. "Doesn't matter where I sleep. I have a suite of rooms up on the top floor, which is probably far enough away from the omegas, but close enough if we have a repeat of last night. As there is only me living in the house and it has a dozen bedrooms, Oakland and Brier can move from the cabins, too." Ethan turned to Oakland. "Will that work for you?"

"Yes. It contains them in a smaller space, something they're used to. I underestimated how something so normal for the ranch hands would impact the omegas, despite reassurances. The smooth transfer here, and the ease with which they appeared to like it here, should have had me on guard." Oakland's expression was grim.

"No one can understand fully what damage those fucking alphas did, so you can't shoulder this blame, Oakland. Dad still hasn't confirmed from what we've found in Amatus's records how long Cace, Ivo, Eric, and Otis remained imprisoned for. They aren't sayin' and pushin' isn't the answer. They've been through so much, it's only to be expected there'd be relapses. Maybe we should count ourselves lucky they had a week without issue."

"We knew it wasn't gonna be easy," Ethan muttered, staring at the doorway leading to the hallway. "They taught us a valuable lesson: don't make any fucking assumptions when things look to be going smoothly!"

"You got that right," Brier said wearily. "I need a shower and a hot meal."

Oakland scratched at his jaw. "You do that, and take a couple of hours to catch some shuteye. I'll watch over the omegas."

"You need to rest, too," Ethan pointed out, frowning. "You've not slept either. Brier, you'll find the beds ready for use down the end of the hallway on the second floor. Last three doors, pick whatever room you want. They all have bathrooms attached."

Brier's lips parted, then shut as Oakland growled, "I'm fine."

Rue shook his head, noticing how Brier became watchful of his boss. "Nope, you both can go and get some food and shuteye. I'll grab Monty from Silas's office, and we'll set up our laptops upstairs in the room next to the master suite and work from there for today. The omegas seem comfortable around me and Monty, so it shouldn't create an issue. They've also had a busy night, so I'd say they'll be out of it for a while. Take the opportunity while you can."

"It's my job—"

"To be rested enough to respond effectively." Rue held up his hand when he could see Oakland was going to argue with him. He had done plenty of ops in the army that involved a degree of sleep deprivation. Oakland had way more experience than Rue, but that didn't mean he was going to shut Rue down. They all needed to be on their A game. "This is not up for discussion. Be sensible, Oakland. Take the time to eat and rest. If I have a problem, I assure you I'll get Monty to come get you."

It wasn't until Oakland stomped wordlessly out of the room ten seconds later that Rue believed the other man listened to reason.

Brier walked to the door at a slower pace, halted and then looked back at them. "It's personal for Oakland. For all of us, after all these months... so don't be too hard on him when..."

"When what?" Rue questioned, frowning when Brier sighed heavily, his expression showing how conflicted he was.

The silence lengthened, and Rue thought Brier wasn't going to answer, but finally he muttered, "It's *personal*."

He was gone before Rue could ask what he meant, his emphasis on 'personal' clearly was supposed to convey some deeper meaning. He ran through what he recalled from the last week, but found nothing out of the ordinary to account for what Brier was referring to. Oakland had done his job. One he was exceptional at. Was it that? Did he somehow perceive the omegas' freak out as some kind of personal failure?

"What am I missing here?" Ethan asked, pulling Rue from his thoughts.

"Not a damn clue." He shrugged off the uneasiness in his gut that said there was more to all this, and focused on Ethan for now. "You sure you're alright with moving out of the master suite? Is me being in town an issue?" It had to be asked, as much as he didn't want to face the possibility the answer might be yes.

"We talked 'bout this when you arrived and nothing has really changed. Last night was unexpected, and your being here wouldn't have made any difference to how those men reacted. As for moving, I only went down to the second floor 'cause Silas insisted it was stupid for me to stay up in the attic when the house was empty." He chuckled, pushing the brim of his hat back to reveal his eyes. "I'll move my things back up there once the omegas go to get food." He glanced at his wristwatch, groaning. "I gotta head out, I'm already way behind."

"Shit, can't you take a couple of hours, too?"

Ethan's laughter held a wealth of 'you gotta be kidding me'. "Who's gonna run the ranch? You?"

Rue had enjoyed the ranch experience more than some of his brothers, but he could admit he had no clue where to start with the endless shit that seemed to need doing. "Yeah, sorry. Not sure that would work out so good for you."

"You got that right." Ethan wiped his eyes, grinning widely. "I'm a big boy."

Monty came into the room at such a pace his sneakers skidded on the wooden flooring, a scowl forming as he stared at Ethan wearing...

Was that a 'back the fuck off' look? The thought tickled Rue as Ethan continued eyeing Monty with speculation. Ethan already knew there was something going on between him and Monty, as well as Kendrick, he just didn't bring it up—thankfully.

"I can manage with no sleep, so it ain't no biggy. I'll come back later and check in." Ethan gave Monty a nod, striding out.

"Why the look?" Rue asked tongue in cheek, because Monty was too fucking darling.

Monty sniffed, his nose going in the air, not looking in the least contrite. "This is my normal look, I don't know what you mean."

Rue strolled over and hooked his fingers into the belt loops of Monty's jeans, tugging him into his body so he had to tilt his head back to look at Rue.

"Oh, you don't?" The pouty lips were too much to resist. He waited until Monty's lips parted before he took a kiss they both wanted. It was fast and dirty.

Releasing a breathless and flushed Monty, Rue walked off toward Silas's office whistling, counting in his head.

"Hey... we aren't finished, Mr," Monty aimed at him, the sound of his sneakers squeaking as he gave chase.

He swung around when Monty reached him and scooped him up in his arms, chuckling at how unprofessional he was being during working hours. His brothers would be shocked. Heck, he was shocked. But after the start of his working day, he needed some light-heartedness. "No, we aren't. I thought there wasn't a problem?"

"Ethan was flirting with you."

The chuckle turned into a belly laugh. "Ethan isn't my type." He kissed the pouting lips because he could, free of prying eyes. "You and Kendrick are more than enough for me to handle. Does that satisfy you?"

Monty claimed his mouth, lips devouring his in an ardent kiss that melted his legs. He wiggled out of Rue's arms and spun, heading to the office.

"It does now," he quipped.

Chapter Twenty-Three

Monty

Hearing movement and some frantic whispered words in the room next door, Monty glanced up from his laptop. Rue had gone to speak to Oakland and they'd left the house thirty minutes ago with Brier, leaving Monty alone with the omegas. Rue had said to call him when they woke up, but from what he could hear, he felt like they might not want to see an alpha just yet.

He placed his laptop down and, rubbing suddenly damp palms down his thighs, he walked into the hallway and tapped on the door. It was a jar, except Monty didn't step inside. He waited for an invitation. He hadn't heard all of what had happened when Rue had left him after calling his dad, and he'd concluded it wasn't good.

"Who is it?" Cace called out after some whispered conversation.

"It's Monty... can I come in?"

The door opened, and it took considerable effort not to react to the state of the men in the room and the smell of horse shit. They looked like they had a fight in the mud and shit, some faring better than others. Monty glanced at the bed Ivo, Otis and Eric were in and quickly decided the sheets needed putting in the trash, judging by the color of them. And if they smelled as bad as Cace, then most definitely.

Cace stood silently, wringing his hands.

"I wondered if you guys wanted to go get something to eat... you know, up at the bunkhouse?"

Cace looked at the others, indecision pouring off all of them.

"I was going, so y'all could come with me? Oh, and if you like, we could visit with Cass. He's got these most amazing chickens." He giggled in such a way to suggest he was sharing a big secret, trying to recall how far the men had ventured since they'd arrived on the ranch. "They all have names, and some wear these cute handmade outfits!"

Ivo came to the edge of the bed. "They do?" he exclaimed, signalling they'd yet to venture that far. It was a slow process, but Monty got why.

He nodded enthusiastically. "They do! Some even have tutus on."

"Really?" Eric asked sceptically.

"Totally, I'll show you."

More eagerly than Monty had hoped for, they got off the bed. Monty wondered about mentioning that they should shower first but in the end, he kept his mouth shut. They'd lived in awful squalor, so potentially they weren't bothered by a little horse shit. If they weren't, then Monty could suck it up.

Sitting at the end of the bed, they tugged on their sneakers. The quiet in the room was unnatural and a little unnerving. It had been the same any time Monty spent time with them.

"Can we go see the chickens first?" Eric gave him a hopeful half smile.

It was a total win in Monty's book, when the omega hadn't smiled in front of him before. "Yep. It might even be feeding time for them. They can get loud, but they are so cute." Monty kept up the litany as they left the house with him.

If he noticed how watchful they were of those going about their business, Monty didn't draw attention to it.

He could hear the chicks and Cassidy's laughter before the coops came into view.

"Wow!" Eric exclaimed and, for a moment, seemed to forget he was scared as he rushed to the fence, peering over.

Ivo and Otis were right behind him but Cace remained close to Monty. He was most definitely the more timid of the bunch.

"I promise they won't peck at you," Monty reassured, uncertain if that was Cace's issue as he hung back.

Cassidy glanced up from where he was crouched, and his gentle smile said he knew who the men were. "Hey y'all, I'm Cass. Have ya come to meet my girls?"

The girls in question rushed to the fence in the same way they had greeted Monty when he'd first met them. He held back a giggle at how Eric took a step back, putting his hands behind his back.

Cassidy rose, his gaze on where he walked so as not to tread on any of the Seramas chicks, Monty figured. They were so small, no bigger than the size of a Coke can. He opened the gate.

"Now, girls, let's show a bit of decorum." He smiled widely at the men as they crept a little closer.

"Could you do an introduction of your girls, Cass? This is Ivo, Cace, Otis and Eric." Monty pointed each man out.

Cassidy scratched his chin, looking with affection at the chicks that Monty knew were his babies.

Having not seen Cassidy, spending most of his time cooped up in the house working, Monty had to work hard at not staring at the obvious bulge at Cassidy's waistline that hadn't been there a month ago. Was he pregnant?

"I have several breeds, and the Seramas—they're the smallest and cutest, right? They're like the teacup puppies of the chicken world. Sweet and lovable with curly feathers, aren't you girls?" He picked up the closet chick, and it squawked in answer. Monty had witnessed the Cassidy effect.

The others all giggled, and Monty's smile grew wider at how relaxed they became. They'd even gotten closer, including Cace.

"As you can see, they come in a wild assortment of colors, feather patterns, and feather types. They also make great pets because of their loveable nature."

"Why do you dress them up?" Eric asked, his eyes on Lynda, who stalked majestically towards them in a bright pink and red striped knitted sweater.

Cassidy answered in a stage whisper, "The La Fleche breed, like Lynda and her sisters, looks like Satan had a hand in creating them." He chuckled, nodding at the chicken he was describing. "See the jet-black feathers and fleshy little devil horns? I don't want her to have a complex about how she looks."

There were nods, and Eric, who was displaying the most interest, crouched down next to Lynda, rubbing his fingers together as if resisting the urge to reach out and touch. Lynda appeared to tolerate Eric's closeness more than she had ever done with Monty and his friends. Cassidy had explained Lynda's breed had a tendency to be more aloof around people, and, unlike the other breeds, they didn't follow anyone. Lynda knew who the boss was, and Cassidy had rightly pointed out it wasn't him.

Cassidy stroked a finger over the little devil horns. "Lynda, say hello to Eric."

Lynda needed no more prompting and stalked to Eric, pressing her beak against his fingers.

"Well look at that. She ain't never done that before." The surprise was genuine as Cassidy grinned at Eric. "She likes you."

Eric went pink under the dirt streaking his face. "She does?"

As if to prove it, Lynda flapped her wings to get up and perch on the top of one of Eric's knees.

The smile was heartbreaking with how much joy shone from Eric's eyes as he looked at the others.

"I've made a friend," he said softly, the excitement un-missable in the declaration.

"You have," Monty murmured, blinking away tears.

"I think I see the one with the tutu on?" Ivo murmured to Otis.

"That one's got a blue sweater on," Cace whispered. "Oh, and that one is wearing yellow."

"Where do you get their sweaters and tutus from?" Eric asked, running a finger over Lynda's feathers.

Cassidy grinned, and so did Monty, knowing what Cassidy's response was going to be.

"I make them. I love to knit, and I'm not bad with a needle and thread." He shrugged causally, and Monty noticed how much the men were hanging off his every word. Was he looking to engage the men? It was a smart move, even if he wasn't. "My girls like to look pretty."

"I can sew. Maybe... I could make something for your girls? For Lynda?" Eric offered shyly.

Monty understood what a huge thing this was and what an understatement of his skills. Eric, like the others, had never ending talent with needle and thread. It was why Rue and his brothers had gone to the factory in Drinkwater in the first place. Their work was exceptional.

But the offer to do something that had brought nothing but pain into their lives was huge.

The noise around them increased, almost like the gathering chicks were answering Eric, demanding he do something for them, too.

"Now come on, girls. Is that any way to behave?" The squawking and wing flapping came down a notch at Cassidy's reprimand, drawing more laughter from the men.

After the previous night, Monty took the visit with Cassidy as a high point of the day, and it gave him hope. His gaze roamed beyond the pastures to the vast green, tree topped mountains. Monty hadn't needed to consider his answer about coming back, and if he was truthful, it wasn't all to do with Rue and Kendrick.

Just maybe the omegas would find the peace they were looking for on the ranch, because if they were going to find it anywhere, it would be there.

Chapter Twenty-Four

Kendrick

Kendrick moved around the kitchen with practiced ease, stirring pots and setting the table for supper. Rue had messaged to say they were on their way home, as he'd done every day since they arrived. However, Monty had also messaged earlier in the day, giving Kendrick a heads-up that things hadn't gone well overnight for the omegas. With no real details, Kendrick had imagined the worst and with it came a sinking feeling deep in the pit of his stomach at what that meant for him, for them.

They hadn't talked about 'what if's' relating to problems if the omegas struggled with the transition. Kendrick kicked himself for not discussing it with how it had ruined his day, plaguing him with questions and doubts.

The looming question of whether Rue and Monty would need to move up to the ranch was the one that gave him the biggest headache. It nagged along with his thoughts all day. When he'd run out of things to do to keep his mind off the subject—which he'd failed miserably at—he had given in and gone online to get the full story on the omegas and the situation in Drinkwater.

It sickened him, and it gave him a different perspective on Rue's family. He'd understood in principle that they'd done a good thing when Rue had mentioned it before, but hadn't gotten the enormity of it. Now he understood what they'd done and spent to free those men from purgatory. It could have been nothing less than that, if he believed all that he'd read. Those Drinkwater alphas were monsters. Superior fuckwits who believed divergents were worthless throwaways.

Bile burned the back of his throat, and he had to make a concerted effort to swallow.

When he'd fallen down the rabbit hole, Kendrick had also done a little more research on Derick and Lane Starling. He'd met them once before, when they'd visited Bayfield and came into the bar. From what he could recall Trey mentioning at the time, they had stayed at Vaughn winery, not Silas's ranch, up in the mountains. Why was that? Was the winery's visitor accommodation better than the ranch?

He'd never bothered to take a trip to the winery, even when Trey had gotten an invite. The owners of the winery were three brothers, Thorn, Dacian, and Calvert. They all

visited the bar, but Thorn was the one who frequent-
ed it the most. There was just something off about
the brothers that Kendrick couldn't pinpoint. His bear
wasn't able to determine what species they were, which
was strange in itself because he didn't think they were
divergent.

Determining the species of a divergent was much
harder than a shifter. And even though Thorn liked
to hook-up with huge alphas, nothing about the man
suggested he wasn't an alpha too. He'd once hit on
Kendrick and as attractive as Thorn was, Kendrick had
never been interested in a hookup.

At the approach of a car turning into the drive, he
turned down the pots bubbling on the stove, his pulse
skipping a beat. He rubbed his hands down the cloth
tucked into his front pocket of his jeans and walked to
the front door, a grin tugging at his mouth. He leaned
against the frame watching Rue and Monty gather their
things from the back seat, a habit that he'd picked up
the last few days. If he was acting like the little woman,
he didn't care.

"Hey y'all."

Monty looked like a bright ray of sunshine, coming
quickly up the path, lips puckered for a kiss which
Kendrick was more than happy to give him. It was such
a natural move, it was as if they'd been doing this for
years instead of days.

Monty skipped past him and into the house. Kendrick heard him drop his laptop bag on the cabinet sat at the bottom of the stairs. However, he didn't take his eyes off Rue, watching for signs of what might be coming. He was much harder to get a read from, but his wide shoulders were rigid and his moves seemed stilted as he locked the car.

When he came up the path, his attention was on the ground and not Kendrick.

Kendrick waited until Rue reached him, then blocked his way into the house. One brow quirked up before a furrow appeared between them. Kendrick cupped stubbly cheeks and forced Rue to look at him as he leaned in slowly to brush their mouths together in a light kiss.

Paying attention, he witnessed the moment Rue relaxed, swaying forward, adding more pressure and seeking a deeper kiss. Kendrick kept it light, moving until his mouth was at the corner of Rue's and nibbled gently.

"Hey, honey, I hope you're hungry." He witnessed a stain of red appear over Rue's slashing cheekbones, his nostrils flaring and pupils dilating. Witnessing the clear flush of arousal, Kendrick added, "For dinner."

A chuckle rumbled out at Rue's look of disappointment. Kendrick ran a finger down his nose, tapping the end. "Did you want something else?"

"You," Rue rasped sexily.

The openness and ease of the admission punched Kendrick in the chest. It was worse than the time he'd stepped in between Cranny and Zippy, taking the punch the lion shifter had thrown at Zippy in fury, which would have snapped the omega in two.

"You've got me," he confessed. And he didn't just mean for sex. He wanted Rue to share whatever burdened him. Kendrick wanted everything and that was fucking scary when he wasn't quite convinced Rue wanted the same. The man held so much back—except when he was naked.

He does want the same. His bear was adamant on that score.

Until he says it aloud, you don't know that, he argued back.

"Something's bubbling over," Monty called from inside, stopping any argument happening between him and his animal side.

"Crap." Kendrick kissed Rue, unable to resist the undecided pout that Rue would most definitely deny graced his mouth.

Swinging around to dart back into the house, Kendrick heard Rue mutter, "Giving me another kiss wouldn't have hurt the food."

In the kitchen, amused at grumpy Rue, Kendrick found Monty eyeing the pots, his hands hovering over the knobs on the stove.

"I got it," he murmured, a smidge pissed because he wanted to have everything perfect. These evenings together were flying by and in another week, he'd not be home in the evenings to do this for his men.

"It smells like a little bit of heaven in here. Is that apple pie I smell?" Monty groaned, bending to investigate the oven, his jacket now slung over one of the kitchen chairs like usual.

"It is." Kendrick was fully aware of Monty's sweet tooth. "It's my grandmother's recipe." He met Rue's bemused stare as he strode in, a flush of embarrassment working its way up the collar of his T-shirt at how domesticated he was being when Rue eyed the kitchen and pretty table setting.

"Do you like apple pie?" he asked, working to deflect from the obvious care he took to please both men.

Rue removed his suit jacket and slung it over the back of the same chair Monty's was on. Kendrick noted he had left his laptop bag somewhere in the hallway. Rue went for his tie next, appearing to consider his answer.

"Popi makes a mean apple pie, so I'd say your grandmother's recipe has a lot to live up to."

"Rue's not wrong. Lane is an expert cook," Monty said through giggles. "I've tasted a lot of his baking, it really will be hard to beat his pie."

"I reckon I'll be able to give Lane a run for his money," Kendrick boasted, hoping he wasn't going to make a fool of himself.

Pausing in pulling out a seat, Rue's brows arched in a look of challenge. "That's fightin' talk."

"You bet your glorious ass it is."

Monty's laughter continued as he went to the refrigerator. The ease with which Monty pulled out two beers and an open bottle of Vaughn wine from last evening gave Kendrick's heart yet another solid bump.

"Then what about having dessert first?" Monty fluttered his eyelashes, flashing a pleading look that made Kendrick chuckle as he swung past him on the way to the kitchen table.

"Good try."

An exaggerated sigh was Monty's reply, and Rue's lips twitched as he took the glass of wine Monty poured and offered.

It was all so... homely.

Isn't it cool!

He could find no fault with his bear's assessment. *Yes, it is.*

He drained the vegetables, nodding his thanks to Monty, who placed a beer on the counter by his elbow. Pot roast out of the oven, he placed it on the table. Both men had said they weren't fussy when Kendrick had asked initially, but he still checked every time he served a meal. "Who wants green beans with their pot roast and cheesy mash?"

"I think I've died and gone to heaven." Monty's answer had both men chuckling when it came with a rather dramatic sigh of pleasure.

Kendrick mashed the potatoes with cheese and butter, hiding the pot of Dijon mustard so his men wouldn't see his secret ingredient just yet. Once done, he plated generously and served both men. Back was Rue's bemused expression as Kendrick placed his beer down, taking the chair that had him sitting between both men. They had established their places at the table the first night.

The silence was broken with groans of appreciation as everyone tucked into the food. A companionable quiet reigned yet the nagging thought persisted about what Monty's text meant for the three of them.

He reached for his beer, took a sip and glanced at Rue. "Monty mentioned something happened last night at the ranch. Is everything okay?"

Rue's attention skipped from Kendrick to Monty, who he aimed a look of pure frustration at. It was hard to say if it was from Monty sharing something with Kendrick or connected to whatever had gone down.

When Rue returned his attention to his meal, he shrugged as if that was his answer. A growing ball of anxiety messed with Kendrick's appetite.

Monty tilted his head, not appearing concerned then he mouthed at Kendrick, "*Go on.*"

"You can talk to me. I'm not gonna share outside of these walls what we talk about. I get the need for privacy." Kendrick did gossip, just never about anything important.

There was a long pause, long enough that Kendrick thought he was going to have to come up with a new tactic, but eventually Rue responded.

"It was a shit show, quite literally," he said dejectedly.

"What does that mean for you?" asked Kendrick, keeping the '*for us*' to himself. His fingers clasped the cutlery he'd picked back up tighter when he couldn't get a read off Rue.

"Are you asking about this"—Rue pointed his fork between them all, frowning— "because it could mean we're gonna move into the ranch?"

Kendrick came to the conclusion that he was way easier to read than Rue, who had understood his concern straight away. Unsure if he would be able to keep the fear from his voice, Kendrick simply nodded in reply.

"I did suggest it to Ethan when he explained what happened last night—" Regret laced Rue's voice as he spoke, except he was quickly cut off.

"You did?" asked Monty, frowning.

"Yes." Rue sighed, placing his knife down and pinching the bridge of his nose.

"And what did you decide?" Kendrick asked hesitantly. He knew that it was the right thing for Rue and Monty to do as they were in Bayfield because of the omegas, but that didn't stop him from hating it. He wanted to find some middle ground with Rue so he could feel free to talk openly about what was going on for him. But he also wished he'd kept his mouth shut when he could have lived without the possibility that what they had going was ending before it began.

Monty forked more green beans aggressively, chewing them like they'd offended him. His attention remained on Rue, waiting the same as Kendrick for him to answer.

"Ethan believes it would have made no difference me being in the house, other than having been able to help with the search—"

"Okay, you've lost me. Search?"

Rue groaned and ran through the events of the previous night. Kendrick then got the reference about the shit. Two of them had buried themselves in manure to prevent scent tracking. One had hidden with the horses, and the fourth omega had gone in with the pigs.

"It took considerable effort to coax them into the ranch house, which is where they'll now be living. They trust Oakland and Brier so they'll be the only two alphas sleeping near them. Ethan has moved back up into his suite of rooms on the third floor of the house for the time being. I called Dad and after a lengthy discussion, everyone thinks another alpha in the house would be a bad thing."

All of it made sense. What Kendrick couldn't gauge was why Rue appeared upset by this. Wasn't he happy to stay here? The possibility made him anxious. It was unnerving and as much as he wanted to take a mental step back, he couldn't with Rue's obvious distress.

"I admit I'm glad not to have to leave," he confessed, sounding pained, stealing Kendrick's breath. "Only the guilt in feeling relief, when it was a miscalculation on our part? Fuck, what do I do with that? They have suffered so much. This was supposed to help, not make things worse. Should we have brought them? Was I so focused on coming back for you that I didn't see the pitfalls?" Food forgotten, fork on his plate, he ran agitated hands through his hair. Dipping his head between his shoulders, he did his best to avoid eye contact.

At Monty's sound of distress, Kendrick placed his own cutlery on his nearly empty plate, reaching to give Monty's hand a reassuring squeeze. One he wasn't feeling, because Rue's confession about wanting to be here for him was a double-edged sword. Guilt cut deep into Rue—fuck, all of them.

Kendrick rose and crouched by Rue's side. He reached out and took hold of his hands, tugging them from his hair.

"Look at me, please." Kendrick's knees hit the floor with a thud, thrown off balance by the abject misery Rue was unable to hide from his eyes as their gazes clashed.

Monty jumped up and skirted around the table to wrap an arm around Rue's shoulders as far as he could manage, placing a hand on Kendrick's neck to connect the three of them. The bond—the glue—between them. Kendrick wasn't sure if Rue even noticed that was what Monty was to their throuple.

He blew a kiss at Monty and got a sniff as he furiously blinked glistening eyes. "I don't think anyone can truly understand what those men went through." He made sure Rue was his only focus as he continued. "But, something tells me that you might have some idea."

The eye widening and paling cheeks were answer enough.

"Honey, I'm not asking you to spill your secrets right now, unless you want to. Just understand that carrying guilt won't change things. It can eat at the heart of a person. What you and your family did and continue to do, allows those men to be free. Don't ever forget that. They'll find their way because you've given them a chance to have a different path. A safe path, even though it might take time for them to realize." Entwining their fingers, he brought a hand to his lips and brushed a kiss over the knuckles. "Make that your focus. Let that be your guide, not the guilt."

A gusty breath hit his face as Rue fought an internal battle. Kendrick sucked in a lungful of air, held it and counted to five before releasing it, waiting for Rue to see what he was offering. "I'll share something with you,"—he glanced at Monty, wearing a sheepish grin—"a selfish part of me is also relieved you both don't need to leave my home. When Monty messaged, it was my biggest fear, losing this."

"I'm selfish too," added Monty, back to sniffling. "And I agree with Kendrick. You didn't see the omegas with Cass today, Rue. They might carry the burden of life's injustices on their backs, but they wanna be free. The ranch, I can see now, will—when they are ready—give them just that!"

Monty placed a kiss on top of Rue's head and moved back to take his seat. It took two attempts before the smile stuck. "I think it's time to check out Kendrick's apple pie, see if he over egged the pudding."

Kendrick went with a mock outraged look when Rue released another gusty breath, a myriad of emotions there to see.

"Pie sounds good," was his quiet reply. It didn't look like that was what Rue was going to say initially.

Kendrick considered maybe he was wrong and shut away the disappointment. He could be patient; these men were worth it.

"I'll have you eat those words!" he stated emphatically, all teeth and sass.

When he stood up, he did the same as Monty and kissed Rue's head, inhaling his warm scent. Stepping back was hard, except he knew they needed to keep it light for the time being, so he went over to the oven where the pie was warming.

"I'd rather eat..." Monty's pause was all for effect. "Pie."

Rue chuckled, as did Kendrick, shaking his head but loving Monty's attempt to lighten the mood. "Honey, I'll prove you wrong on that score later, too. Now ice cream, cream, or crème anglaise?"

Rue stacked their dinner plates, placing them off to the side. "Cream is my favorite." He smacked his lips together for effect, making Monty groan and slip a hand under the table.

Using an oven cloth, Kendrick pulled out the pie and placed it in the middle of the table. Brown and glistening with the encrusted sugar, cinnamon and spiced apples scented the air. He met Rue's gaze over the pie and gave him a salacious wink.

"Cream it is."

Chapter Twenty-Five

Derick

"We need to go."

Derick eyed Lane. The set of his jaw said he wasn't going to be dissuaded of the notion. "My love, let's give Rue the chance to figure this out on his own."

He hadn't even finished speaking before Lane was shaking his head. "Derick, don't you think we've given him enough time to figure himself out? To understand that he's ours. We love him unconditionally and that he can be loved in that way, not just by us but by others too?" Lane stamped his foot in full rant mode. "He's holding on to the past in such an unhealthy way. Unless he unburdens himself, he's never going to be able to love with his whole heart."

Derick agreed with his husband. He did. Because Derick carried some of the guilt of that. He'd taken a misstep somewhere along the way. The result was Rue's lack of belief that he deserved happiness. "Yes, love."

Derick had come to that conclusion when Rue had rung to talk through what had happened with the omegas. When Rue had suggested he move into the ranch house, it hadn't taken long to notice his reluctance. It had taken another ten minutes before Rue confessed to staying in Bayfield, at Kendrick's home. Derick had listened and heard the anguish his son hadn't hidden for both the omegas and for having to return to the ranch. Clearly, he didn't want to, but felt that his commitment to his job required it.

"Don't yes love me in that tone." Lane flounced to the walk-in closet, and Derick groaned under his breath at hearing Lane rummaging around in there.

Where Derick had gone wrong was telling Lane about the conversation with Rue. What Derick hadn't expected—though why, he wasn't sure—was Lane's sudden need for an impromptu trip to Bayfield to meet and vet Kendrick.

They had met him once before. Derick's impression had been a flirty guy who didn't take life too seriously. Had he said that aloud? Of course he had, and now Lane was on a mission to find out if Kendrick was just out for a good time when Rue was more invested than Derick suspected he'd ever admit to. Again, had he said that to his husband?

He sighed at his own stupidity when he couldn't decide if he had done this because he wanted to check in on Rue.

Ever since Lane had discovered that Rue was interested in a throuple relationship, he wanted to show that he supported that. He seemed desperate to demonstrate that nothing would change how he felt for Rue, but Lane's protective instincts were strong. Derick loved his husband for it, but it was also frustrating when Lane got it into his head that he needed to fix whatever problem any of their sons had. Lane's idea of fixing things right now was to head to the ranch and spy on their youngest son's boyfriend—or whatever Kendrick was.

And it's not what you want to do?

His wolf half wasn't wrong, and he went into the walk-in closet after his husband, resigned to the fact he might have to manipulate the situation to his favor. "We'll stay at Vaughn's winery in one of their cottages. It's our wedding anniversary next week—"

Lane grinned. "You old romantic," he interjected, stopping what he was doing to sway sexily towards Derick, his expression making Derick's pulse quicken.

"No, we have Emmy tonight." He held up his hands only to find them full of his husband's ass in the next moment when he expertly leapt at him.

"Then you'll need to be quick." Lane nipped at his mouth, a gleam of lust directed at Derick. "Won't you?"

Chapter Twenty-Six

Alphaholes

Silas: *Rue, has something happened that you haven't mentioned?*

Rue: *Why???*

Silas: *Dad and Popi are heading your way. Something about their anniversary, so they are planning a trip.*

Booker: *Shit. They never said a word to me! When are they leaving? I'm gonna need someone to have Emmy. Frey's po-*

tentially gonna have a heat in the next week or two.

Silas: *Exactly, they never mentioned it when I went to dinner with Ziggy the day before yesterday. So, I'm thinking something is up.*

Laken: *That's a 'you' problem, Booker.*

Kodi: *No, it's a fucking us problem. Remember the last time!*

Laken: *How can any of us forget? Oh yeah, Tay escaped last time. Now Silas doesn't have to deal, living at Ziggy's. What I don't get is why we all must stay home and put up with this shit?*

Jupiter: *It's our burden in life to carry the weight of Booker's big ass.*

Booker: *How many times did you say you'd love a bigger ass as a teenager? You forget how good a memory I have, Jup.*

Kodi: *Fuck, remember when he cried when the company brought out the new range of slouch pants and they wouldn't stay up over Jup's ass.*

Taylin: *I remember! Didn't poor Bessie go find a belt to stop being traumatized by Jup's underwear?*

Booker: *Fuck, I forgot that part of it.*

Jupiter: *As I was the best bet for having Emmy, you can swivel, dickweed!*

Booker: *You love Emmy Jup, so you'll only be denying yourself...*

Kari: *Next week is the Milan fashion show, Jup. You won't be home, or had you forgotten? Though how is beyond me after all the damn prep.*

Jupiter: *Nope, not forgotten, just giving Booker a false sense of hope for being an asshole.*

Dad: *Why is it y'all seem to forget I can read? Silas, it was a surprise for Popi, hence why I never mentioned it. It's our fortieth wedding anniversary, and he loves staying at the vineyard. Booker, Bessie is more than happy to assist with Emmy. I would have discussed this with you when you got home this evening.*

Silas: *Oh.*

Booker: *Right.*

Rue: *You aren't planning to come to the ranch then, Dad?*

Dad: *Popi will of course want to come and see you.*

Rue: *Of course.*

Chapter Twenty-Seven

Rue

Rue dropped his head to allow the hot water to pound the back of his neck, easing some of the tension he'd pretended wasn't there after reading the Alpha-hole chat. He hadn't mentioned anything to Kendrick or Monty about the planned 'surprise' visit of his parents'. He should have known better than to talk to Dad about moving back into the ranch house.

Had he let slip more than he'd intended? Yes. And now he was paying the price for that. He was sure Dad would have mentioned a trip to the Vaughn winery during their last conversation. He hadn't, and no matter what he'd said in the chat, Rue couldn't see any reason Dad wouldn't have told him about the visit. It was easy to come to the conclusion that the trip was booked after their conversation. Which meant Dad had to have mentioned something to Popi. Didn't it?

Rue had been going around in circles all day trying to figure it out. And with that came the panic because Popi would want to come to the place Rue was staying at. There was no doubt this was going to open up a whole can of worms. He wasn't prepared for it. Fuck, he wasn't sure he ever would be when he was having a relationship—and it was a relationship—with two men. All the hallmarks were there. They shared a damn house together. *Did everything together*. Even with Kendrick returning to work the next day, there was no way to avoid it. They couldn't play pretend, when he suspected Kendrick and Monty would be hurt by a suggestion to hide their relationship in front of the two people that mattered the most to Rue.

Rue released a whimpering groan of despair.

"Everythin' okay in there?" Kendrick's voice could just be heard over the water.

Rue couldn't tell if he heard concern, and he was too chickenshit to look out the glass wall. He'd come straight up for a shower when he got home to avoid this very conversation.

"Mostly," he hedged, not wanting to lie, but needing some more time to figure out what the heck to do.

All day, that's all I'm saying.

I don't need your input. Rue didn't need his animal side getting in on the act, and closing himself off to prevent this kind of conversation hadn't really worked. His animal side had nagged.

Giving my opinion is not nagging.

You keep believin' that!

The blast of cool air against his wet skin got him swallowing back the desire to be left alone. A large, naked body brushed against his, and he bit back a moan and the urge to tilt his ass as Kendrick's arousal touched the back of his thigh.

Sex right now won't solve anything.

Say's who?

"Talk to me," Kendrick murmured, his lips gently touching the pulse pounding at the junction of his neck and shoulder.

Such a simple touch, yet Rue felt the weight of it. Kendrick had a knack of making him feel... safe. With it came the need to talk, off-load, that was strong enough Rue found himself unable to hold back. "Dad and Popi are coming to visit."

Rue noted just the barest hint of hesitation before the lips nibbling on the cord of his neck leading to his ear continued, causing a rush of blood to his head.

"Is this a problem... for us?"

This right here was why Rue respected Kendrick. He never shied away from tough subjects. In the past two weeks, Rue had come to appreciate Kendrick's bluntness. It prevented barriers being built through miscommunication. Monty was very similar to Kendrick in his approach, and Rue had to question why he found it attractive in both men when he wasn't like that. When talking was so difficult for him, why would they want someone like him?

Stunted?

Hiding?

"Why do you want someone like me?" he blurted out in frustration at his own lack, his gaze fixed on the tiles in front of him, tension holding him still.

"Strong, beautiful, caring, passionate... loving. Why wouldn't I want someone like that?"

Rue swung around, chest heaving at the raw honesty, water flicking everywhere as he kept some distance between them. The shower stall was easily big enough for three. Just then, he needed space. He desperately wanted to believe Kendrick. To let the man carry his burden, if only for a moment. Only he couldn't.

Their gazes held, and Rue searched for answers. The frightened child he'd been sat in the center of him, forcing him back from the cliff edge he dangled on when Kendrick showed him his generous heart once more.

Would Kendrick still feel compassion towards him when he knew he'd done nothing to protect his family from being slaughtered? When he was the sole reason they'd lost their lives?

Rue didn't think so. He believed that if he told anyone, then the world as he knew it would disappear. Popi and

Dad would disown him. They were good people. The best. Rue had worked hard to match their goodness, he had. Except, a part of him remained sure that the secret he carried would destroy everything.

Kendrick took hold of his jaw in a firm grip, his brows tugging together. "What is going on in your head? I can see your pain. Let me understand, please, so I can help. I want to help."

A violent shudder ran through him at Kendrick's anguish. "I-I... It's... fuck, I don't know how to do this."

Kendrick kissed him softly. The merest touch of lips that held such hope. "I do. Monty does. Let us show you."

"Why?" he questioned in pain, his eyes aching as they blurred. "Why, when I'm not worth it?"

"You are."

"You don't know what I did," he whispered brokenly, his heart squeezed hard enough by the guilt, he couldn't catch his breath. His eyelids dipped to hide his shame.

"Look at me, Rue." The commanding voice was the same one he used in the bedroom, and Rue obeyed. "Tell me what's hurting you."

Softer, yet no less commanding. Rue released a sharp exhale, and words tumbled out of his mouth like a shaken bottle of soda. The words spewed out of him.

"I got my parents and brother killed." He tasted salt on his lips, only then realizing he was crying. "Wade was five, defenceless, and I did nothing! You hear me? I did nothing to prevent it. It's all my fault. My existence caused the sweetest boy to be murdered, and I did nothing."

The words bounced off the tiles as he bellowed at the grief tearing him apart. Kendrick wrapped his enormous arms around him, surrounding him in his warmth. Rue fought to escape, mewling like a broken child.

"I got you. I got you..." On and on Kendrick repeated the words, his arms never letting go, squeezing and forcing him to still. The fight drained from him, and he collapsed against Kendrick, shaking violently, each gut-wrenching sob that tore from his throat purging the pain trapped inside.

"What on earth..." Monty's voice faded away, and Rue didn't have the strength to determine if it was him crying or possibly Kendrick's expression that stopped Monty speaking.

"Can you grab a couple of the bath sheets for me?"

The shower shut off, and the steam cleared with the door open. Kendrick murmured softly to him, but Rue heard nothing above the blood rushing in his head at having opened a valve, releasing all the pressure. Groggy and with a woolly head, his mind shut down and, much like a child, he let himself be guided, too hollowed out to do more.

Moving sluggishly, he barely registered the fluffy cotton draped over his shoulders. The scent of freshly laundered towels came as both men dried him where he stood, the tears continuing to drip off his cheeks and chin.

He closed his eyes so they couldn't see his shame as he perched on the end of the bed, directed by Kendrick.

"No, Rue. Don't shut us out, please." Gentle hands touched his face, stroking away the tears as he blinked blurry eyes at Kendrick, bent at the knee. "If you do that, you're telling us you don't want what we're building here. Is that the case? If so, this stops now because my heart is already invested. Do you understand?" The tremor in Kendrick's voice made it very clear just how serious he was.

Rue dashed the back of his hand across his eyes, regrouping impossible with how exposed he felt. "I've n-never s-shared my s-secret with *a-anyone*."

If that didn't reveal how serious Rue was about these two men, nothing would.

"Anyone?" gasped Kendrick.

"Not even Dad or Popi," he managed without stuttering, though barely more than a whisper.

"Fuck." Rue wasn't sure what he read in Kendrick's expression before his mouth became captured in the sweetest of kisses. Was he somehow being rewarded for telling the truth? That couldn't be right. Had Kendrick misunderstood what he was confessing?

The mattress dipped behind him and Monty shuffled until he was plastered to Rue's back, clinging on like he was getting a piggyback ride.

"Can you tell me what's wrong, too?" Monty sounded small, something he'd never been before.

"Rue, have you eaten today?"

He shook his head, too exhausted to do more. The thought of food was too unappealing.

"I'll make us subs, and we'll eat them in bed."

Rue didn't have enough energy to argue. He allowed himself to be lifted up the bed until he was nestled in the vast mountain of pillows Kendrick's bear had a soft spot for.

"Monty, you climb up and snuggle while I grab everything."

Monty didn't need to be asked twice, and he quickly tugged off his clothes, throwing them haphazardly in all directions before clambering over the covers. He didn't stop until he was laid across Rue like a blanket.

Monty rested his cheek against Rue's chest, right over his heart. Fingers ran soothingly up his chest and down to his waist repeatedly, lulling Rue into drifting on the edges of sleep. The darkness was a welcome shield from what would come next.

Chapter Twenty-Eight

Monty

When he'd run upstairs at the sound of anguished, bellowed cries, he'd nearly pissed his pants in fright. He'd never heard such pain-filled cries. One look at Kendrick's devastated expression and Monty couldn't get his mouth to work to ask what the hell had happened.

Rue had been off since that morning, looking preoccupied. He knew it wasn't work as they'd been through the long list of things he'd been tasked with and they were all under control. When they'd left the house that morning, everything was the same as usual.

So Monty's mind raced with a thousand and one possibilities to what would have Rue looking broken. Unhinged. His eyes were those of a victim. Fuck, they were so much like the omegas they'd brought to the ranch, it was terrifying. What had set him off? What had he said to Kendrick?

He snuggled into Rue, giving comfort but also seeking it when he was scared about what it all meant. He used his fingertips, sliding down Rue's side, feeling his breathing even out.

He kept quiet, despite how many questions were darting around his brain. He'd understood the warning look from Kendrick, even when he didn't get the reason for it. Monty could hear the slow steady beat of Rue's heart while also listening to Kendrick move around in the kitchen below. Both sounds helped to keep him from unravelling.

He must have drifted off to sleep with Rue when a light touch to his shoulder brought his groggy gaze to Kendrick's.

"How long did I sleep for?" he murmured softly, aware the man beneath him was sleeping.

"About an hour. You both looked so peaceful, I thought I'd leave you for a bit."

Rue stirred, and a warm hand slid over Monty's bare backside. "Sorry," he mumbled sleepily.

"It's cool," Monty answered, slipping sideways, noting the velvet throw Kendrick must have covered them with as he nestled into Rue's side, tucking the throw over his ass.

Rue's body relaxed against him, yet still there was something about the stillness that was... watchful. Almost as if he were waiting for an attack.

Kendrick grabbed a laden tray off the dresser drawers and came back to the bed to sit at Rue's side. He had slipped on a pair of shorts at some point. He stretched out his legs and placed the lap tray down onto his thighs. "Meatball subs. Hope that's okay?"

At their nods, Kendrick handed over the laden plates. Monty could see the tension around Kendrick's eyes, but his expression didn't reveal any of what was going on in his head, leaving Monty in the dark.

They ate in silence, the food delicious despite it no longer being warm. They shared a can of soda, and that was enough to suggest to Monty, whatever conversation they would have, Kendrick wanted them all clear-headed.

Plates cleared and the tray placed on the floor, Monty felt the tension in Rue's muscles increase.

One for always facing the hard stuff head on, Monty inhaled the familiar scent of the men who meant more to him than he'd ever have thought possible. "Can someone tell me what happened in the shower?"

Monty heard the air whistle through Rue's teeth and witnessed his whole body stiffen. He gave Kendrick a pleading look, unsure what he was asking for when he was flying blind.

"Rue, do you think you can explain to Monty and me what happened to you as a child?"

Rue wasn't a fidgeter, so Monty's nerves stretched to screaming point at how Rue plucked at the velvet throw, his gaze transfixed on the seam like it was the most fascinating thing in the world. He watched as the man seemed to cave in on himself—shrink.

Monty chewed the inside of his cheek to stop himself from prompting Rue when it was evident he was finding this situation difficult. Monty's chest hurt. The struggle to take a breath was real.

Kendrick shook his head when Monty gave in fifteen seconds later, his lips parting to speak. He closed them and sucked his lower lip in between his teeth, clamping down on that sucker to do as Kendrick wanted—give Rue the time he needed.

Seconds felt like hours as the silence continued, and Rue never once looked at either man, making the sub he'd eaten plunge unpleasantly around his guts.

About to demand somebody say something with how his mouth watered with the desire to vomit, Rue spoke.

"When I was about ten, my parents, who were divergent, got asked to join a crash. They were so happy that they didn't question why a crash without divergents would suddenly accept them. Then, not long after Mom got pregnant, the crash was super excited until my brother was born."

His actual parents, he's talking about his actual parents. A brother? He had a brother before...

Kendrick made a noise in the back of his throat that was more wounded animal than human and effortlessly lifted

Rue onto his lap so that his back pressed into his chest, wrapping an arm around his middle. He spread his legs to allow Rue's to sit between his thighs. Then Kendrick tugged Monty to their sides.

It wasn't rightly comfortable, but Monty didn't move. He nestled closer, terror growing as Rue's breathing became labored.

"I didn't know at the time but there was a blood test being developed to identify divergent children. I'm sure Mom and Dad would never have agreed to them testing Wade if they had known."

Wade. Tears burned his nose as they slipped down his cheeks when his mind skipped to what was coming, without his permission. *He had a brother called Wade... before.*

If Rue heard his hiccupped sob, he saw no signs of it as he continued to speak stiltedly, stopping and starting.

"They wanted me... wanted to breed me with other crash members. Their numbers were failing due to infertility. They weren't concerned that my parents were divergent because they saw me as a miracle. Strong." He stared straight ahead, his own tears dripping off his chin unnoticed. "I wasn't strong, or I'd have been able to stop them... stop them from coming and stampeding through my home... through my family until they were nothing but pulp on the floor. I wasn't enough... to save my brother."

The anguish brought Monty up to his knees. His cry came out as a croak of distress at the words plowing into him harder than a battering ram. He straddled Rue's lap facing both men, unconcerned that he was crushing anyone, when they'd been in the position before. He took hold of icy cheeks, his lips trembling as he worked to hold on to the riot of emotions Rue's distress caused, or the bloody visual that wanted to paint a macabre picture in his mind, one that Rue had lived with.

Used to shield himself behind.

Oh, goddesses.

Monty could suddenly see exactly why Rue held back. "You answer me this." He came in so close he could feel Rue's ragged breaths hitting his wet skin. "How many of them were there?" The urgency pushed him to prove Rue wrong.

"It does—"

"No. No, don't dismiss it. How many?" *I wasn't enough.* Did he believe he wasn't worthy of... love? It chilled Monty to his very core, despite the rage that fired his soul to seek out the motherfuckers and... there was nothing worse he could think of.

"Ten..."

"Rhino's?" Monty shuddered, but persisted, needing Rue to hear himself. Fuck, ten rhinos on a rampage, he couldn't even imagine the carnage. The nightmares such an act would cause for the boy Rue was.

"Y-yes."

Kendrick moved to grip hold of Monty's waist, bringing them closer together. Monty didn't look away from Rue, but he felt the restraint Kendrick was using to stop from hurting him. The fingers dug in as if trying to keep hold of something, to stop the need to crush something. It was how Monty felt.

"As an adult, do you believe you could defeat ten rhinos at the same time?" He had to make Rue see beyond the past pain. The hesitation gave him hope.

"I... no," Rue whispered, barely loud enough for Monty to hear.

"No. You couldn't save them, but I'm damn positive your parents would be happy you escaped. That's important to so many people." Monty leapt off the cliff without a backward look. "To me." His hands trembled as he held Rue, kissing him softly.

"I love you. You're enough for me."

Chapter Twenty-Nine

Kendrick

Kendrick's mind wasn't on what he was doing, and it was evident when he'd gotten orders mixed up twice. Trey, who was busy up the other end of the packed bar where Paddy was, kept throwing looks of concern that said Kendrick was being obvious about the worry he was carting around like a packhorse. Coming in right on time for work hadn't prevented that. It seemed he wasn't as good at hiding his erratic emotions as he thought.

"Yo Kendrick, can you give me three fingers of Bourbon," Cranny called to him. The lion shifter looked how Kendrick felt, troubled.

He grabbed the bottle and poured liberally. "That bad?" Kendrick eyed the other man as he placed the glass down in front of him. "What did Zippy do now?"

Kendrick hazarded a guess with how often he had to separate the two of them over the last two years and the sour expression that came at the mention of Zippy's name.

"Motherfucker is an asshole who needs a personality transplant..."—Cranny reached for the glass and downed the contents—"or another fucking job far from me. Another." He pushed the empty glass at Kendrick.

It was band night, and the last thing Kendrick needed was Cranny on a tear with a full bar, so he checked over Cranny's shoulder to see if his nemesis was in the bar. He poured another drink after seeing no sign of Zippy.

"Thanks." Cranny nodded and placed cash on the bar before taking his glass and walking dejectedly towards the pool table.

"What's up with Cranny?"

Kendrick glanced at Trey, picking up the cash. "Don't you mean 'who' is up with Cranny?"

"What did Zippy do now?" Trey pulled a pint, chuckling. "Breathe?"

Kendrick shook his head. "Who fucking knows with that pair! As long as they keep the anger outside of the bar!"

Trey nodded, the smile disappearing. "What's with you? You've hardly said a word all night? You've had a two weeks' vacation, shouldn't you be happier?"

Trey was looking at the glass he was filling, so he missed Kendrick's frown. Had he been quiet? Why should he feel happier? He'd left his men at home, and he was here! None of that was making him happy.

"Just got stuff on my mind and the band is rock-ing it loud enough to make talking hard," he stated the half-truth, hoping his friend didn't pick up how maudlin he was being.

"I call bullshit. You came in right on time, which means you were avoiding me. Whatsup, really?" Trey enquired, finishing serving the customer and moving to the next in a fluid move developed over years of practice.

Fuck it all. Like he could pull the wool over Trey's eyes. As Trey served drinks, it gave Kendrick a moment to con-sider his answer while they had an audience. The mu-sic was loud, but it wouldn't knock out all conversation if someone was paying attention. Everything about the night before left him conflicted. Rue's discussion about the dreadfulness of his past was difficult to deal with when there was nothing he could do to change what happened. If that wasn't enough, there was the stress Rue hadn't hidden about his parents coming to Bayfield. Which they hadn't discussed, so Kendrick had no idea if Rue was going to bring up the subject of who he was dating. Then the big pile of shit got topped off with Monty's declaration of love. Monty hadn't been in a throuple before, and that left Kendrick unsure of his footing to gauge what, if anything, Monty had in mind about continuing this relationship.

Because the raw honesty of his declaration meant Monty had held nothing back in that moment.

Kendrick respected Monty, who'd succinctly made his point to Rue about the past being beyond his control. A point that Rue couldn't deny. No teenager could have defeated ten rhinos. Fuck, no adult could. Not when they'd done a surprise attack.

Rue had given them the full story after Monty had declared his love. The love was like a healing dressing that, after the purging, closed over the wound inside Rue. One he had allowed to abrade his heart. And, fuck, if Kendrick wasn't proud of Monty for achieving it.

In all of that though, where did it leave him?

He wasn't some insecure dude, he never had been. Only right then, it was all he was feeling when he didn't know what part he would play long term in a relationship where two people were so in love. Rue might not have said the words back to Monty, but the love was evident to Kendrick when Rue looked at Monty when he thought no one was watching.

Paddy wandered towards them, his easy grin aimed at Kendrick. "Band's killer."

"Yep," he replied, not in the mood for small talk.

Kendrick took the opportunity to move on when a woman waved a fifty in the air, and Trey got beckoned by a regular at the other end of the bar.

The busyness meant he could avoid Trey prying for the rest of the night. As Kendrick worked, he kept his eye on the door. Monty, having discovered there was going to be a band playing, had mentioned coming in when Kendrick had left them just after dinner. Rue hadn't said yes when Kendrick had asked.

Was he distancing himself? Regrouping to prepare for his parents coming? In Kendrick's opinion, that was exactly what Rue was doing. It would be what he would do if the positions were reversed and he didn't want to answer questions.

Normally he'd push for answers from Rue, just... *insecurity was a bitch.*

He smiled, chatted, and wished like hell the evening was over. It was a first for him. A first he didn't like.

An hour later, when he locked up and shoved Trey out the door when his friend had checked his phone every two minutes for the past hour, Kendrick wiped down the bar, clearing away the last few glasses.

Paddy took the stacked dirty glasses to the dishwasher. "I can finish up if you wanna head."

"You sure?" Kendrick asked, head tilting as he eyed Paddy picking up something, just not sure what.

"Yep, I ain't got anyone waiting for me at home." He winked cheekily. "And you got two someone's waiting for you, lucky bastard."

Did he sound annoyed?

Kendrick's gaze narrowed on Paddy, who had swung around to the dishwasher, giving Kendrick his back. Was he just overthinking things because of all that was going on inside his head? "Cheers. I'll owe you one."

Paddy chuckled, glasses clinking as he filled the machine. "Sounds good to me."

Kendrick shook off the odd feeling he was missing something and headed to grab his truck keys and jacket. Out the door seconds later, he sent the guys a message in their group chat.

Kendrick: *On my way home… x*

He stared at the message, thinking of adding more, then decided against it as he hit send. In the truck, he reminded himself to focus on what he wanted, not what he didn't want. His phone remained silent, making the latter part harder.

He drove home listening to a local rock music station to keep his mind off his problems. The hard, pulsing rock was a total waste when his head wasn't playing ball. As he pulled into the drive, he noticed the downstairs lights were off, but his bedroom lights were still on. His pulse leapt as he got out of the truck and headed into the house. After removing his jacket and boots, Kendrick locked up, checking the windows and back door as usual, giving himself time to get his thoughts in order before heading upstairs. His mind was on how he was gonna approach the elephant—rhino—in the room.

At the entrance to his bedroom, he halted, breath catching at the sight of the two naked men lounging on the bed. The covers were neatly folded at the bottom. Both men were resting against the head of the bed watching him... waiting. An invitation to play.

His blood hummed with desire, appreciating how different both men were. Despite that, they fit perfectly—with him. Would that always be the case? He searched Monty's expression for clues. Desire was there, but more than that Kendrick couldn't determine. He met Rue's heated gaze, one full of need, and the ball of anxiety he'd not acknowledged since his confession loosened in his gut.

He didn't want to head back down the path of what ifs, when both men had other plans, he could more than get on board with. So he shut down his thoughts before they could take hold and derail what was going to happen before it began.

Both men were off the weekend, so neither had to get up for work the following day. Kendrick wasn't due to start his shift until five the next afternoon. That gave him time to give them what they wanted—him in charge.

He stepped into the bedroom and kicked the door shut behind him, never taking his eyes off his men, his hands going to his belt buckle. "So, we wanna play, do we?"

Rue's semi hard cock thickened, his eyes glinting with lust. Monty grabbed his shaft and pumped it twice before Kendrick shook his head, lips curling into a wicked grin. "Who's in charge, honey?"

Monty groaned in complaint and let go of his hard cock. It was all for show, his eyes revealing how much he wanted this. Kendrick whipped out his belt and side-stepped the end of the bed, walking to Monty. He looped the belt, his heated gaze pinning Monty in place. "Hold out your wrists."

Rue inched closer to Monty, his gaze on the belt as Kendrick slipped the loops over Monty's outstretched wrists. The sound of leather rubbing on metal made Monty groan and shift on the sheet. A blush of pink rose up his chest when his gaze drifted to his leather encased wrists.

"Whose idea was this?" His voice deepened as he tightened the loops, pulling Monty's hands together.

"Mine," offered Monty, "but we both wanted it."

"We missed you," Rue added, his chin quivering.

Kendrick heard the whoosh of his erratic pulse in his ears at the confession. He inhaled deeply, needing a moment to pull himself together with what they were doing to him.

Only when he was sure his hand was steady did he offer the belt end to Rue. "Take hold and make sure he doesn't touch until I say so."

The scent of their arousal was all Kendrick could smell in the warm air before stepping back, breathing hard. The sexual tension zapped electricity against his skin, but it wasn't the only thing causing it.

Rue's hand shook as he grasped the belt, his heavy-lidded eyes already begging for more.

Kendrick walked to the big armchair. Removing his shirt, he threw it on the floor before shifting its position to ensure his view didn't become obstructed with what he had in mind for the night's entertainment.

Once happy, he sat and took his time removing his socks, stretching out his long legs in front of him, the tension in the room palpable. He rested back against the soft fabric cushions and tapped at his lower lip, eyes narrowing on the bed. His mind visualized where he wanted both men.

"Rue help Monty off the bed and come to the end, facing the pillows."

Monty whimpered and shivered when Rue's idea of helping was to tug the leather until Monty was on his knees at the edge of the bed, then scoop one arm under Monty's butt and lift him up and off, striding to where Kendrick wanted them, still holding the leather belt binding Monty's wrists.

Eyes glittering at the show of strength and bulge of biceps, Kendrick growled in the back of his throat and reached to slide his zip down to release the pressure off his shaft. Rue's strength—steel wrapped in silk. Soft skin covering all the hard muscle was such a turn on when he could effortlessly show off his power.

On his feet, Monty visibly vibrated as he glanced at Kendrick, ensuring his attention returned to the omega. Monty was a quick study and judging by his knowing smirk, had easily figured that Kendrick had plans that involved tormenting Rue.

"Rue, spread your legs wide and brace a hand on the end of the bed. Let's give Monty a view of what's his for the night."

Rue released a curse, but did as he was told, his left arm tensing when Kendrick continued. "Monty kneel behind Rue and thread the leather up between his spread thighs. Rue grasp it and don't let go. We wouldn't want Monty coming too soon."

Monty's hands got tugged up, bringing them closer to Rue's balls, and having to follow, his face was barely inches from the ass he was about to play with.

Perfect.

"Do you remember the first night you were both in here?"

"How could I forget," Monty whimpered. In the position he was in, he could twist to glance at Kendrick, but his focus was on the ass in front of him. Monty fidgeted closer to the man who visibly tensed.

Rue's head hung between shoulders, which rose and fell in quick succession, then he released a self-conscious whimper.

A feverish light in his eyes, Kendrick came forward to get a better view. "What's Monty doing to you, Rue?" He could see, but he wanted Rue to tell him.

"Smells sexy and edible," Monty mumbled, his face pressed into the crack of Rue's ass before Rue could reply to Kendrick. Monty trembled and didn't wait to be told what to do next.

"Arggghhh... f-fuck... d-damn..." Rue stammered, coming up on his toes, his calves straining as he lifted his ass higher, encouraging Monty to move that frisky tongue of his.

"Eager, Monty, for a taste of our honey?" Kendrick rasped through the tightness of his throat at the sight of Monty's neck arching back, his chin pushing under Rue's balls to get his tongue to Rue's asshole without the use of his hands to pry the cheeks apart.

Rue's ass was a thing of beauty, perfect round globes of firmness.

Monty made a noise that could have been assent as his tongue tickled Rue's hole, teasing it with small, measured swipes. By now, Rue's legs were so wide Kendrick could see them straining as his ass cheeks parted for Monty.

"Is he tickling your hole, honey? I can see it fluttering. Do you want him to go deeper? Monty, spear that pretty hole open."

Rue mewl-growled, his legs trembling as he worked to hold the position. The hand gripping the leather strap landed on the bed, forcing Monty to shove his face into Rue's ass.

Seeing he could suffocate Monty, who didn't seem that worried with the muffled slurping noises, Kendrick demanded, "Rue, lift the hand holding the belt off the bed."

It took several seconds and Kendrick asking again to get him to comply. Rue's asshole glistened with spit, the pink rim relaxed enough for Monty to jab at it and his tongue to sink in effortlessly.

Both men were sheened in sweat, gleaming in the lamplight and looking the picture of debauchery. Their lewd noises were their own aphrodisiac as Kendrick's gaze remained riveted on the pair.

"That's it, Monty, open up that sweet hole. Get him ready to take your cock. And when you're balls deep, I'm gonna fuck you so hard I'll feel Rue come."

Rue made a pained noise. Monty's was a more garbled gasp, his body reacting to the idea. More pre-cum dripped over Monty's thighs, which shone with his desire. Monty hadn't topped Rue, but he'd made a passing comment that suggested he'd enjoy sandwiching between them, with Rue under him.

Their reaction was enough to have Kendrick shaking from the strength of the pulse thundering through his veins at just how much he wanted this.

Chapter Thirty

Rue

"Monty is going to fuck the cum right out of you." Kendrick was right next to him. When he'd moved, Rue couldn't say, not with Monty eating his ass with such enthusiasm. Kendrick's lips brushed his ear as he growled, "While I'll do the same to Monty, so he can fill your ass full of cum. Breed you until you're ours."

Oh, Goddess, don't come. Don't fucking cum. He wanted it so bad. Whereas his rhino half was in a muddy wallow state, blissed out to the point of giving zero fucks at being topped by an omega.

The air was thick with the scent of their lust, and Rue couldn't get enough air inside him to make the band constricting his chest release. His whole body trembled with how taut his innards were. There was nothing he could do about it with the tongue taking him apart while the dirty talk held him right on the precipice. He wanted to leap off, yet he battled with fiber in him, desperate for the pleasure to continue. To never end.

His fingers slipped over the leather as he fought to hold back the desperation of needing to come. Once, Kendrick had eaten him out and turned him into a gibbering mess. This was more intense with Monty's over the top enthusiasm; it was destroying him. The jabs were precise, spearing into his hole, Monty widened and wiggled his tongue until Rue felt the burn, then he'd withdraw and lap at the quivering muscle. The delicate tonguing was maddening with how the nerves danced under Monty's clever mouth. Then came the damn sucking, which sent the maddening desire swirling through his sack, right to the tip of his cock. Agonizing pleasure!

"How deep is Monty? Is he hitting that secret spot, driving you wild, honey?"

Rue's head lifted with effort to glance at the unrepentant man tormenting him, and he begged, "S-stop... c-can't take a-anymore." He gritted his teeth together at the next full body shudder wracking through him from head to toe when Monty's tongue did indeed meet his prostate. Most definitely spurred on by Kendrick.

Rue's cock jerked hard enough his eyes crossed and his arm gave out, his face mashing into the bedcovers. The slippery leather fell from his hand in the urgency to grab his balls and tug hard enough to make his eyes water.

He heaved into the covers, eyes closing as tremors ran through him at gaining a small semblance of control. But for how long, who the fuck knew.

The tongue disappeared from his ass, and he received a stinging blow, forcing him to lift his head. He sucked in one ragged breath after another, his swimming vision forcing him to realize he was oxygen deprived.

"Did you nearly come undone, honey?"

Rue couldn't speak with how dry his mouth was as he panted, but he gave the unrepentant man a hard stare that did nothing when they both knew how much he loved being taken apart like this.

"Come on, honey. Let's give Monty his reward for all his hard work opening up that tight hole of yours." As Kendrick spoke, he moved behind Rue. Next thing he knew, large hands slipped under his armpits, hooking to lift him up the bed.

He groaned at Kendrick's cock branding his butt cheek before he found himself plonked onto the bed, his feet dangling off the end. Monty scampered on, straddling Rue's thighs as Kendrick moved out of the way. Used to having Kendrick do this to him, the difference in weight and size was very noticeable. It took Rue a few seconds to adjust and figure it wasn't bad, just different.

"Lube, I need lube." Monty's demand brought a chuckle from Kendrick.

"Bossy top, I like it."

Rue groaned and shoved his face into the closest pillow, his thighs tensed to stop the hard pulse of desire causing his cock to leak when humping the bed would give him the friction to make him come. He didn't want that. Fucking hell no, he wanted what Kendrick promised.

Monty crowded over Rue's back, his damp skin rubbing against Rue's as he whispered, "All the times I watched Kendrick fuck you, I imagined what it would be like to feel your ass squeeze my cock." When Rue twisted his head to meet Monty's mischievous gaze, Monty's lips pressed against the rim of his ear, and he could smell his own musky scent. "I want it so tight that you leave an imprint on my cock, do you hear me?"

"I fucking sure as hell do," Kendrick rumbled, lube landing next to Rue's head.

Monty released a sexy purr and picked up the lube. "Good, 'cause I'm gonna squeeze you as tight as Rue does to me."

Rue's groans became pained, the same as Kendrick's. His heated gaze met Rue's. "Rue, you up for the challenge?"

Was he? Right then, he wasn't sure with how aroused he was. He'd be fucking lucky to last ten seconds when Monty got his dick inside him. Except he nodded because these were his men, and he'd do anything for them.

Anything, even if it meant embarrassing himself.

A wiggling Monty moved off, and Rue eagerly spread his legs. The pillow muffled his moan as slick, nimble fingers slipped between his butt cheeks, zeroing in on his asshole, and air hissed through his gritted teeth at the gentle probing.

"I don't need to be stretched," he grunted as the finger sank deep, hitting his prostate in an electrifying move that had him right back on the edge, looking down into a pleasure oblivion.

"I'm in charge," Monty rasped sexily. One finger became two, and Rue scrabbled to think of something, anything that would give him a distraction when his hips gyrated, seeking more. Needing something bigger in his ass.

"You look so beautiful, both of you." Kendrick sounded punch drunk and Rue moved his head to glance in his direction, seeing him climb on the bed and slide behind Monty. "Lift up, sweet cheeks."

Monty continued to thrust his fingers into Rue's ass even as he came forward and lifted his ass into the air for Kendrick. They looked like train cars all lined up, just with a small one in the middle. Rue couldn't see from his angle what the bear was doing behind Monty, but he knew how thorough Kendrick was when fucking.

Noises of pure filth poured from Monty, yet he didn't become deterred from prepping Rue, who was thrusting to meet Monty's every touch.

"Need... more... need... more," he pleaded as the tell-tale tingling at the base of his tailbone started again, zinging through his ass and under his balls, drawing them tight. He buried his head into the pillow, eyes squeezed shut, rocking and pleading.

"Pleasepleasepleaseplease." The words ran into each other as the fingers slipped free and hands gripped his hips tugging him up and back until he felt the pressure of slick skin rub against his hole.

"Push out," Monty gasped breathlessly, clearly as affected by whatever Kendrick was doing to him.

Rue did as he was told, too far gone to wait any longer. He needed to come in the worst way. He felt the welcome stretch making his toes curl and his cock throb. One touch to his dick and he'd go off like a detonator. Monty wasn't as patient as Kendrick, but then he wasn't as big either. The second the head was past the protective rim of muscle, he slammed home. A good solid six inches of hard cock.

"Mother of gods," Rue sobbed out in relief when Monty didn't wait and thrust like his life depended on it.

"That's it, squeeze my cock." Monty's voice was wrecked.

Rue's cock bounced, the air brushing over the head was torment when it gave him no relief. He went to slide a hand under him, only for Kendrick to stop him. "No, honey, that's our job."

He muttered a curse between the groans, moans and whimpers at the pounding his ass was getting. He tilted his hips, and Monty hit his prostate dead on. Pounded on it until Rue lost any ability to think beyond the need to come. The whooshing in his ears was all he could hear as his back arched. His ass clamped tightly, yet Monty continued to pulverize it. Sudden weight pushed him into the mattress, the air leaving his lungs. Monty mewled in broken whimpers, but he didn't stop, forcing the cum right out the end of Rue's cock in painful spurts as it rubbed against the cotton sheet. The force was all Kendrick, except Monty was unrelenting. What did it matter who was fucking him through the mattress when it was the best sex of his life?

White spots danced before his eyes, spasms of pain-pleasure coming with each forceful jerk and splatter on the bed beneath him until he lay limp and exhausted. His brain switched off much the same as him turning off a light.

Sounds of murmuring infiltrated past the sexual haze he'd drifted into—more likely passed out cold from—and Rue realized two things at once. He was lying on his back, not his front, in a wet patch, and someone had cleaned him up.

He squinted in the direction of the voices, the lamplight making his eyes water.

Monty sat in Kendrick's lap dressed in Rue's T-shirt, whereas Kendrick remained naked, looking flushed and sexy.

"What time is it?" Rue's voice was rough like sandpaper as he glanced at the closed curtains, rubbing at his eyes.

"Look, he lives," Monty said, giggling. "I thought we'd killed you the way you passed out."

He shuffled a little closer, sliding a hand over Kendrick's thigh and touching Monty's knee when Monty didn't conceal all his worry. "You just fucked my brains out, is all. Maybe you both did."

"Kendrick sure gave my butt something to think about for the next few days," Monty stated dramatically as he shifted and winced on Kendrick's lap.

"I know that feeling." Rue grinned at Kendrick. "I think next time we should be the ones pounding Kendrick's ass. What do you say, Monty?"

The light that appeared in Monty's eyes left Rue catching his breath and his cock twitching. When he glanced at Kendrick, Rue lost his ability to grab hold of his thoughts. The man looked positively wicked as he grinned at him over Monty's head.

"I think that can be arranged... if you're up for the *challenge!*"

Rue did not know what was going on inside Kendrick's head, but fuck, he wanted to find out. "We should invest in some full-length mirrors to surround the bed so none of us miss out. What do you think?" He wasn't sure where that came from, and he blushed at the eyebrow raise Kendrick wore.

"Jeez," Monty groaned, hand dropping onto the T-shirt, pressing down on his cock, "my ass can't take another pounding, but talk like that makes me wanna try."

Rue's rumbles of tired laughter met Kendrick's booming chuckles. "Mirrors, you say? I believe I can organize that. But would that be before or after your parents' visit?" It was asked with humor, yet Rue didn't miss how the light of amusement disappeared from Kendrick's eyes.

His own narrowed, searching for answers, but finding none in Kendrick's guarded expression. "They're staying at Vaughn Winery for their anniversary. Do you want me to invite them to stay here?"

There were three spare bedrooms, except Rue didn't think that was what Kendrick was getting at. More, it was about their relationship, the dynamic.

"The winery is much nicer for an anniversary," he replied noncommittally.

Rue nodded in agreement. "It is." He didn't look away from Kendrick, but he sensed Monty's gaze on him. "I was going to ask whether you wanted to go to dinner, both of you, with my parents." He'd planned on discussing this tomorrow—it was already tomorrow. "I know the winery has a restaurant that's supposed to be good... if you fancy it?" Did it sound lame? *Come officially meet my parents?* Was he being presumptive?

"Count me in," Monty said when Kendrick remained silent, staring at him, a furrow developing between his brows.

"Great," Rue responded, his heart rate tripping fast enough he felt his hands tremble.

"I'd... love to," Kendrick murmured softly. "It would be my pleasure to *officially* meet your parents."

There it was—the flash of love. It took out all Rue's self-control. He rolled onto his side and rested his cheek on Kendrick's knee, blinking back the tears and sucking in a breath.

"And mine," he whispered. *And mine.*

Chapter Thirty-One

Monty

Monty was only half paying attention to Ethan as he stamped across the carpet complaining about... he wasn't sure what. His focus was Rue, who was tapping at his laptop, nodding occasionally to what Ethan was saying.

The weekend had been... this was why he couldn't concentrate. After last Thursday, where Rue had lost it and revealed what haunted him, he'd been *different*. Yes, they'd lived together for a couple of weeks, could essentially call themselves a couple—throuple—but it hadn't felt truly real until the weekend. Was it declaring his love for Rue? Releasing himself from the fear of letting it slip out unintentionally. Kendrick orchestrating him topping Rue where he'd epically lost control? He still couldn't quite believe Rue had passed out. Monty didn't know, not for sure, which, if any of these things made the difference.

Kendrick had been different, too. There'd been a tension about him that hadn't been there before Thursday. Monty had given this a lot of thought, and he had to wonder if it was because of his declaration of love for Rue. Had Kendrick felt excluded? Monty sure would, he didn't need an in-depth soul searching for that. The guilt left him conflicted because he did have deep feelings for Kendrick, he just wasn't ready to declare it as love because wasn't it too soon? It had taken months of knowing Rue before that realization happened. Could he trust himself when the sexual chemistry clouded everything? When Kendrick was near, everything seemed brighter inside Monty, his skin hummed with it. Was that love or sex? Could it be both?

"—what do you think, Monty?"

He blinked Ethan into focus and chewed his thumbnail, searching for anything to give him a clue about what he was talking about.

"Can you repeat that," he asked, feeling his skin warm when Ethan chuckled and Rue made a snorting noise like he was swallowing back laughter even though he was still tapping at his laptop. The man could clearly multitask where it would appear Monty couldn't.

"The omegas getting jobs outside of the ranch. Good or bad idea, what do you think?"

"Do they want to? What does Oakland say about this?" Monty had spent time with them every day after the visit to Cassidy the first week. Rue had encouraged this because they seemed more relaxed with him. As far as he could recall, there was no mention of them saying anything about a job off the ranch. He believed Oakland would never approve, and possibly Ethan, the way he hung around a certain omega. Then there was Brier...

"This isn't Oakland's choice, it's theirs." Ethan's teeth gnashed on 'theirs', wearing a mutinous scowl.

Okay, touchy subject.

Monty scratched his jaw, weighing his words. "If the omegas want to do something beyond here, then I'd say they've considered it seriously, so we need to do the same. They had their freedom taken from them,"—he swept his arm around the room to make his point—"aren't we showing them they have gotten it back?"

"Yeah... you're right," Ethan muttered more to himself than them. Monty was positive of it with how he looked to be staring off into space.

"If Oakland can assess risk like he did here, I think it could be good for them," Monty added. "But I can sound them out this afternoon, if you like. We are helping Cassidy."

Monty got a buzz of excitement recalling what was happening later. The afternoon's visit was the grand reveal of Eric's chicken outfits. It might not be fashion week in Milan, something he was missing out on, but it was to the omegas, judging by how they'd been bubbling with enthusiasm at the coming reveal. Monty needed to check his phone had enough charge so he could video it and share it with the others.

"That would be helpful," Ethan finally answered. "They like Cassidy."

He didn't sound impressed, but Monty couldn't say why. Everyone loved Cassidy. "They do, but it's the chicks they love."

"Really?" Ethan sounded genuinely surprised, which meant none of the omegas had spoken about what they were up to. Why was that?

Monty shook off the feeling of sorrow that wanted to blanket his earlier excitement at all the reasons they hadn't shared, with an alpha they appeared to trust, what they were up to.

"Yep. If you maybe slip by the coops this afternoon, you'll see." He didn't think it was a bad thing to encourage Ethan. He hoped the omegas saw it that way when he nodded in agreement.

"Can we now get back to business?" Rue asked, brows raised, the laptop no longer his focus.

Monty gave him a cheeky grin, one he'd never have considered giving back in Hazardville. "Of course, Mr. Starling."

Ethan chuckled and gave them a small salute, heading out of Silas's office.

"You wouldn't be giving me cheek, would you, Mr. Gibson?" Rue aimed for stern and managed it for a whole two seconds before he allowed a smile to slip free.

Monty glided over the carpet and shimmed in between the desk and Rue, the rolling office chair moving back with Rue's help. Seeing the invite, Monty straddled Rue's lap and waggled his eyebrows.

"Now how to answer?" He slipped his arms around Rue's neck, inching closer until their lips were close enough that he could smell the coffee Rue had recently drunk. "If I said yes, you might consider *punishing me* for insubordination."

The gray of Rue's eyes twinkled with amusement. "I could." A smile that could melt ice formed. "Or I could just let Kendrick know how naughty you're being and let him decide on how to *punish you.*"

Monty grew light-headed at the threat, but not because he was worried. The blood from his head had descended south in a sure-fire hurry. He ground down and kissed Rue with a hunger very much not appropriate for the office.

Through the pounding blood in his ears, a distant sound came from behind him. Releasing Rue to drag in a breath, he heard a smothered cough-laugh and his eyes widened. Just as Rue's cheeks suddenly filled with color, Monty got a sinking feeling, squirming as he twisted his head to look over his shoulder.

Why now?

Why did it have to be them?

Derick and Lane stood in the open doorway. It took two seconds to figure out who had made the noise, when Derick's expression didn't give Monty any clue as to what he thought about their current predicament. Lane looked highly amused, so that was something.

Only Rue wasn't the only one blushing with embarrassment. The dose of reality that they were supposed to be working and the two men—though retired—were still probably paying Monty's wages hit him hard. That was enough to cool his ardour and get him sliding off Rue's lap.

"Mr. Starling—"

Lane raised a hand, chuckling as he came into the room. "When have I ever been Mr. Starling? And I do believe we are way past that when you were sitting on my son's lap, about to—"

"Popi," Rue said in warning.

Derick sniggered and looked almost relaxed as he strolled in. Monty then noticed how casually dressed he was. He wore clothes more suited to a cowboy. Monty had seen him in slacks and a polo shirt in his home the one time he'd gotten invited to talk about Emmy, but this was something else. Although Monty wasn't into men so much older than him, he totally got why guys would be. Derick exuded power wearing a suit. Dressed as he was, he most certainly continued to exude that, but there was also a sexiness Monty hadn't noticed before. Thigh hugging jeans, cowboy boots and a rugged shirt... they really worked for him.

When it struck that he was enjoying the view a little more than was decent when he was dating Derick's son, Monty shoved his hands in his pocket and shifted his attention to Rue who hadn't moved from behind the desk, like he didn't know how to act.

Monty gave him a 'get up and help me' look.

Rue rose gracefully, going to Lane. "Dad, Popi, this is a surprise. I thought you weren't supposed to arrive until tomorrow?"

Monty blinked in confusion. Rue hadn't mentioned that, had he? Had he booked the restaurant for the official introduction?

Like you need that after you were lap dancing on Rue when they arrived.

Go away.

Seriously? Like I can. His otter was cracking up in his head, rolling around laughing. Monty forced himself to remain still while Rue hugged Lane, then Derick.

"We thought we'd come a day early and spend some time on the ranch with you."

Lane's words brought a lump to Monty's throat he couldn't swallow passed when he didn't need to look at Rue to know he'd frozen in place. Hadn't he told them he was staying in town? Monty was back to blinking in confusion as he looked between the three men, working to sort through what he might be missing.

"Popi... I..." Rue shifted his attention to Derick. "Dad..." Rue shook his head, clearly mystified—maybe—by the whole situation.

How often did one get caught mounting their boss and kissing them?

"Stop teasing Rue, my love. He's already had one shock today."

Monty couldn't decide if the shock was their arrival or them catching Monty sitting on his lap in a very unprofessional manner during work hours and joking about it.

Praying for some sort of miracle that allowed Monty to disappear so Rue could have whatever conversation that needed to be had, a tap at the open door had Monty groan in relief before he could stop himself.

Ivo didn't take his eyes off Derick as he hovered on the threshold of the room.

"Hey Ivo, this is Derick,"—Monty pointed at the man in question—"and Lane Starling. They're Rue's parents," he explained, when Ivo didn't so much as blink.

Monty, hating the fear Ivo wasn't able to hide, walked over and slipped an arm around Ivo's waist without thinking about it.

Ivo leaned into him, saying shyly, "Hi."

Lane's bright smile held sadness as he came forward and offered his hand to Ivo. "So lovely to meet you. I don't suppose you know where they're hiding the cake, do you? Last time I was visiting, I couldn't find any. I mean, that's such a disgrace, no cake in the cupboards. Do I have to make my own?"

Monty could see what Lane was doing, and it reinforced just how amazing this man was. "I made a batch of brownies over the weekend, and I left some in the kitchen."

A smile appeared as Ivo glanced at Monty. "Are they the ones with cherries in?"

He giggled at the enthusiasm. "Of course. I added some mashed banana too."

"Really," Lane questioned, coming to slip an arm through Monty's, joining the three of them. "Lead on, I must try them." He glanced at his husband. "I'm sure Rue can entertain you for a while."

Lane guided them out of the office and down the corridor into the kitchen effortlessly enough. Ivo wore a bemused look. As they entered, Lane's gaze swept the countertops, a frown appearing.

"Where did you leave them, Monty?"

Monty gave Ivo a quick squeeze of reassurance, then headed over to the cupboard that was used for kitchen implements. From what Monty had noticed, he was the only one who used them because everyone ate at the bunkhouse. Pete and Orion were skilled cooks, and not having to think about what to make daily was great now Kendrick was back at work.

Not thinking about that. It was part of the reason he'd ended up baking while Rue watched a baseball game. He understood Kendrick didn't have the same kind of nine-to-five job as him and Rue. When in Hazardville, it was somehow different. Living with Kendrick didn't mean he had to like it when he was out in the evening, so he'd occupied himself in the kitchen. It was the first time Kendrick got to benefit, as usually he was the one cooking. Not that Monty hadn't been baking. He had, just up at the ranch for the omegas. Something that Rue had encouraged. The kitchen here was well stocked, so the cowboys had benefitted from his culinary skills too.

"I hide them in here. You have to if you don't want the cowboys sneaking in and eating them all."

"Monty, your brownies are exceptional, so you can't blame them," Lane enthused, the warm smile allaying some of Monty's doubts that Lane might consider Monty wasn't right for his son. Lane and Monty had always had a great working relationship, but one never knew when it came to family.

Ivo's giggle was pure magic. "They are. Just yesterday, Zippy and Cranny nearly came to blows over the last brownie from the batch you made last week."

He said it so innocently, Monty's head jerked in Ivo's direction, knowing just how bad the two cowboys were with each other. What startled him was how calm Ivo was over it. "They did?"

He came to where Monty placed the tub on the counter, Lane coming with him. "Yeah... Oakland stepped in and ate the brownie, stopping the argument."

"He did?" Lane asked, surprise filling his voice.

Monty offered the brownies to Ivo, who nodded in response, taking one out of the tub. "He said he doesn't eat sweet things, but secretly I think he does, the way he devoured it. Monty, do you think you could teach me to make them?"

"Of course. Maybe you could teach me to sew?"

The clatter of boots alerted to someone coming. Otis arrived first, pursued by the others. None of them looked at Lane as they zeroed in on the tub Monty held. It was extremely flattering.

"Brownies. I knew I could smell them." Otis was across the room so fast that if Monty had blinked, he would have missed it. He reached into the tub and snatched out a brownie, giving Monty a solid whack to his heart at the joy written on his face when it went straight to his mouth.

"Is this why you didn't come outside where we were waiting?" Eric questioned, elbowing past Ivo to get to the tub, holding a large brown sack in one hand.

It was all so normal, Monty got an ache at the back of his eyes with the urge to cry. He was helping; it made all the difference after leaving these men in purgatory.

Monty sniffed twice, not quite meeting anyone's gaze in case they noticed his eyes were sheened with tears.

Lane dashed a hand over his own eyes before reaching to nab a brownie. "I better grab one before they all disappear," Lane said gaily, not looking directly at anyone but somehow including all the men, who then appeared to notice him.

They were getting much better at being in places with strangers—just not alpha strangers. "This is Lane Starling, Rue's Popi. His dad is in the office with him," he advised softly, so no one else got a shock if Derick appeared. "This is Eric, Otis and Cace." Monty did the introductions despite knowing Lane knew the names.

It helped him stop thinking about whatever conversation was happening between father and son while he was out of the room.

Categorically not thinking about that.

"Hi," Otis mumbled around a mouthful of brownie.

"Hi." Lane glanced at Eric. "Why were you waiting outside? Is it something to do with the bag you're holding, Eric?"

"We were off to see Cass—"

"Have you got what you made in the sack?" Monty interrupted Eric, forgetting himself in his excitement, dropping the tub to come around the counter, keen to see what Eric had made.

He pulled the sack to his chest, pouting, which was hard when he was still chewing on the brownie. "I want to show Lynda first."

"Lynda?" Lane questioned, looking between the two men. "Is there a Lynda working at the ranch?"

Monty bit the inside of his cheek to hold off laughing at Lane, who looked bewildered. There were only men employed on the ranch, so Monty got it.

"Of course," Eric stated. "She's a La Fleche chicken." The way he spoke, it was like it made total sense to him.

Lane nodded, a twinkle coming to light in his eyes. "I see. What are we showing Lynda?"

Eric blushed to the roots of his hair. "I made her and some of the other chics outfits, like the ones Cass makes for his girls."

Monty saw the second the penny dropped as Lane's smile widened. "Cass is a treasure the way he looks after his girls. I bet he's super pleased with the offer."

Eric eyed Lane with suspicion, but he must have decided a second later that Lane was being genuine as he offered a timid smile. "He is, and he's letting me dress some of his girls. Lynda might not let me, but he said she likes me,"—his rail thin shoulders moved up jerkily—"so maybe she'll allow it."

It was heartbreaking how hopeful he sounded. Monty prayed to whatever chicken god there was that Lynda played ball and allowed Eric to dress her.

Monty really wanted to see what was in the sack and for Lane to witness first hand what his sons had done for these men. "Shall we head over there now?"

The eagerness didn't miss any of the men who all giggled, including Lane.

"We can," Eric answered before shoving the last of the brownie in his mouth, then dusting off the crumbs on his fingers down the leg of his jeans, heading towards the door eagerly.

Monty was right behind him, and could hear the others following.

They weren't as skittish about walking around when men were busy dealing with horses and other general tasks, and he grinned at Lane, who beamed back.

They made it to the fenced off area where the coups were, the sound of clucking and squawking growing louder at the sight of Eric. Lynda was the fastest to reach the closed gate, as if she knew exactly what Eric was there for.

A grinning Cassidy came right behind her. "Eric, what you got there that has my girls flapping their skirts?"

Monty noticed Cassidy was way more careful with his footing now that his belly protruded out enough that he couldn't see his boots.

Eric grinned so big it transformed his face. The gauntness was much less obvious, as was the pain in his eyes. "I have some outfits for my—your girls," he quickly corrected.

"I'd say the way Lynda's behavin', she's your girl now," he said affably.

"Cass, oh my gosh, no one told me you were pregnant!" Lane exclaimed, greeting the man like a long-lost friend, going in for a hug when Cassidy opened the gate to come out.

"I've got a mate now." Cassidy beamed. "Trey made an honest man of me."

Ivo nudged Otis and whispered, "What's he mean?"

Otis shook his head. "Heck if I know."

"Eric, are you gonna put me out of my misery?" Monty asked without thought.

He froze at his own stupidity, about to apologize when Eric did a ta-da move, opening the bag and pulling out some tiny dresses.

Monty's mouth fell open, as did Cassidy's.

"Oh my," Lane said in awe. "They're gorgeous."

They were. The hand stitched dresses came in rainbow colors. Some had pretty frills. Others had scalloped edges with hand-painted designs on the silk. There were so many different ones, Monty didn't know where to look first. The intricate detail and tiny, precision stitching, fuck Monty couldn't even dream of achieving that in any lifetime.

"Eric... they are precious."

Cassidy released a choked sob, drawing everyone's attention. "Don't mind me, it's pregnancy hormones. Though I gotta say, Eric, you got skills, man. I can only dream of ever making something so fancy."

"I helped with the painting," murmured Cace, looking abashed when it appeared he hadn't wanted to be left out, but didn't then want everyone staring at him by how he fidgeted and looked at the ground.

Eric's head bobbed enthusiastically. "He did, he's the one with talent. Look here, these are all the chics. See? He drew them first on paper, then painted them on the silk with the special paints and brushes Brier bought for him."

"Why, damn, it is." Cassidy, who seemed to have gotten himself under control, gave Cace the brightest smile, tears shimmering in his eyes. "You guys are the best. Do you think, Cace, I could have the pictures of my girls? I'd like to put them on the walls of my new home."

"You would?" whispered Cace, eyes so big they consumed his face.

"Heck, yeah." Cassidy rubbed at his round belly. "The baby likes the idea too with how it's kickin' me."

"Does it hurt?" Ivo was eyeing Cassidy's belly as if trying to see the kicks.

Cassidy held out his hand to Ivo. "Wanna feel?"

There was an obvious hesitation before Ivo placed his hand in Cassidy's, stepping closer as Cassidy pressed the palm of Ivo's hand against the side of his belly.

His lips formed a perfect O as he stared at where his hand was. "That's gotta hurt!" he exclaimed.

"A little when it hits me in a rib, but mainly it's reassuring me they're happy rolling around in there."

"I never thought of it like that," Ivo murmured thoughtfully.

Monty wondered if he was thinking about the omega that died giving birth to Emmy.

As if Lane had the same thought, he came closer to Eric. "Are we going to try the outfits on for size?"

"Please," Monty added. "I'm so excited to see how they look."

Eric handed out outfits, keeping one with the silk paintings on it in wild fuchsia. He sat right down in the dirt and patted his thigh, looking longingly at Lynda. "Wanna try the dress, Lynda?"

The chicken in question hopped straight up onto Eric's lap and lifted its wings.

"She ain't never done that to me." Cassidy shook his head, sighing dramatically while grinning widely. "Traitor."

Everyone laughed, including Eric, who lowered to kiss the top of Lynda's head.

"Don't listen to him, he doesn't mean it," he said, getting more laughter as the others, including Lane, sat down in the dirt to dress the chickens.

Monty pulled out his phone and started videoing; he couldn't wait to show his friends because this was the best day ever!

Chapter Thirty-Two

Delicious & Vicious

Frey: *The video Monty, I can't stop crying!*

Hollis: *It was beautiful, seeing them all so happy.*

Bowie: *I'm a little jealous we didn't get to be there. Did you see the design on the material? What was that Monty? I couldn't zoom in close enough to see.*

Monty: *Cace drew pictures of all the chickens and then painted them on the silk. Gods, he's amazingly talented. Cass* is having the pictures framed for his new home. Did I tell you he's pregnant?

Bowie: He is? Wow, he'll be such a good daddy.

Isley: I wish we could come visit. And Bowie, you're so right, Cass will be wonderful.

Lennon: Yeah, it would be great to be there rather than here! It's nice to be heading to Milan in two days and everything, but with how difficult Kodi is being, I'd rather be somewhere else.

Hollis: I'm coming to your office, Lennon.

Lennon: Don't bother, I have a meeting in two minutes, and I'm fed-up of moaning.

Ziggy: Can we help in any way?

Lennon: Monty's video helped... a lot.

Bowie: I made pineapple upside down cake.

Ziggy: You did? I'll grab you a slice, Lennon, and leave it in your office.

Lennon: Thanks.

Wilder: As we're all going to Milan, maybe we need another night out together.

Hollis: No sex clubs!

Ziggy: Are you sure?

Wilder: You're no fun, Hollis.

Hollis: I am, ask Taylin.

Lennon: He's your mate, he should think you're fun, right? But a night out would be great.

Isley: Yeah, some fun away from Misery Is My Middle Name, would be good.

Lane: It sounds like I need to have words with my sons when I get home.

Lennon: Please don't, he's bad enough now.

Isley: I second that. Laken has grumpiness down to a fine art.

Bowie: How is grumpiness art?

Ziggy: He just means that Laken has had a lot of practice at being grumpy.

Lane: I've also got lots of practice with my sons' behaviors. I'll speak to them, but don't worry, they won't know why.

Chapter Thirty-Three
Alphaholes

Jupiter: *Booker, what did you do to make Frey cry?*

Booker: *What? I didn't do anything. That means one of you assholes has to have upset him. When I find out, I'm gonna kick ass!*

Rue: *It's probably the video Monty sent to all the PAs. It's very emotional.*

Silas: What video? Why is he videoing stuff at the ranch? And why is it emotional?

Rue: It's the omegas with Cass and his chicks. Eric made little outfits for them, and Cace did some neat designs on them. Popi went with them and sat in the dirt in chicken poop! I get it, they were so fucking happy.

Silas: Popi sitting in poop? No way!

Rue: Get Ziggy to show you the video, seeing is believing!

Jupiter: That's some breakthrough with them, if they are being creative. I can totally see Popi getting involved, despite the poop.

Rue: After the disastrous night they had after the first week here, it was great to see them acting like the other omegas on the ranch.

Silas: *What are you talking about? What disaster? Ethan never mentioned anything when we spoke.*

Rue: *I spoke to Dad about it when it happened. Not sure why Ethan didn't mention it. Although he has been extra busy with all that's needed to keep the omegas safe. Maybe that's why.*

Silas: *Maybe… Dad, is everything okay at the ranch?*

Rue: *Hello, I'm right here!*

Silas: *That might be so, but you never said a word either, and it is my damn ranch.*

Laken: *You're not there, and Rue is, so why have a go at him? It's not like we have to report to you daily, for pity's sake! He coped perfectly well before Dad and Popi retired. He doesn't need you to wipe his nose.*

Silas: Who got up your butt?

Jupiter: No one, I'd say, with how uptight he is!

Dad: Silas, everything is fine, in fact better than fine from what I've seen. Jupiter, if I had a cent for every time you wound up your brothers, I'd never have had to worry about running out of money in ten lifetimes. Laken, clearly something is playing on your mind, so stop avoiding me. We will talk when I get home.

Booker: You guys need to see this video…

Jupiter: Are you blubbering?

Booker: I'm on my way to your office, let's see how you react!

Kari: This I gotta see.

Jupiter: *Then it's a good job I just left to go to the airport to head to Milan.*

Kari: *That's okay, I'm sharing the plane. You won't escape!*

Chapter Thirty-Four

Rue

He sat staring at his laptop screen, not seeing the email he'd been reading before he'd gotten the alert for the group chat. His phone sat on the desk, and he breathed out a sigh of frustration at Silas and Laken.

Laken was acting in ways Rue hadn't witnessed before. Yes, Laken bitched the same as the rest of them, but he'd never had a proper pot-shot at one of their brothers on Rue's behalf before.

Laken hadn't been around when he'd packed to come to the ranch, and now he wondered if that was on purpose. There was most definitely something off, especially if Dad thought Laken was avoiding him, too. Rue's guilt sat like a lead ball in his gut, reminding him how wrapped up in his own shit he'd gotten, not paying attention to what was happening with Laken.

Was it a PA thing? They were like falling dominos. Had Laken complained about Isley? Rue couldn't rightly remember. Was it something else? It was hard to say for sure. He eyed his phone with trepidation at the prospect of searching through the group chat to discover if Laken had given himself away.

Should he just message Laken?

Mention his worry to Dad?

He shook off the notion of asking Dad about Laken when it would be like throwing him under the bus. He'd hate it if Laken did that to him. Keeping secrets from Popi was hard when he got into pump mode while feeding them their favourite treat. Dad just got a look that said he wouldn't take any messing, making it impossible to hold water around him. None of them wanted to disappoint Dad. If he asked questions, then they knew they were in trouble. It was why Rue was more than a little relieved when Popi rang, derailing their earlier conversation. Rue had known it was going to get heavy; he'd seen the way Dad had watched him before Popi and Monty left with Ivo.

Rue knew his fate. The earlier derailing, only temporarily, gave some breathing space to get his thoughts in order. Being caught so spectacularly, kissing his PA, by his parents, was not how he envisioned he'd introduce his 'boyfriends'. It didn't matter that they already knew something was happening between them. If he were honest, he kind of had a romantic notion of how he'd do it.

Dang it all, he'd booked a table for dinner housed in the hotel at Vaughn winery, asking for a secluded table, flowers and their best champagne for Thursday evening, Kendrick's night off.

Now he considered their early arrival, he should have realized they'd pull a stunt like this and come early. Particularly if he'd reflected on the call he'd had with Dad since he'd been on the ranch.

He groaned in frustration and buried his head in his hands. His parents seeing him get down and dirty while he should be working, what was he thinking?

He hadn't been!

His fingers ran through his hair. He had never gotten caught kissing someone before, it felt weird. Like he was being naughty somehow.

It's not naughty to kiss our little otter. When are we going to see him in his shifted form? I want to meet him, and our bear.

Otters are tiny compared to us. You don't want to frighten him off.

Rue felt the eye roll his animal side was pulling. *Fear, what nonsense is this? He reamed your ass like a pro. He's not frightened, you are! And are you forgetting he loves us?*

What rubbish.

He loves us, his rhino argued.

I'm not debating that. He wasn't. Nothing about the confession felt fake. The way Monty had looked at him, like nothing else existed, couldn't be faked. *I'm not frightened.*

Then why are you avoiding addressing what's wrong with Kendrick?

"Still here, good. We can finish our conversation," said Dad as he came back into the office alone, striding to the desk looking every inch a cowboy.

Great! Aloud he hedged, "Dad, I've got a shit ton of work to finish."

Dad's silver eyebrows rose while taking the seat opposite him. "I'm sure it can wait when you're able to take the time to be... *distracted.*" He lounged in the seat, crossing his denim-clad legs, aiming an affable smile at Rue that didn't fool him one bit. He was about to be interrogated.

"Dad..."

"Rue, talk to me."

There was the concern that melted away any resistance he had. "What are we talking 'bout?"

"The shadows of your past... they're no longer there in your eyes. Do I have Kendrick, Kendrick and Monty, or Monty to thank for this?"

If someone had used a cattle prod on him, he wasn't sure he'd have reacted so violently, shooting forward in his seat, mouth hanging open in shock.

"W-what..." he choked out, unable to say more when he'd built himself up to talk, but this? Rue held Dad's gaze,

searching for answers. "You know about my b-brother...
don't you?"

"I do."

"How?" he croaked out, feeling the need to move but
knowing with certainty his legs would not hold him up.

"When you came into my family, I needed to make
sure we could protect you, so I used an investigator,
and he gathered information."

They know. They know. "W-why..."

"Why didn't I say something?" Rue's nod was stilted,
his brain trying to play catch up to why he'd never considered they'd investigate what happened that night.
"I was waiting for you to talk to me about it. When we
sent you to the therapist, they advised me to let you
come to me. I listened, and I let you down." Dad ran a
shaky hand over his mouth. "I'm sorry for that, son."

Rue released a shuddery breath, and what struck was
the lack of condemnation. Sadness yes, he witnessed
that, could hear it, but not condemnation. Same as
Monty and Kendrick.

It was the same.

For years he'd held on to the guilt, using it to beat
on himself. Had talking to Kendrick and Monty allowed
him to stop, to step out of the shadowy, painful past?
Because how was it this easy? He didn't know. Yet
here it was, his worst fears exposed, and there was no
rejection.

He searched Dad's expression, seeing nothing but love. Love he'd given freely and without strings. The strings attached to it were all Rue's. He struggled to blink away the tears gathering in his eyes as he got up and strode to Dad, grabbing his arm to haul him up. There was a flicker of surprise before Rue pulled him in and gave him a crushing hug. The air expelled with force out of him when Dad returned the hug just as hard.

Never one to show affection, Rue clung on and gave in to the need. "I'm sorry. I'm so sorry, Dad. I didn't trust you and Popi."

Dad squeezed tight and kissed his forehead. "You have nothing to be sorry for. You're my son, I love you, and nothing will change that. What happened to you was a crime. Same to your birth parents and brother." Dad eased his hold to be able to look Rue in the eye. "Through tragedy came a gift to us, you. If I could have given you back what was stolen, I would have. I'd have sold my soul to prevent the trauma you and your family suffered."

A sob tore from Rue's throat. "I don't know what I did to deserve you and Popi after—"

"If you're gonna say it's your fault, I might just have to paddle your ass. Nothing about who you are can justify what the crash did to your family. *Nothing*!"

The steel in his voice came wrapped in silk, but it was still there.

"I love you, Dad."

For the first time, Rue witnessed tears in Dad's eyes. "I love you, too. Never forget that." Another tender kiss to his forehead, and Rue gave in and rested his head against the solid chest that smelled like home. "Now, shall we talk about Kendrick and Monty?"

"Daddddd!" he groaned, but with some amusement.

"What? It seems you've found men who see beyond your walls, and I couldn't be happier for you."

Rue tugged back, resigned yet relieved, too. He wanted to talk. "I told them about... *everything*."

The smile of approval that lit Dad's eyes made it hard to swallow. "I figured. They must be very special to you."

"They are... Monty... he loves me."

Dad nodded like he expected nothing else. "And Kendrick?"

"Hang on... you knew? About Monty?"

"Let's just say the omega wasn't as discrete at hiding his adoration when he was around you."

Rue frowned. No, he hadn't missed that, had he? "Huh! Seriously?" It was best not to think too hard on the subject, because otherwise he'd have to consider his brothers could have noticed too!

"Yes, you were just in denial. He's perfect for you."

"Honestly, I don't think I want to have this conversation."

He didn't like how Dad laughed, shaking his head at him. "Then we can talk about your alpha, Kendrick."

Back was Rue's frown. "I didn't mention he was an alpha." As he was watching Dad closely, he didn't miss the slight wince, and he quickly added up what was going on. "You had him investigated, didn't you!"

Good God, what if Kendrick found out?

It took a second before he nodded, and Rue let go to take a step back, unsure how to react.

"I have met Kendrick once before, Rue, just to be clear."

"He never mentioned it." Rue had to wonder why.

"Maybe he forgot, is it relevant? What is, is that I protect what I love—my family. When you have your own, you'll understand there is nothing you won't do to prevent harm coming to them. I needed to know that the man my son is serious about is worthy of him. I won't apologise for it."

Rue should be furious. But to have someone want to protect him from harm, how could he be mad about that when it was Dad? Then he considered his brothers' mates. "Did you do the same to Hollis, Frey, and Ziggy?"

He had to know if it was just him.

"Of course I did." A sheepish look came and went.

"Oh my God, they don't know, do they? Silas, Taylin, and Booker? You didn't tell them."

Dad shrugged, not looking at all comfortable. "They never asked. If they had, I would have told the truth."

Rue believed him. "You trust me not to tell them." It wasn't a question.

"I do."

That right there was why he couldn't find it in himself to be pissed off. Honesty. Dad and Popi never shied away from the hard questions. It just wasn't who they were. "You're right. I won't unless they ask me."

"I expect nothing less." He returned to the seat. "Now, when are we officially meeting Kendrick?"

Rue chuckled. "I've booked a table for dinner on Thursday. It's Kendrick's day off."

He took two steps back to Silas's desk, then swung around, giving Dad a serious look. "I don't want to know what you found out about Kendrick, okay? I trust him."

"Good."

That one-word reply said everything, leaving Rue with another idea. One he had been playing around with, looking at possibilities, and it seemed this was the right time to bring it up. "Can we talk about where I need to be based?"

"I see..." Dad's head tilted, a shrewd look in his eyes. "I hope he realizes how lucky he is."

Rue grinned widely. "I believe he does."

Chapter Thirty-Five

Lane

"My love, it doesn't do to look so smug right before we're heading out for dinner. Rue will notice and figure out you've been meddling."

Lane fluttered his eyelashes at his husband in the bathroom mirror, returning to sorting his hair, unconcerned. He wanted to make a good impression, despite having met Kendrick before. This time was different because it was never on his radar that his son would need two mates, not one.

Lane easily readjusted and was excited to get to know Kendrick the way he had Monty. What he remembered about Kendrick was a charming smile and friendliness, the kind that wasn't forced.

"I mean it, Lane, you have to tread carefully," Derick warned, kissing the side of his neck, his whiskers brushing against his skin, warming it and causing a shiver of desire.

"I'll behave." *After chatting to Kendrick.* He kept that to himself, having already pumped Monty when they'd spent the afternoon baking. It was the perfect chance, and one Lane had used while no one else was around to stop him. He'd always had high hopes for Monty and Rue. The moment he'd met Monty at his interview, he'd felt he'd be perfect for Rue. Witnessing Monty sitting on Rue earlier in the week was exactly what he wanted to see. Open affection, something Rue tended to avoid at all costs—he needed that.

Monty had confessed to being honest with Rue about his feelings. The omega had no problem sharing, and he'd used Lane as a sounding board about his feelings for Kendrick, once Lane had assured Monty he had no problem with this new dynamic.

It was important that Rue, who carried a shield to protect his emotions, had men who would see past those barriers. It warmed Lane's heart how much Monty loved his son.

He didn't need to brag.

So here he was, needing to understand where Kendrick fitted into their lives. The easiness between him and Monty — would it be there with Kendrick? Lane needed to know that Kendrick could offer Rue the balance it seemed he needed. Lane just had to be clever about how to get the answers.

"I can hear your brain whirring, my love. Can't we just enjoy a meal and the company?" Derick stood back and twirled Lane around to hold his gaze, searchingly. "Please don't frighten Kendrick off with your not-so-subtle questions."

"Me? I couldn't frighten a fly. And I'm the epitome of subtlety."

Derick's deep bass laughter filled the bathroom. "My love, you're more frightening than a pack of starved wolves! As for subtle, a sledgehammer against a brick wall springs to mind."

Lane's laughter joined his husband's. He wasn't wrong on both counts, but he had a suspicion that he'd need more finesse with Kendrick.

He reached up and smoothed down the silk tie, eyes twinkling. "Darling, I learned from the best. I also know I won't be alone in finding answers..."—he eyed his husband—"if you haven't already done so." There it was in his eyes. "Did your investigator find anything?"

A flash of annoyance made Lane chuckle. "I'm not the only one who is obvious." He came up on his toes and waited until Derick met him halfway. "Now kiss me. It is our anniversary, and I've got a present you'll enjoy later."

"A present?" Large hands roamed down his back, coming to rest on his bottom. Derick lifted him up so their bodies were flush against each other. It was a move he'd done a thousand times before, but it still had the ability to make Lane's heart flutter with the show of strength.

"Hum," he murmured against the heat of Derick's mouth. "Something special that you'll enjoy unwrapping."

Derick groaned, pupils dilating. "You're a tease, my love."

Lane wore a sexy smirk as Derick released him, shaking his head, eyes traveling down his body as if searching for clues to what lay beneath. "And you love me for it when it's all you'll be thinking about throughout the meal. Now shall we go?"

Derick took his hand and guided him eagerly out of their cottage.

The sun was setting, hitting the vines. Their sweet scent perfumed the air, adding to the romance of the evening.

Lane paused to appreciate the view with the man who was his world. "It's a perfect night for romance."

It really was.

Chapter Thirty-Six

Kendrick

How had he gotten to the age of forty-two and never experienced the nerves of meeting 'the parents'? Kendrick couldn't say, but fuck, he sure as hell felt them now. He tugged at the tie that felt like it was strangling him, one he'd just finished tying not ten seconds ago. He couldn't remember the last time he'd worn one. In fact, he'd had to go out and buy one. A feat in itself when he couldn't remember ever going into the one posh shop they had in town that sold such things.

Rue had told him not to bother, but Rue lived in suits mostly and no doubt his parents did too. Accordingly, Kendrick had sucked it up and gone shopping to buy one, along with a new shirt. He eyed the gray silk and tried not to think too hard on the cost for something he was likely never to wear again. Would he?

He had every intention of having a future with both men, so suits could most certainly get tucked in there. When nearly a week back at work Kendrick felt stressed from the separation, how the fuck would he feel when they had to return to Hazardville?

Christ, the very idea caused a flare of panic to grip his throat, making him want to rip off the tie. Being reasonable, he understood that Rue and Monty had important jobs. That they had to work Monday through Friday and occasional weekends. Kendrick's job wasn't important. It paid the bills for him.

How would life be if they made a commitment to each other? Kendrick was not averse to being home. Cooking, cleaning and taking care of his men's needs. Dang, the vacation proved how much he loved it. It was a thrill, which he missed now he was back at work. He could be a househusband. And wasn't that a shocker. He'd come to that conclusion late on Tuesday when all he wanted was to tell Trey he was done, and hadn't that given him lots to think about.

"Are you coming?" Monty shouted from the bottom of the stairs.

"Not in the way I want to," he muttered under his breath, before shouting back, "I'm coming."

He'd not gotten three steps when he heard Monty coming up the stairs, the thud of his footfall revealing his impatience.

He appeared in the bedroom doorway. "We're gonna be late," he stated, looking smart in a suit Kendrick hadn't seen before. Slim fitting, in brown, he had paired it with a cream shirt open at the throat, no tie in sight.

"Why aren't you wearing a tie?" Kendrick questioned, frowning as he let Monty drag him out of the bathroom.

Monty shrugged, looking sideways at Kendrick, not stopping. "Don't you like what I'm wearing?"

Kendrick witnessed the smile dim and dragged Monty to a halt halfway down the stairs. "You look gorgeous." To make his point, he cupped his cheeks and kissed him hard on the lips until they were both breathless.

"As much as I love to watch you pair kissing, can we get a wiggle on? My parents are always early for everything."

Kendrick glanced at his watch and groaned at seeing they were indeed going to be late. "Why didn't either of you shout me earlier?" he questioned, taking Monty's hand to rush him down the remaining stairs.

"I was boxing up the Nutella cheesecake I'd made for Lane and Derick."

"What about us?" blustered Rue, looking outraged at the suggestion he wasn't getting any, causing Kendrick to smirk. But he swallowed the laughter seeing how serious Rue was at being denied.

Monty skipped to Rue and patted his shoulder as he passed to pick up the box he'd left on the table in the hallway. Kendrick's attention went to the impeccable cut of the expensive jacket Rue wore. It moulded to his shoulders and tapered down to his waist, highlighting the leanness of his hips. Kendrick cursed, realizing he should have bought a new damn suit, too!

"I made two, so don't fear. You'll get *dessert later*." Monty's comment brought his attention to him.

How he said it suggested he'd be dessert, and Kendrick wished they could stay home.

"Ready to head?" he said instead, holding out a hand to Rue. When he met Rue's gaze, his apprehension made it impossible to consider doing anything else.

He came to him, and Kendrick kissed him as he had done to Monty, reaffirming his feelings. To leave Rue in no doubt he was in this relationship so deep there was no sky to be seen.

"Aren't we leaving?" Monty's laughter brought them apart.

"Yep, I just needed to even the kissing balance."

A look of interest appeared as Monty glanced between the two of them. "There's a kissing balance? No one told me. Now I'll need to keep track. I wouldn't want to be missing out."

Heading out the door, Rue rolled his eyes. "There's no chance of that. You miss nothing."

The easy banter continued as Kendrick drove them up into the mountains, a road he'd rarely traveled, paying attention to road signs.

A rustic building with traditional style Italian shutters sat far away from the main house, where the Vaughn brothers lived together. The hotel was a later addition but remained in keeping with the older buildings. The small cottages they'd also added for anyone wanting a more private stay were at the back of the property and overlooked the vines.

Kendrick parked his truck in the designated area. He'd barely taken a breath to calm down his erratic, beating pulse when Lane and Derick strolled into sight. He admired the striking couple, their ease with each other as they strolled towards the truck, hands linked. Though both men were in their sixties, and despite silver hair, both appeared youthful and full of life.

Kendrick got out of the truck as Rue and Monty opened their doors.

Lane's attractive smile widened and his pace increased, pulling, it seemed, his husband with him in his eagerness. Derick's gaze was assessing as it met Kendrick's, and he gave a slight nod of acknowledgement.

It removed some of the tension within him for reasons he'd explore later. "Good evening, lovely to see you both again." Kendrick stepped forward with confidence, offering his outstretched hand.

Lane ignored it and came in for a hug, their size difference obvious as he barely reached the middle of Kendrick's chest. When he spoke, Kendrick blushed hard enough to feel it travel down his chest. "My, aren't you big."

Kendrick froze, his gaze darting to Derick's, who wore an amused expression. "My love, stop teasing Kendrick."

"Dad, please let go of my boyfriend. You're going to scare him off."

Kendrick's eyes darted to Rue at the ease of his declaration. "No, he won't. No one will do that, honey." If they were setting out intentions, then he was on board—fully.

The light in Rue's eyes made his heart thud painfully against his ribs. Lane surely felt it.

He patted Kendrick's chest after letting go, his eyes twinkling with laughter. "I believe you and I will be great friends." He glanced away at the group standing watching them. "Vaughn has the most amazing champagne, a 72 vintage. I think we need a bottle to celebrate."

"I've ordered a bottle for the table," replied Rue.

Lane hooked his arm through Kendrick's, guiding him towards the door like the force of nature he was. "Tell me about yourself, Kendrick. How long have you lived in Bayfield?"

"And we're off," Rue muttered loud enough for Kendrick to catch before they stepped into the plush reception area of the restaurant, the scent of perfume and wealth greeting them.

Kendrick heard laughter, but he couldn't say who it belonged to. "Twenty years, and I've worked for Trey most of that time," he explained before Lane could ask. "I've always known any relationship I was in would be a throuple. I bought my four bedroomed house with that in mind," he confessed, mentally ticking off what he deemed important questions.

He was distracted from saying more when they were met by the maître'd, who greeted them with warm enthusiasm. "Good evening, gentlemen. Can I take the name of the booking, please?"

"Starling," Kendrick supplied before Lane.

The maître'd nodded, then promptly escorted them to a secluded table in the corner of the room. Plant positioning ensured no one overlooked the table, not that Kendrick knew anyone else in the nearly full dining room. The suit he wore was most unquestionably the right thing to wear in such opulence.

"Nice," Lane murmured, bringing Kendrick with him. "You can sit next to me."

He helped seat Lane and took the chair he indicated to his left. Derick sat on the other side of him, and Kendrick heard Rue curse.

He gave Rue an 'I've got this' smile when he sat across the round table from Kendrick, tension evident in the stiffness of his posture.

Monty laid a hand on Rue's shoulder, bending to whisper something in his ear, bringing a light to his eyes that Kendrick knew well. Intrigued, his brows rose in question at the two men. Rue licked his lips, sharing nothing of his thoughts as Monty sat next to him, looking rather pleased with himself.

Kendrick listened as the wine server brought the champagne, explaining the flavor notes, and offered Rue a taste. He nodded his approval, and the server moved to pour wine into gorgeous flutes. The wine was so fucking good, Kendrick moaned in delight. The bubbles tickled his palate as the delicious sweetness of the grape hit his tastebuds.

"Wonderful," he murmured, nodding his approval of his man's taste in wine.

"What's in the box, Monty?"

Lane's inquiry had Monty slide the white box between the wine glasses and around the flower centerpiece that none of the other tables held. Had Rue ordered flowers for them? A glow of romance he'd never experienced before warmed his chest.

"I made a Nutella cheesecake for you and Derick for your anniversary."

Damnit all! Why hadn't Rue mentioned this to him? It explained the champagne and the flowers.

Rue gave him an apologetic head tilt while Monty directed the conversation to all things baking and took the pressure off Kendrick from having to answer anything more personal. It gave him some breathing room to watch the dynamics between Lane and Monty.

What struck was how easy they were with each other and the genuine affection Lane had for the other man. Their relationship was much more than employee and boss. They were friends, too.

"Kendrick is fabulous in the kitchen too. His grandmother's recipe for apple pie is amazing," bragged Monty, making Kendrick fight to stop squirming in his seat with both Derick and Lane looking at him with interest.

"Better than mine?" Lane questioned Rue.

"How do I answer that?" Rue looked at Dad.

"Carefully," said Derick.

This brought laughter, and it somehow relaxed everyone. The meals they ordered were so delicious that the conversation slowed, but the questions didn't stop. Lane was the culprit, with an occasional one from Derick.

Understanding it came from concern made it easy to ignore the intrusiveness he'd not experienced to this level before. Love. Love between father and son, husband and husband, even employer and employee. Somehow, he fit into their mix with ease.

"Have you witnessed Rue on a stampede yet?"

"Dad, not you too," groaned Rue, his skin decidedly pink in the flickering candlelight and lamps lighting the room.

Caught off guard, Kendrick probed, "A stampede? I haven't seen Rue's rhino or Monty's otter." He was intrigued by Derick's assumption, not Lane's. "Does he stampede often?"

"My darling, our boy loves a good stampede." Lane's expression was one of mischief as he gave Rue a cheeky wink.

"I need to see this," Monty said as Kendrick spoke.

"He does?"

"I haven't needed to act like that in some time," Rue muttered, the embarrassment darkening his cheeks further.

Derick hid his mouth with his napkin, coughing—laughing.

To shift the attention, Kendrick grinned at Rue. "My bear would love to meet your rhino," he twisted to look at Monty, "and your otter."

His bear went from not paying attention to fully alert.

"He's the cutest thing when he's swimming."

"Which one?" Kendrick glanced at Lane, unsure who he was referring to, brows arching.

"Actually, both, but I meant Monty. We had a pool party last year, and as it's saltwater, Monty let his otter out. Such fun to watch him play in the water."

"Was this before we came home? I've never seen your otter." Rue was looking at Monty, pouting.

Kendrick had to pick up his napkin to hide his quivering lips, much the same as Derick.

"It was. If we can find a pool, we'd love to play,"—Monty looked between both of them—"with you both."

"Won't that be fun?" Lane looked innocently at them all, but Kendrick didn't miss Derick's eye roll or the huffed-out breath as Kendrick choked on his own saliva.

Rue appeared to give in to his own amusement and met Lane's stare. "You have no idea."

Kendrick's lips flapped open as everyone else burst out laughing at the double entendre.

Derick patted his shoulder once he'd got himself under control. "If you can't beat them, I suggest you join them."

He could find no fault in Derick's logic.

Chapter Thirty-Seven

Monty

His bear was persistent. "Come on, get a shake on."

"Where are we going?" Monty had less than four hours' sleep after Kendrick's return home from his bar shift. The week, with the added pressure of entertaining Lane and staying on top of his work, left Monty with plans of lounging in bed until Kendrick had to go in for his lunchtime shift. How was Kendrick so bright and breezy this early on a Sunday?

"It's a surprise," Kendrick advised, giving Monty no clue at the bland expression he was looking at.

He huffed noisily while encouraged out of the house so Kendrick could lock up.

Monty caught Rue's jaw cracking yawn, but he wasn't complaining. "Do you know where we're going?"

His eyes narrowed at the nonchalant shrug before Rue climbed in the front passenger side of the truck when Kendrick hit the fob to open the doors, shaking his head. "Nope."

Eyeing the large bag Kendrick placed in the trunk, Monty's forehead wrinkled. "I like surprises, I do, but I'm tired. Can't you tell us what we're gonna be doing?" He nodded to the trunk as Kendrick shut it. "That bag looks pretty full and *heavy*."

Kendrick traced a cool fingertip down the side of Monty's face, then slid his hand around to cup the back of his neck, squeezing gently. "I have it on good authority that you *love* surprises." Cool lips pressed against Monty's. The presence of the orange juice Kendrick had drunk made his lips taste sweet.

Monty slipped his hands into the short, gray silky strands of Kendrick's hair and clung on, sinking into the kiss.

"Hey, if we're gonna do the kissy thing, can't we do it in the house?"

Monty moaned in complaint as Kendrick released him to glance at Rue, who had opened the passenger door and was peering out.

"Sorry, you know how tempting Monty is."

Rue's returning smile was all agreement. "Does this mean we're going back inside?" Now he seemed hopeful.

Kendrick immediately shook his head. "No, I've worked hard to sort this out."

Rue shut his door, and Monty grumbled under his breath but got into the back of the truck.

"Will this be better than sex?" he questioned suspiciously as Kendrick started the engine.

"We'll find out soon enough."

Did he sound confident?

He watched closely, looking for clues as Kendrick drove through town. The sun crept slowly up the side of the enormous mountain towering in front of them, which held the valley where Vaughn Winery sat. "Are we heading back to the winery?" He couldn't see what was up there besides wine, and it was way too early to be drinking wine.

"Yep."

Rue looked sideways at Kendrick, but Monty couldn't make out his expression from his seat. "I didn't think there was much up there to be visiting, unless we're doing a wine tour?"

"Nope."

"You're good at these non replies," groused Monty, resting his head back on the seat, seeing as Kendrick wasn't going to give in and tell them what they were doing. Monty was too tired for guessing games and closed his eyes. He figured he could catch a twenty-minute nap before they reached their destination.

The lack of movement roused Monty, and he blinked sleepily, seeing they were back outside the hotel, only at the main entrance. The towering, dark-haired figure standing in the open doorway caused Monty to whistle in appreciation. "Who is that?"

"Your boyfriends are right here," muttered Rue in a pissed off tone.

Monty released his seatbelt and came forward to poke his head between the seats, first kissing Rue's cheek and then Kendrick's. "I'm spoken for, not dead."

He hopped out of the truck, grinning at the man whose gaze swept over him. Monty got the impression he missed nothing. The guy's eyes glowed... red. Holy shit. He glanced at Rue, looking to see if he'd noticed, but he was busy shutting the trunk.

"Thank you for this, Dacian." Kendrick strode with the bag held in one hand, the other outstretched to Dacian.

When he looked at Dacian, the red was gone. Had he imagined it? He was tired; it was making him see things.

Monty followed Kendrick's lead, walking to Dacian, smiling. He had met none of the Vaughn brothers. He'd heard quite a bit about them and Ledger, mate to the oldest brother Thorn, who had recently given birth to twins. Dacian and Calvert, he was told, were twins. Two that looked like Dacian, the gods had surely been shining a light that day!

Dacian focused sea-green eyes on him, and something about his expression set off a bout of nerves at the intensity that made him feel Dacian was... looking directly inside him. *Weird.*

"And who is this?"

The velvet smooth voice compelled Monty to answer. "I'm Monty."

He sensed Rue moving before an arm slipped around his waist, tugging him almost off his feet and into Rue's side.

"Hey," he muttered as he staggered.

A sudden tension crackled in the air as Kendrick flanked the other side of him, the pleasant smile replaced by hostility. "Monty and Rue are my boyfriends."

All my days! Where had that come from?

Dacian didn't seem at all phased by that as he stepped closer to Monty. He caught his aftershave and not much else as he tried to determine what kind of shifter Dacian was.

Dacian leaned in and sniffed deliberately at Monty's jacket.

Rue and Kendrick nearly squashed him in between them, and Monty had only one place to go to escape the squishing, backwards. Except looking at Dacian, he felt the compulsion to stay exactly as he was.

Most definitely weird!

He isn't a threat to us. His otter was adamant.

I don't think he really needs to be sniffing at me like that. I had a shower!

Then Dacian stepped back, and the feeling disappeared. His expression revealed zilch of what the heck that was all about. Then he smiled and back was the 'wow factor'. The man was drop dead gorgeous, for sure. Monty could appreciate it, but no one could match his men.

"It's lovely to meet you, Monty." Dacian glanced at Kendrick. "I've had the staff set everything up to your specifications. No one will bother you, so it's your choice whether or not you wish to lock the doors."

Derailed by what Dacian said, Rue wore a perplexed look, one Monty suspected he wore as well, as Dacian raised a hand as he turned. "If you'll follow me, I'll show you to the pool area."

Pool?

Swimming.

They were going swimming.

We're going swimming, his otter replied gleefully, attempting to shift before they'd gone more than a few steps.

Behave, I'll let you out once I've seen the pool.

Then hurry up.

Monty did, his sneakers moving silently as they walked through the hotel lobby that was all elegance. The corridor Dacian led them down was empty. The walls had painted murals depicting the different seasons of growth of the vines. Dacian came to a large set of decorative double doors and opened them. They led into a small, opulent area with an ornate table with a red velvet seat behind it. There was one other door, leading to the pool, he supposed. Yet, the scent of oils and herbs made it obvious the area housed a spa, somewhere beyond the door, as well as a pool.

"Through the door, to your left, you'll find the changing rooms. Enjoy." Dacian offered what could only be described as a tight-lipped smile before he went out the door they'd just come through, shutting it quietly.

"What was that about?" whispered Monty, still no clue what Dacian was beneath all the polish and dashing suit.

"No fucking clue," Kendrick growled. "He was sniffing you like he was about to cock his leg and pee on you."

"Yeah, I picked that up too."

Monty's otter wasn't interested in silly talking, and his shift was upon him before he could reply. *Hey!*

Swimming. He wriggled out of the pile of clothes and lifted his tiny paws to Kendrick, wiggling his bottom. *Swimming, come on take me swimming.*

"Why aren't you just the cutest!" Kendrick scooped him out of the clothes one handed and brought Monty to within reach of his whiskered jaw.

His otter tapped impatiently on Kendrick's cheeks.

"He's as impatient as Monty. I think he's ready to get in the pool," chuckled Rue.

"Then let's give him what he wants." Kendrick glanced at the clothes. "Can you grab his things?"

Wiggling impatiently, he squeaked to get Kendrick moving. His laughter had Monty shaking in his hand as they walked through the door into another area, this one with several doors. Kendrick strode to the one marked with blue waves on it. The scent of salt water got his otter giddy with excitement. He squeaked and vocalized his pleasure and impatience.

Kendrick walked to the loungers at the side of the pool and placed Monty down. He scampered down the leg of the lounger and across the pale green iridescent tiles surrounding the pool, and dived into the water.

It was warm and heavenly as he flipped over onto his back, floating, watching his mates strip off.

His teeth gnawed at a paw. *We aren't biting anyone.*

Mine.

I agree. It's polite and the right thing to ask first.

Then ask.

I will.

When?

I can't now. Can I?

His otter considered this, and Monty chuckled at how he was reluctant to shift to get him to do what he wanted. *When we get home.*

Monty didn't answer when his otter side had other things on his mind. A nude Kendrick, stretching out his arms, tilting his neck from side to side, right before his bear emerged. His otter flipped over onto its front and swam to the shallowest part of the pool, the same direction Rue headed in.

Excitement got his otter vocalizing loudly at Rue coming into the shallows, rolling his shoulders, then there was his rhino. The water reached the middle of his vast body. The rhino lowered its head when Monty's otter lifted its paws as far as it could to keep afloat. Its large horn right there for Monty's otter to grab hold of, he scampered up to sit on top of Rue's head, clapping his paws in delight.

The sound of Rue's trumpet bounced off tiles and glass. Monty's otter squealed and clapped harder, looking at Kendrick with begging eyes. The bear rumbled and lumbered to the edge of the pool, slowly coming down the first three wide steps before sitting on the second to top step. Half in and half out of the water, he was wearing what Monty's otter considered a beautiful grin. All sharp teeth and sass.

Rue's rhino lowered his head and Monty's otter moved to cling on to his horn, seeing it was a game when Rue's rhino ducked his massive head under the water and came up fast enough to splash the bear.

Water dripped off the gleaming brown and honey colored fur. The bear's eyes narrowed and an enormous paw hit the water, causing a tidal wave to swamp Monty's otter and hit Rue's rhino directly in the face.

Monty howled with laughter while his otter squealed its delight. His otter let go of the horn and scampered down the back of the rhino's head, along his back and swung off his tail, flying into the water barely splashing anything, but he didn't notice.

The rhino trumpeted, and the bear roared. They were music to the otter, who surfaced and climbed up the back of the rhino's tail, running back the way he'd come, to cling to the horn, encouraging his rhino to splash their bear.

This is the best surprise.

Monty couldn't disagree; it was.

Chapter Thirty-Eight

Rue

They'd had such a fun morning. Monty's otter was utterly adorable. His attempts at splashing them failed epically, but it didn't stop the little guy bringing much hilarity. They'd spent two hours playing before Kendrick had shifted and lay on his back, floating with Monty's otter resting on his chest, gesticulating with his paws as if they could understand him.

Rue's rhino had just enjoyed watching them as they chilled in the water. It had been longer than Rue could recall since they'd spent so much time in his rhino form. It made him all the more reluctant to let him shift back when Kendrick pointed out that he had a shift at the bar, and they needed to leave. It had grumbled and complained, blaming Rue for not asking for what he wanted after he'd discussed with Dad the potential of staying permanently in Bayfield and getting his blessing.

The reasons for being home no longer held for Rue, and Dad had rightly pointed out Rue could use their private jet to take him to and from places he needed to visit for work. If Rue had notions of Kendrick traveling with him and Monty so they weren't apart, he'd kept them to himself for now. Planning was what Rue was good at, he just needed to figure out all the logistics. It wasn't very romantic to place all the facts down. It would, however, prove he was serious about staying—with both men.

The smile he had worn since they'd gotten into the pool to play, dimmed watching Kendrick slip on his jacket to leave as he followed him into the hallway.

"Why the droopy lips?"

He didn't answer, just kissed Kendrick hard until they were both breathless. "Thanks for this morning, it was wonderful."

Since they'd gotten home, the part of him that had played let's pretend that Kendrick wasn't going anywhere, had to give up.

"It was fun." Kendrick kissed Rue once more and glanced towards the kitchen, where Monty was banging around. "Monty, I gotta go."

There was the sound of Monty's bare feet slapping on the floor before he appeared, flushed, breathless, with smudges of flour on one cheek and his hands. He puckered up, putting his hands behind his back, but Rue didn't miss the look of disappointment.

Rue watched the care that Kendrick took stroking his thumbs over the sides of Monty's jaw before he kissed him with the same depth of passion they'd shared.

"I'll be back by eight." He nuzzled the size of Monty's mouth, looking at Rue. "Maybe have a nap, you pair, so we can have some naked playtime later?"

Monty fake yawned. "After someone had me up most of the night and then wouldn't let me sleep in, I might still be too tired." He lied badly.

A smile that should be outlawed graced Kendrick's gorgeous face. "Then I'll need to work *extra hard* to keep you awake."

Monty and Rue groaned in unison. Rue's sweatpants formed a tent at what that meant.

"See ya later." Kendrick was gone, the door shutting softly behind him, and Rue's shoulders sagged dejectedly.

"It sucks he has to work," Monty muttered huffily and then stomped off back to the kitchen.

He wasn't wrong. It fucking sucked big time. Had Kendrick felt like this when they left him to go to work? He hardly worked early in the morning unless there was a delivery.

Rue strolled into the living room and plonked himself down, analyzing Kendrick's behavior. The harder Rue thought on that, the more he would suggest Kendrick got a real kick at doing stuff in his home when they left for work. His gaze swept the cosy living room. The place was dust free and tidy considering there were three of them living in the house and one being messy Monty, duly nicknamed by Kendrick. He'd go as far as to suggest their man got a lot of pleasure out of taking care of *them*, not just the house.

The meals he prepared, even when he couldn't eat with them, were there in tubs in the refrigerator waiting to be heated. Little sticky notes with messages on. Most with little hearts for a signature. Had Rue tucked a couple in his sock drawer? Why yes, he had.

Was Kendrick hiding his feelings about what he wanted from them long term while living day to day like this wasn't going to end? Rue wasn't a fool not to notice that once he'd faced his fears, what they had going was serious. They were in a poly relationship. He'd looked into how that worked for marriage. Legally, Rue could have paperwork created to protect both Monty and Kendrick's rights regarding him and vice versa. They could have a ceremony just for them and their families.

Was he jumping the gun? Diving in but potentially finding himself disqualified from the love race.

He didn't think so when he'd clocked more than one sour expression when Kendrick mentioned he had to leave them. Kendrick liked his job, so it wasn't a work thing. Rue thought it was a 'leaving them' thing.

Rue chewed his lip between his teeth as got up and paced in front of the large screen TV, his mind whirring. Dad and Popi had always worked, even when they'd had children. Bessie was the linchpin that made it all run smoothly, for sure.

He tripped over his own feet as he lurched at the obvious. Could Kendrick be that for them?

Pulse hopping around like he only had one leg, he stared unseeingly at the room. Rue hadn't considered having a family of his own. Was it possible now? The past barriers to happiness were smashed by love.

He sucked in an unsteady breath and shut his eyes. Could he have it all? He could if he went with what his heart wanted.

Shaking out his hands, his gaze travelled in the direction the noise was coming from. He was moving before it fully registered as something else struck him. Monty hadn't had a heat. He calculated the time they'd been working together. Was he taking heat blockers? If he were, did that mean he didn't want children?

Compelled to find out, Rue went stomping to the kitchen. "God Monty, have you been having a baking duel with the invisible man?" Laughter boomed out of him at the frightful mess that would have given Kendrick a heart attack.

Monty at least looked embarrassed as he eyed the counters covered with dirty pots, goo and some substances Rue wasn't willing to guess at. "I'm making several batches of cookies. Different flavors for the omegas," he answered, sniffing indignantly. "What do you want?"

The demand, said in a petulant tone, made Rue wary about his reasons for coming into the kitchen. Then his brain went on the fritz. Why else would he blurt out, "When's your heat due?"

"My heat?" Monty pushed back his bangs, seemingly missing that his hands were covered in goop. "Erm... sometime in December, why? Are you planning a work trip?"

He was frowning as he shifted two bowls of cookie batter to one side, making room for Rue had no clue what, with the sheer number of tubs scattered about.

"No... just curious as I couldn't remember you requesting time off."

Monty shrugged that off, concentrating on what he was doing. "I only have two heats a year and they're December and January, mating season for otters. It's a little inconvenient having them so close together, but then I get ten months in between without worrying about it. Anyway, it's on the heat calendar," he pointed out distractedly, eyeing the bowls.

"Yeah," Rue replied awkwardly at not thinking about checking that first before starting this conversation. Yet he couldn't seem to leave it be when he wanted to know if Monty wanted children. He was endearing with Emmy. "Do you... have you..."

Monty glanced at him, his brows tugging together. "Have I what?"

"Wanted a family of your own?" he blurted out, blushing under the scrutiny of Monty's stare. He was never good at this kind of conversation, so why had he thought this was a good idea?

Monty grabbed a cloth and wiped his hands before tucking it into his sweats pocket, much the same as Kendrick did when he was cooking.

"My kit was quite large, and I was the youngest, so I was pretty much left to my own devices with my parents running the grocery store they own." He came to a halt in front of Rue. "I was lonely often. Not neglected as such, just wasn't anyone's focus unless I was working in the shop. No playtime, no fun stuff, just tired parents always too busy for me. I don't want that for my children... I love my work, and it would be selfish to have a child and not put them first. So, having children hasn't been something I've considered will be in my future."

Rue hadn't realized just how lonely Monty must have felt for this to be the reason not to have children. His parents had been selfish. Selfish. The word struck Rue's heart.

"You don't want children?" Rue pushed to clarify, his stomach knotting that with his own past issues, he'd somehow missed this vital part of Monty's past. They'd all talked about their families, but Monty clearly hadn't burdened them with how he truly felt as a child, left to his own devices.

"I never said that." Monty's head tilted, holding Rue's stare. "What's this about?"

"If someone was there while you were at work, taking care to make sure our—*the* child wasn't lonely, showing they were loved every day, would that make a difference? Like Frey and Booker have with Emmy."

Monty left teeth impressions on his lower lip, his expression full of so many emotions. "I'm not sure. Emmy comes to work with Frey and Booker, so they can see her anytime they want."

Rue exhaled gustily. "Okay, consider this, though it is a more nebulous concept. Just hear me out. Popi and Dad have always worked, and I've never felt neglected, and I'd say my brothers would say the same. They found a balance, which your parents don't seem to have done or considered they needed. Maybe after having so many children by the time you came along, they didn't consider the age gap between you and your siblings and that you were alone." He was trying to be reasonable in his thinking, despite thinking Monty's parents were selfish assholes.

"You could say that Bessie was in a throuple with my parents, being at home with us, loving us as a parent would." Monty's look of morphing alarm had Rue add quickly, "Not a traditional throuple in any genuine sense. My parents love Bessie, she is a part of the family, taking care of the home while my parents worked. Even now that my parents are retired, she's there taking care of us."

"In this scenario in your head, who do you see as Bessie? Kendrick, because he takes care of us like Bessie?"

Rue was nodding before Monty finished speaking.

"Would it not offend Kendrick to even suggest that he quit work and look after us... a baby full time? A house-husband?"

The latter was whispered with hope, and Rue's heart trembled in his chest at hearing it. "A husband. Two hus-bands," Rue murmured, leaping off the cliff edge without a safety net.

"Are you proposing," gasped Monty, staggering back, eyes wide.

"It wasn't on today's agenda, and I'd like something a little more romantic than doing it in this mess." He went for humor; it was that or blubber when he couldn't figure if the alarmed expression Monty wore was good or bad.

Monty jabbed a finger. "You're proposing to me... to Kendrick... you love us!" he squealed, leaping at Rue, who was the one staggering back as he attempted to fend off a grubby Monty who peppered his face with kisses. "This is the best day ever!"

Rue sighed for show as he took hold of a wiggling Monty. "I haven't proposed yet!" He didn't deny the love when it would be a lie.

Monty held the sides of his head, transferring goo, and gave Rue a gleeful grin. "No, but you're gonna." He gave him a smacking lipped kiss, then wiggled out of his arms. "My otter has decided you're ours already, you and Kendrick. And this morning he was thinking of biting you both." Monty looked very bashful as he kicked at some imaginary thing on the ground. "He insisted I bring it up, so this is me bringing it up."

Rue's lower jaw dropped open, his heart racing so fast he felt a wave of dizziness when his rhino released an ear drum shattering trumpet in full agreement to the claiming. "I—"

Yes. The answer is yes.

Do you mind? I was trying to talk!

Monty peered at him, nose wrinkling adorably. "Is your animal being bossy?"

"Yes, he is!"

"So does he want to?"

There was so much hesitation in the words that Rue swept Monty up off the ground, uncaring he was spreading more mess, to look Monty directly in the eye when he answered, so there was no misunderstanding. "Marriage and mating, in my mind, go hand in hand. We do one, then the other will also happen. Clear?"

Monty pressed their foreheads together. "Very clear." His lips twitched. "So when is the proposal happening? Would that be before or after my heat?"

"Which would you prefer?" He couldn't have made himself clearer, what he was offering, and Monty kissed him with all the love that filled Rue's heart until it felt bigger than the world surrounding him.

By the time he needed to breathe, Monty wore a flush of desire with a dreamy expression. "I've some thoughts on that."

"On what?" Rue's brow wrinkled in confusion.

"You're so good for my ego." Monty giggled in delight. "Kendrick. And how we approach things with him."

"You do?"

His grin matched the mischievous one Monty sported. "I do..."

Chapter Thirty-Nine

Kendrick

"How did the pool date go?" Trey's inquiry brought Kendrick's attention to his friend from the cash register. He was leaning his hip against the counter at the back of the bar, staring at him with interest. The Sunday lunch crowd had ensured Kendrick dived right into work, which prevented him getting twenty seconds to chat with Trey. It helped stop him grumping at having to come to work, a state he'd only been in since his return from vacation.

"Monty is so fucking cute and playful in his shifted form." Kendrick had gotten Trey to reach out to Thorn Vaughn to ask about using the pool privately as a surprise introduction for their animal sides.

"And Rue?"

Kendrick motioned for Trey to wait while he went to give the customer their change. He checked to see if anyone else needed serving. Seeing no one, he walked back to Trey and mimicked his pose.

"Huge and playful, it turns out." Kendrick had been amazed at just how playful. His bear's side was cheeky, but so was Rue's rhino. The man was far more serious, not that Kendrick minded at all. Monty balanced things out.

Trey laughed and slapped him on the shoulder playfully. "I can see your bear loving that."

"Of course..." Kendrick frowned, recalling Dacian's behavior and what his bear didn't love. "Peculiar thing when we got there, though. Dacian came to greet us and got all up in Monty's space."

He hadn't really talked with Rue about the way Dacian had acted, bar mentioning it when they entered the pool area. He'd set it aside after seeing Monty in the pool, but that didn't mean he was going to let it go. Kendrick planned to go back to the winery without Monty or Rue and make a point that both men were taken, even if Dacian seemed more interested in Monty. There was no harm in laying it out so there was no misunderstanding.

"He did? I find him a bit more reserved around folks. You know, distant, though he's friendly enough when you talk to him."

"He took friendly to a whole new level this morning with Monty! Do you know what kind of shifter he is?"

Trey shook his head. "Never figured it out. The brothers don't have a scent that gives any clues."

"Yeah, I noticed." And wasn't that odd?

"Anyway, what's with you? When you came in, you weren't your normal sunny self. It wasn't the face of a man who'd had a fun outing this morning with his boyfriends. What caused it?"

"You know how you felt about the time apart from Cass,"—at his nod, Kendrick rubbed a hand over the back of his neck—"I'm feeling the same. I hate leaving them." He hit the center of his chest with his other hand. "It's like a mule has kicked me, right here."

Trey's sigh said it all before he uttered, "You're gonna resign, aren't you?"

"I'm thinking about it. I own the house and have some savings. They're here for what, six months, if I'm lucky?" He really didn't want to dwell on that, when it would lead down a spiral of despair.

"I don't wanna waste the time I could have with them working." Laying it out helped put it into perspective for him, but he could see the worry in Trey's eyes. "Don't stress, I'm not gonna just abandon you." He wouldn't do that, they were friends first. "The new guys are working out great."

"They are," Trey agreed. "What about dropping your hours? Do fewer evenings? Have the weekends off?"

Kendrick could see Trey trying to work it out to meet both their needs, and he was grateful for it. "That could work temporarily."

He would not commit to long term when he had no clue what that would look like for him. Monty and Rue had a life elsewhere. This was temporary for them, and he needed to keep that at the forefront to push him to live in the now. "I can assess who can do what to cover you and me." Trey would need more time when Cassidy gave birth, and the days were counting down.

"I'll take that." Trey shifted off the counter to go when someone called his name. "Just keep me in the loop."

"Will do."

It was all he could think about throughout the rest of his shift. The crossover into the evening went smoothly with Paddy coming in early, giving Kendrick a chance to leave half an hour earlier than planned.

When he pulled up outside the front of his house, he ran a hand over the middle of his chest. The increased thudding at coming home to two men who held his heart in their hands, whether they knew it or not, let him know how invested he was. The shadows flickered from the TV beyond the window, and he got out of the truck hurriedly, imagining himself snuggling on the couch between his guys before he took them to bed like he'd promised.

Entering the house, the homely scent of cookies greeted him. It was with mixed emotions that he shut the door. Monty baked when upset or happy. Earlier, when he'd left, he'd say it was the first and not the second that had the house smelling like a bakery at Thanksgiving.

"I'm home," he called out, despite knowing they'd have heard him come in. He kicked off his cowboy boots and shrugged out of his jacket, hanging it up before heading straight for the living room when no one appeared.

In the open doorway, he stopped, frowning at finding the room empty. He listened out, but heard nothing from above. The TV was on low, and he went and switched it off. Were they both asleep?

He went into the kitchen to check he hadn't missed something and found it empty and spotless. He suspected that was Rue's doing with the number of tubs filled with cookies on the counter. Messy Monty could create a disaster zone without trying when he was baking.

Checking the house was locked up, cuddles looked like the only thing he'd be getting tonight. He had no problem with that. Retracing his steps, he headed upstairs.

He heard Monty giggle and Rue shush him, and he was grinning before he opened the bedroom door.

Dang it, how did I get so fucking lucky?

Monty lounged like a sexy siren in Kendrick's chair—naked and on display. Rue was sitting in the center of the bed, looking sexy as fuck, all flushed and aroused, his cock at full mast.

"What's this? Did you think to get this party started without me?" Kendrick didn't think so. They were waiting for him. Entering the room, he reached to unbutton his shirt, his senses firing in all different directions at the intention rolling off both men. What was he missing here?

"Absolutely not," Monty informed him, a devilish light sparking in the depths of his eyes. "But you aren't in charge tonight. We've decided that I am."

He didn't miss the 'we' and, as aroused as he was by the sight of his men naked, Kendrick's cock went from semi-hard to full fucking mast at the intention behind Monty's bold statement. Kendrick's eyes narrowed with speculation on Rue before switching to Monty, playing along.

"Is that so?" He undid the cuffs of his shirt, coming to a stop at the side of the bed.

"It is. But first, I've a question—"

"We've a question," Rue interjected, chuckling.

"We've got a question," Monty stated with an eye roll at Rue.

"And what's that?" Kendrick had his shirt off, dropping it to reach for his belt.

"Where do you see this relationship going?" Monty's voice was full of nerves that weren't there a moment ago.

Kendrick's own danced under his skin like ants had invaded his body. It was difficult to hold still when he once more looked at Rue, assessing what they were after. His guarded expression gave little away, but the tension in his body betrayed him. Then Kendrick looked closely at Monty. There was the love that he'd declared to Rue, aimed directly at him.

It took a second to release the air from his lungs and find the ability to speak. "I talked to Trey today about quitting to spend time with you both." He shoved open his fly to release the pressure off his erection, but his attention never wavered from the two men in front of him. "I don't want to waste any of the time we have while *you're here*. Does that answer your question?"

"How would you feel about a more permanent arrangement?" rasped Rue, the words barely more than a whisper. He pointed between himself and Monty. "With us."

That he was the one to ask was all the declaration Kendrick needed about Rue's true feelings. "I'd ask, 'where do I sign up for that'?"

Monty nodded towards the bed. "Right there. You with mine and Rue's dick inside you at the same time so I can fuck you both and we claim you the way we want."

Kendrick bent forward, breathless, hands hitting his knees with how dizzy he felt. His dick hurt at the visual while his ass clamped tight at how that would feel when neither man was small.

"Fuck," came the raw curse through a voice box that tried to mince the word.

"Is that a yes?" Monty questioned, sounding far from certain.

A hand touched his shoulder, and he wheezed out a breath, nodding vigorously.

A dark, sexy chuckle came from the man on the bed. "I think we've rendered Kendrick speechless."

Lifting his head, Kendrick fired an incendiary look at Rue.

"When I fuck into you, my dick up against Rue's, know this: I'm going to own both of you for eternity," Monty growled right into his ear.

Rue and Kendrick groaned in unison, both sounding pained.

"I've created a monster," Kendrick complained when Monty skipped to the end of the bed. When Kendrick felt able to stand upright without embarrassing himself at the loss of blood to his head when it vacated to another part of his anatomy, he straightened. It seemed his body was fully on board with Monty's plans for the rest of the night.

Monty patted the mattress. "Climb up, big boy, and straddle Rue's lap facing the end of the bed." He waggled his brows and held up a tube of lube, his expression sparking some concern when it was pure naughtiness. "*We* need to prep *you*."

He was in so much trouble when he was ready to bust a nut already, and they hadn't touched him. He finished stripping and climbed onto the bed, lifting a knee over Rue's thighs to settle it on the bed, facing the other way. Not waiting for Monty, he came forward, resting his hands at the sides of Rue's calves, getting on to all fours and receiving a mutter of approval from behind him.

The mattress dipped as Monty climbed up next to him, and he felt the heat of both men's stares on his backside. A first for him to have this much attention on his ass.

He braced his arms and clenched at the first touch of a slim, slicked finger swiping over his taint and moving so slow.

"So beautiful. Look how it twitches, Rue."

His head hung down between his shoulders, and he released a shaky moan at the knowledge they were going to fucking torment him first. Rue cupped his balls and cinched them.

"We wouldn't want you coming too soon."

Rue's rumbled words were their own tease. Then he got in on the action. A thicker digit dueled with the slim one, spreading the slick over his sensitive flesh. It was maddening, the exploring. The teasing. He fucking loved it.

Two fingertips explored and moved in tiny circles until the lube warmed before the tip of a finger pushed in past the tight rim of muscle, making his belly quiver. Their touches created a shower of pleasurable sparks to run deep inside his clenching hole.

"Push out." Monty's request was barely audible.

Kendrick breathed in the scent of their arousal, and his own, then pushed out. As soon as he did, a second finger pushed in. The burn, though expected, punched the air from his lungs when paired with the urgency to come. One touch to his dick and he'd be done for, despite Rue making his balls ache with his hold.

"Gimme a sec," he huffed, sucking in a breath, eyes closing to focus on anything but the need to come.

Except that didn't work when it left him feeling everything when neither man moved their fingers. Instead, they used their other hands to slide fingertips around the stretched rim, pushing just enough to make him aware of what was to come.

Hot breath touched the slick skin before Monty said seductively, "So slick. Your skin feels like satin. Let's see if it feels that way against my tongue."

Kendrick grunted, straining to hold back the desire to hump the bed at the tongue lapping at fingers and hole. Monty's moans of delight vibrated inside Kendrick's ass causing the muscles to ripple, adding to the violent urges decimating him. The man was a menace.

"A-arghh," he cried out as the tongue slid in between the fingers inside his ass, increasing the burn, which was morphing into a carnal need. The kind Kendrick had never achieved with anyone else. Mind blown, he shook and begged, "Hurry the fuck up! Someone get their dick in me," he ground out between aching teeth that clenched and unclenched.

"You're not in charge tonight,"—Monty jabbed his tongue deep, the fingers moving in the opposite direction, then the tongue reversed and the fingers sank back in—"I am."

In—out—tongue jab—in—out—tongue jab. It was maddening. It was nothing like he'd expected. It was everything he didn't know he was missing. They were taking him to a place he'd never visited, a place where the need to have a cock in his ass consumed him. Left him no place to hide the wanton passion to be fucked just like Monty promised.

"Fuck me like you promised." His demand, rough with desire, did fuck all to get what he wanted. His hips rolled, his arms and legs shook in their attempt to hold him up and get what he wanted. *More. Deeper. More. Deeper.*

He was unsure if the chant was in his head or he was voicing it, everything narrowed down to the clawing need. His cock swung through the air, its warmth teasing the wet head leaking pre-come. Rue continued to cinch his balls to stop him coming when two fingers became four. Monty's mouth was unrelenting in taking him apart.

His ass was dripping with spit and lube, he felt it run over his balls. Lewd noises came from behind him as Monty slurped and sucked like he was at a damn ass eating competition.

Rue's growl lifted the hairs on Kendrick's body. "He's ready. I'm fucking ready. Monty, get your cock ready."

At last!

Only Monty didn't immediately stop. No, the little shit wiggled his tongue in deep and pushed the fingers against Kendrick's prostate, causing an earthquake of want to erupt through him and bring with it the inclination to scream in frustration when his balls felt they were going to explode, despite Rue's effort to stop him coming.

"Now... now... fuck me... *now*."

As if they'd heard how close he was to breaking, fingers and tongue disappeared, leaving him mewling at how empty he suddenly felt. He had no time to complain when Rue manhandled him until the broad head of his cock slid over his hole.

He whimpered in pathetic relief when Rue grunted out, "Fuck, you have no idea how much I want to pound into your ass when it looks so fucking perfect sat over my cock. Your hole, all slick and slightly open, ready for us."

The fuckers were out for revenge when Rue's observations added fuel to the raging fire burning him whole. Sweat coated his skin from using all his strength to impale himself on Rue's cock. His punishing grip was welcome when it gave him something else to focus on.

"M-motherfucker," Rue snarled, the air punched once more from Kendrick's lungs when Rue ground into him. He didn't care his ass was on fire, not when the satisfaction at getting what he wanted overrode common sense. He placed his hands over Rue's and used the strength in his thighs to lift up, fighting against Rue's tight grip to slam back down.

"*All my days!* Look how much you want it. Want to have Rue buried in your ass. Is it everything you imagined? That thick cock splitting your ass open? Giving you the perfect dicking of your life?"

Monty's eyes were fervent with desire, the words spilling from his lips painted visuals he didn't need with how that same dick was indeed taking him apart.

Kendrick worked to drag in a deep breath to gain some semblance of control. It was minimal, but enough to lay back against Rue's heaving chest, the cock in his ass stroking against his prostate wanted to short circuit his brain. The violent urge to come had him freeze, eyes widening. Monty picking up the right cue. It was now, or Kendrick was going to lose his shit—cum before he'd gotten what they promised.

Monty grabbed Kendrick's cock with both hands and squeezed until it was more purple than pink, but it staved off the imminent combustion. He wouldn't last a minute at this rate. Lowering but true. They had him wound up tighter than a coiled spring. His head a mess and his fucking dick had taken charge.

He licked his dry lips, exhaling noisily, nodding at Monty. "Okay, get your fucking cock inside me now!"

He stretched out his legs, moving them over the top of Rue's, essentially pinning him to the bed with his weight.

Rue's groin cupped Kendrick's ass, shaft position not fully in with the new angle, but it opened Kendrick's asshole for Monty, who couldn't take his eyes off where he was joined with Rue.

About to demand he move, Monty grabbed the lube bottle off the cover and poured the contents over his cock. It dripped everywhere as he chucked the bottle over his shoulder and rose to step over the limbs, placing his feet next to Rue's hips. His cock waved in Kendrick's face before he slut dropped and rocked his slick ass over the head of Kendrick's cock.

"Christ," he wailed—whimpered—in distress. Violent shudders made his ass clench hold of the cock in it.

Rue, who was tracing his teeth up the side of Kendrick's throat, growled, sending shivers through Kendrick at the animalist sound. Kendrick's ass squeezed tighter, gaining several hissed curses, right as Monty lifted off Kendrick's dripping cock to move and settle himself onto Kendrick's thighs.

The lube made his skin slippery, overstimulating Kendrick to the point of madness. He didn't know if his lungs, cock and heart would ever function right again. Monty reached between his spread thighs and angled the head of his cock under Kendrick's, lifting his balls to push the head of his erection against the base of Rue's dick.

"I'm not gonna last long," Kendrick whistled through his teeth, sweat sliding down the back of his hairline. It was a miracle he'd held on this long.

"Me neither." Rue sounded frantic.

"Then bear down and hold on for the quickest ride of your life."

If he'd hoped that the stretch would take the edge off, he was wrong. Monty's determination made it impossible to hold on to the moans of distress with how he wanted to come doing as directed.

Driving slowly inside, Monty didn't stop until Kendrick felt so full he was sure he could taste dick at the back of his throat.

Rue's grip would surely leave bruises. "W-why h-haven't we done t-this before," Rue stuttered, the body beneath Kendrick feeling like he was sitting on stone.

Then Monty's thighs gripped around theirs, angling his bottom forward, his cock pushed Rue deeper, and Rue's cry was cut off as he sank his teeth into Kendrick's throat.

"Bite me," Kendrick demanded, wheezing, looking at the man who he wanted as his forever, same as the man behind him.

Rue went wild, hips jerking erratically when Monty surged forward, nowhere near Kendrick's neck, and bit him right above his heart. Monty's hips pistoned crazily, doing exactly what he'd said he'd do. He fucking owned them.

They owned him. As his cognizance expanded, and his dick erupted, spraying cum everywhere, Kendrick found himself taken to another plane.

What. A. Fucking. Ride.

Chapter Forty

Monty

The scent of Kendrick's cum, and the feel of it splattering against his skin sent Monty into a tailwind of gut-wrenching pleasure. He swallowed deep, the blood sweet, and he groaned in bliss. His hips did not stop for a second, even when Kendrick's ass took hold in a vice clamp move that made his eyes cross and Rue's cock expand as he writhed before warmth bathed Monty's cock, triggering his own orgasm.

There were noises, mewls, groans and moans, but who was making them, Monty couldn't comprehend. His entire body buzzed with a new awareness that he'd only read about when a person claimed a mate. This was only the beginning, he needed more. Was greedy for it all after Rue and then Kendrick had offered him their hearts—forever.

At that thought, his teeth released, and he gasped, "bite me," of the two men in front of him. Shuddering, manhandled, his cock slipped out of Kendrick, cum dripping down Rue's cock. Kendrick dragged him up his sweat and cum soaked chest so he was within reach of both men. His limbs weak as a newborn otter, they weren't after obeying him as he attempted to help Kendrick.

Kendrick slipped his hands under Monty's ass and hauled him higher, positioning him so his head was between Kendrick's shoulder and Rue's head. Lips trailed down one side of his neck while on the other side, Kendrick's lips parted on his shoulder. The sharp sting of teeth piercing flesh at the same time had his still semi-hard cock stiffen, and creamy ropes of cum smeared Kendrick's already messy chest.

Exhilarated, Monty squirmed in their hold at the tug of their mouths sucking his life force. Did they feel the strength of the connection that coursed through him?

Tongues lapped at the bites, and his cock did its best to respond to the erotic feel when the marks tingled. When he watched Rue tilt his head in offering, his eyes pools of want, he twisted to look at Kendrick.

"Rue's turn," he murmured enticingly, finding enough energy to move, with help from Kendrick, who groaned as he lifted Monty to the side to free Rue's cock and allow it to slide out of him. More cum dribbled out of Kendrick's ass.

Fuck, that was sexy. Monty wanted to bury his face down there to suck and bite. Seeing he could be derailed, he looked back at Rue who wore a well-fucked expression.

Rue lifted his arms when Kendrick moved to the other side, and they moved into Rue's sides together. His eyes gleamed with need, the same as Kendrick's.

Monty looked pointedly at Rue's budded nipples. At the unspoken question, Kendrick's eyes glowed with wickedness, and he nodded. They moved together, lowering and closing their mouths around the firm buds. Monty sucked, enjoying Rue's distinct taste.

Rue shivered beneath them, his chest pushing up. He met Kendrick's heated stare, their hands reaching for Rue's cock as it thickened, and they bit true. Rue's blood filled his mouth and cum covered his knuckles as he pumped Rue's cock in tandem with Kendrick.

"Y-yes," Rue sobbed out a cry, his body moving as if electrified, making it hard for Monty to stay put. Teeth embedded in the flesh and his hand holding the cock were the only reason he didn't topple off Rue completely.

He wasn't sure how long they stayed like that. Monty's own body was in a state of drugged blood haze. He felt different. Felt, at a cellular level, that everything had changed. It was a sense more than an actual feeling he supposed. He was too tired right then to get his brain to function and work through exactly how he was feeling. But elated ranked pretty high.

When Rue shifted beneath him, Monty mustered the energy to flop onto his back, cum covering most of him, making his skin gleam in the lamplight. His eyelids fluttered in an effort to stay open. To enjoy how his mate's blood flowed through him. Moving in his veins, changing everything. Wasn't that just wonderful?

His breathing deepening and his eyelids growing heavier by the second, he murmured, "I'm the bomb. The dick bomb."

There might have been tired laughter, only his brain had already shut down while his body adapted to a new reality—matedom.

Bleary-eyed, Monty squinted at the man who was carrying him—he looked at the open door—to the bathroom. The sound of the shower roused him further. Inside, he could see Rue was already under the spray. Monty's lips tugged into a smug smirk at the mating marks gracing his chest. He looked like he'd gotten nipple tattoos. Kendrick's mark was decidedly bigger than Monty's, but his wasn't small either.

Kendrick stepped to the shower door, and Rue opened it so Kendrick didn't have to put him down. As tired as he was after their antics, they'd have to wash him too.

"Just hold me under the spray, that'll do."

"Have you seen the state of you?" Kendrick's chuckles rumbled through Monty.

"Don't care. You wore me out." He groaned, eyes closing at how nice it felt with the heat of the water penetrating his aching muscles. Topping was hard work!

Soapy hands cleaned his chest as Kendrick continued to hold him under the water. Monty floated in the tenderness. No one, not even his parents—that he could remember—took such good care of him.

"I could get used to this," he murmured.

"Good, because you're ours now, to treasure forever."

Monty hadn't considered himself a crybaby. Of course he cried. Many situations warranted it. The omegas from Drinkwater. His friends finding their mates. Emmy when teething, and he couldn't help. They were genuine reasons. Blubbering all over Kendrick's massive chest all because they were going to treasure him... yeah, crybaby right here.

He turned his face into Kendrick's chest to hide the tears. He was the cocky one. The upbeat one. Most definitely not the one who acted like a crybaby.

"We've got you." Rue was there, his nose pressed against Monty's cheek. "It's been an emotional day for all of us."

"Then why aren't you crying," he mumbled accusingly, moving just enough to catch sight of Rue's eyes.

The man holding him shook with silent laughter as Rue looked to struggle to keep his own laughter in check. "I cried out a lot while you were fucking me."

Feeling slightly mollified by the answer, Monty nodded. "You did and Kendrick begged," he made sure to point out.

Kendrick kissed his head. "I did, and I can't wait to do it again."

"Good, because we will be. Now I know how good it feels to be in charge, I'll be wanting to do it more often. You're right, you have created a monster."

"Is that because you're the dick bomb?" Kendrick asked, eyes gleaming with mirth.

Shit. Had he said that? All my days, he had. His cheeks flamed, though he hoped that could be attributed to the hot water.

He met Kendrick's gaze with confidence. "Did you come like a bomb exploding?"

"I most certainly did."

Rue's chuckles increased as he went back to washing Monty.

"Then I've the dick bomb."

Kendrick kissed him. "How can I argue with that?"

Monty yawned, his jaw clicking at the stretch, water filling his mouth. He spat it out away from Kendrick. "What time is it?"

"About midnight."

Monty groaned and complained. "You could have left me to sleep. I've work in the morning."

"So have I," Rue pointed out.

"Yes, but I spent the day baking, and remember, I was the one doing all the work in the bedroom."

"How can we make it up to you?" Rue asked, his soapy hands sliding between his legs and over his groin.

His cock tingled and perked up, making him groan, but for a different reason than tiredness.

"I suppose if you both did all the work, I could manage another round," he supplied on a breathy moan.

Chapter Forty-One

Rue

Rue sat in Silas's office, staring at his phone. His thoughts circled around on who to call first to share his news. He swiped to open the screen, and he went into the video chat app, and pressed Laken's name. He would call Dad and Popi next. First, he wanted to let Laken know, before anyone else, that he had two mates.

Six rings later, and Rue thought that Laken must be in a meeting that couldn't be interrupted. He was about to end the call when a dishevelled-looking Laken appeared on the screen.

Rue, in all the time he'd known Laken, had never seen him—but once—anything but put together, so this was a sucker punch that he'd once taken from Booker. It knocked him right off the reality perch he sat on about his expectations of Laken.

"Holy fuck, are you home with a hangover when you're supposed to be at work?"

Was that high-pitched voice his? It fucking seemed so when Laken grunted, and a glass of what looked like water appeared on the screen in front of Laken's face. He downed it in greedy gulps.

Rue stared wide eyed at his brother, at a total loss at witnessing behavior he'd never have believed of him. "Have you taken some vacation time? Cause I'm pretty sure you're supposed to be at work."

"Not when I can't fucking concentrate," he snarled, placing the glass down on something with a clatter. "He's everywhere I fucking turn, I can't escape!" Unfocused eyes skittered about as if searching for whoever Laken was talking about. "Smells like Popi's cinnamon rolls."

Clearly, he wasn't as sober as he should be at ten am on a workday when he sounded like a starving man in desperate need of said cinnamon roll!

Again, Rue acknowledged the gut punch and unnerving feelings seeing his *sensible brother*, in his view, allowing himself to get drunk enough that he couldn't get up for work. Or to talk so freely about something so personal when the man never talked about his dating history, making Rue wonder if he did indeed date.

The behavior right then was making it obvious who Laken was referring to. He was clearly home and hiding from Isley to Rue's mind, but he chose not to make assumptions.

"Escape who?" He didn't mention the cinnamon roll part.

Laken blinked groggily at the screen and appeared to try to focus his eyes. "My iddy-biddy PA.. Who else?" He groaned and ran a hand over his unshaven jaw. "How can someone be so small and take up so much room in a brain?" he demanded, only Rue suspected he wasn't asking him the question. "Do you know how small a sugar glider is? They can fly right into the palm of your hand when they're pissed off and refuse to let go of your fingers!"

Rue struggled to stop himself laughing aloud at how Laken knew that and instead asked in all seriousness, "How long?"

"How long, what?" replied Laken, sounding confused.

"Have you been in love with Isley?"

"I'm not," he spluttered, sobering before Rue's eyes. "He's the bane of my existence." There was absolutely no truth in that statement when Laken wore a lost expression Rue hadn't seen in years.

"Do you wanna talk about this?" he asked in a tone that brought Laken's haunted gaze to the screen.

Laken unenthusiastically shook his head. "Nah... not now."

"I'm just at the end of the phone when you're ready," he said softly, understanding the denial when it came with fear of the unknown. He'd been in that place.

Laken pinched the bridge of his nose. "What did you ring for?"

"I wanted you to be the first to know I'm mated." He said it like he was ripping off a plaster, fast and without hesitation, practicing for what was coming.

The phone clattered to the floor, and Rue got an upside-down view of Laken as he grappled to pick it back up, wearing a look Rue hadn't expected to see—jealousy. Rue recognized it from looking in the mirror when he thought about how lucky Taylin, Booker and Silas were. God forbid he ever admitted that aloud though.

"You are!" Laken appeared fully on the screen, croaking, "Who is it?"

"Monty *and Kendrick*, the guy from the bar." He had mentioned the hook-up to Laken after he questioned where he'd been after he'd not shown up for work. Laken was good at not prying, so he was the easiest for Rue to talk to.

"You claimed them both."

He wore a flabbergasted expression causing Rue to snort in amusement. "If you could see your expression."

"I can, you dork. We're on video chat." Back was some of the amusement he was used to sharing with Laken.

"You threw me off with this hobo look you got going this morning."

"Drop it," he said sharply, then sighed dejectedly. "Ignore me. I'm happy for you, genuinely."

"I know you are." He did. "And that's why you were my first call."

The hand he was dragging through his disheveled hair, stopped. "You haven't rung Dad and Popi?"

"Didn't I just tell you I wanted you to be the first person I shared the news with?"

"Right. I'm honored, but you know I'm gonna gloat about this, right?"

"I wouldn't expect anything else. So, if you wanna drop that nugget in the group chat, go for it."

For the first time since he answered, Laken looked more like himself when he grinned. "Hang on."

Laken disappeared from the screen, and Rue figured what he was up to before he got a notification from the alphahole group chat.

"Is Kendrick planning on moving to Hazardville?" Laken questioned while his phone blew up with notifications.

"I'm moving to Bayfield permanently." They had actually managed to fit in some talking this morning, despite how tired they all were from being up all night. Monty, regardless of his complaints of being tired, had gotten a second, then third, wind last night, resulting in Rue's ass feeling Monty's *dick bomb* too.

Laken's face reappeared as Rue chuckled at Monty's new description of his dick.

"How's that gonna work? Dad and Popi will not be happy to hear that news."

Directed back to the conversation, Rue informed Laken, "I spoke to Dad about the potential when he came up for their anniversary—spying—visit."

"I figured that might be what they were doing. How did he take it?" Laken was all avid interest.

"They're okay with it." He didn't know what else to say when he didn't want to share the conversation he'd had with Dad.

His phone pinged several more times, making Laken laugh. "You need to go read the chat."

"Will do. Are we good?" Rue had to know.

"We are. I'll see if I can wangle a trip out your way to meet my future brother-in-laws." The sly wink left Rue open-mouthed and gave Laken time to end the call with a quick "bye."

"Asshole," he mumbled good naturedly to the empty room. Somehow Laken knew exactly what Rue would want. Switching to the alphahole chat to see how his brothers had taken the news, he burst out laughing as he started reading.

Alphaholes

Laken: *Another one bites the dust!*

Kodi: *What are you talking about? And where the fuck are you? We had a meeting at nine am!*

Laken: *I asked Charlotte to reschedule it.*

Booker: *What are we missing, Laken?*

Silas: *Clearly something when his reference sounds like he knows something we don't.*

Laken: *Rue is mated!*

Kodi: *No fucking way! Please tell me it's not his PA.*

Laken: *Kendrick…*

Jupiter: I figured.

Laken: How so?

Jupiter: The way he eyefucked the guy at the bar, same as he was doing to Monty. Does he have two mates? Laken, spill. You seem to have all the goss?

Kodi: Wait up. Two mates? Who would be that fucking crazy?

Laken: Rue.

Kari: Good for him.

Kodi: Is it fucking really? This will give the remaining PAs damn ideas. That leaves me, Laken, Kari and Jupiter as the only single ones now! Did some fucker put something in the water? I don't wanna catch whatever this is.

Jupiter: *Why are you freaking out? You do have a choice, and mine is to remain just as I am.*

Silas: *Jup, I can't wait for the smug smile to get wiped off your face when you fall. It will be epic. And Kodi, I don't think you got anything to worry about, no one would want your overreactive ass.*

Kodi: *Thank fuck!*

Jupiter: *Hell will freeze over first, so be prepared because I know you hate the cold Silas.*

Booker: *How's this gonna work when he comes home?*

Rue: *I'm mated, which means I won't be coming home. Kendrick is happy in Bayfield, and so am I.*

Dad: *You better call your Popi before he hears this secondhand, son.*

Rue: *On it.*

Taylin: *Someone wanna tell me why you aren't all ragging on Rue's ass like you did me?*

Jupiter: *You're just special.*

Taylin: *Fuck off. I can hear your sniggers through the wall, Jup!*

Rue ignored the continued back and forth, closed the app and dialed home. His breath came in fast puffs at what he was about to do.

"Hello, Starling residence."

"Hey Bessie, is Popi about?"

"Sweet boy, how are you?"

"I'm good Bessie."

"Is that Rue on the phone?" Dad's muffled question came from somewhere in the background.

"It is, he's after Lane."

"I'll speak to him first, if you could get Lane from the nursery?" There was some rubbing at the speaker before Dad came on the line. "Congratulations."

Rue released an undignified sniff as he was hit by a wave of emotion at how pleased Dad sounded.

"Thank you, Dad," he choked out.

"What is it?"

Rue braced at hearing Popi and then Dad muttered, "Good luck."

"Rue's on the phone. He wants to speak to you."

"What... why... why are you smiling like that?" Rue heard before there was an almighty screech. "Rue, are you mated? Oh my, I couldn't be happier. This is just wonderful news. I can't even..." Then started the sobbing that left Rue at a loss when he'd not gotten a chance to say a word.

"Give me the phone, my love." The sobs increased, and he realized Dad was holding Popi.

Rue choked back his own emotions when Dad came back on the phone. "Your Popi's just a little emotional right now. He'll ring you back when he's pulled himself together."

"G-good... r-right," he stammered, working on holding back the urge to join Popi for no damn reason. None whatsoever—except every damn reason: love.

Chapter Forty-Two

Delicious & Vicious

Monty: *I have something to share…*

Frey: *You're moving permanently to Bayfield!*

Monty: *What the heck? How do you know that… no, forget I asked. Booker!*

Bowie: *Moving? Why are you moving to Bayfield? I thought this was a temporary thing.*

Isley: There's got to be more to it. Was that what you wanted to share?

Ziggy: You're mated!

Monty: You guys are thunder stealers!

Bowie: Why would we steal thunder, if that was even possible??? I don't get it.

Frey: Us sharing the information before Monty, Bowie. That's what stealing thunder means. We stole Monty's thunder when he wanted to tell us his news, instead of me and Ziggy got to say it first.

Bowie: Oh…

Lennon: Is it Rue or Kendrick?

Frey: Good question Lennon.

Monty: BOTH.

Ziggy: *Over here fanning myself! Go you. I bet that was epic!*

Monty: *I don't want to brag, but I'm the bomb… the dick bomb.*

Bowie: *I'm not even gonna ask.*

Hollis: *I'm with you, Bowie. I do not want to know. I'm already traumatized by Frey's oversharing to go there with you too, Monty!*

Wilder: *You lucky sod, Monty. And I want all the details, so ignore Hollis. I'll live vicariously through you as I'm on a sex drought!*

Bowie: *A sex drought?*

Wilder: *I'm getting no peen at all… big sigh.*

Hollis: Wilder!

Wilder: You're getting all the peen, so don't use that text tone with me.

Bowie: I'm so lost. Text tone? Is that a thing I've missed?

Wilder: Don't worry Bowie, I'll come explain it after. So, Monty, how does it feel to have two peens to play with?

Monty: Like I won the peen lottery... twice!

Hollis: How did I end up here? How? Can we please go back to work... you know, the thing you're paid to do, and stop talking about penis.

Ziggy: Yes, boss. But we should have a video call, all of us, to celebrate Monty's mating. We can have cocktails and cake in our own homes. Wouldn't that be fun when we haven't sorted another night out?

Hollis: *A great idea when we get to avoid sex clubs and much less chance of ending up in trouble. I'll look at everyone's work calendars and send out some dates.*

Frey: *And the heat calendar too.*

Hollis: *Good point. So, will that work for everyone?*

Bowie: *Yes.*

Wilder: *Totally, as long as you don't get bossy and tell Monty not to share... just saying!*

Isley: *I'm in.*

Lennon: *Me too.*

Frey: *Wouldn't miss it.*

Ziggy: *Count me in.*

Monty: *Great, I can't wait.*

Chapter Forty-Three

Kendrick

From his position on the couch, Kendrick leaned forward at the sound of a truck coming to a stop outside the front of the house. When he realized who it was, he was off the couch and hustling to the door with an eagerness he couldn't contain.

"It's about bloody time you came to visit. I got a mountain of presents for the girls." He'd popped in briefly the week before to meet Trey's daughters, and he had left with the promise of a visit from his friend.

He had no remorse over the amount of money he'd spent on matching little outfits, soft toys and things that could entertain a baby. And alright, he'd hidden the numerous parcels that arrived daily up in the spare room. His reasoning was the sheer amount of room they took up, not that he was mortified to have lost all sense on the baby sites with all the cuteness overload—no siree, definitely not!

"It's been a week, and you're acting like its years since you last saw them. My precious girls needed to get accustomed to being in the baby seats. Didn't you, Zinnia?"

Kendrick reached for the bag Cassidy held and ignored Trey's comment as he strutted past carrying both girls in his arms like the proud daddy he was.

"What was wrong with the car seats?"

Cassidy rolled his eyes at his back and stage whispered, "Nothing at all, it's just their overprotective daddy stressing when he has to strap them in."

"I'm not an overprotective, stressing daddy!"

"You'd think he was the one who'd given birth to them," Cassidy said around several giggles as he entered the house after his mate.

They'd barely gotten into the living room when the girls started to fuss.

"Do they need a nappy change?" Kendrick sniffed and felt a pang of regret when he smelled baby powder and what he assumed was baby body wash.

"They're getting hungry."

Trey, who was rocking the girls, stopped and gave Cassidy a pointed look. "You'll need to express the milk. I packed everything in the bag."

"Come on, stop being silly."

"Silly about what?" Kenrick asked, noticing Trey's pensive gaze.

"Breastfeeding." Cassidy took the bag from Kendrick. "Can I use your kitchen?" he asked sweetly, throwing a look that spoke to how ridiculous he thought Trey was being.

"Go ahead. I'll try to talk Trey into letting me hold the girls."

Cassidy was back to giggling. "Good luck with that."

Kendrick went and sat on the couch and held out his arms, giving Trey a hard stare, waiting for him to give in and put his daughters in them.

The sound of his sigh said it all, but Kendrick didn't gloat when he came to him.

"Make sure you support their heads," Trey murmured, being overprotective, hovering parent, he denied being.

"I have held a baby before," Kendrick said in exasperation as Trey faffed around so much that Kendrick's arms started to complain. "Just give me them."

The girls both fussed, letting them know they were hungry, which was why Cassidy was doing whatever it was to express milk. It seemed Trey had an issue with Cassidy getting his chest out to feed the girls in public.

Kendrick couldn't say he understood, but he sure hoped to find out. Monty would go into heat in a couple of months' time, and they'd talked about it and their expectations. He'd not mentioned anything to Trey yet. They'd reduced Kendrick's hours to just three mornings and one afternoon a week, and right now it worked because he was home when Monty and Rue were. He didn't see any point in talking about babies when there were no assurances that Monty would get pregnant during his heat, no matter how much he wished for it.

Trey made a few huffing noises as he finally rested first Zuri into the crook of his left arm and then Zinnia into the right crook.

"Hello sweet ladies, your daddy is just being silly. Uncle Kendrick knows what he's doing, isn't that right, Zuri?" He jiggled her carefully, hoping to get her to settle while they waited for Cassidy to return.

"How can you tell them apart," Cassidy asked, strolling back into the room holding two bottles of milk. "Trey still gets the girls mixed up."

"I don't!" Trey blustered, going red in the face.

Cassidy kissed him before going to where Kendrick sat.

"It's easy. Zuri has this tiny beauty spot right at the corner of her eye. Don't you honey?"

Monty strolled into the room looking windswept. His gaze landed on the girls and a light of delight appeared.

"I thought that was Trey's truck parked out front." Monty hustled to the couch, peering down at the girls as he puckered up for a kiss. "I know someone else who needs some honey love."

After a quick peck on the lips, Monty gave a kiss to each baby's head.

Cassidy perched on the couch next to Kendrick and offered the bottle to Zuri, who instantly suckled and quietened.

"Can I feed Zinnia?" Monty's eagerness got a nod from Cassidy and an arched look from Trey when Monty clearly knew which twin was which.

"Sit next to Kendrick and I'll lift her into your arms." Cassidy moved to allow Monty to take his place.

Eagerly taking off his suit jacket, Monty threw it in the direction of one of the large chairs, not noticing as it slithered to the floor in a heap before he'd even sat down. Arms outstretched, he wiggled his fingers in Cassidy's direction, making him laugh. Messy Monty would never change, not that Kendrick had any issue with it when he was so fucking adorable.

"I can see we won't have any problem finding a babysitter when we need one."

"Why do we need a babysitter?"

Trey's seemingly silly question got a headshake and the comment, "Alphas!" while Cassity effortlessly moved Zinnia from Kendrick's arms into Monty's.

"Who's babysitting? And are we having a baby party that no one informed me about?" Rue stood leaning against the doorjamb looking handsome, arms folded over his chest as he watched Monty with a longing he didn't hide.

Monty didn't take his eyes off Zinnia as she noisily gobbled down the milk, her gaze fixed on Monty. "I was with you, so you have to blame Kendrick," Monty answered absently.

Kendrick winked at Rue and blew him a kiss. "How could I resist these two darlings?"

A week after claiming each other, conversation had somehow turned to children over dinner. That was when Kendrick had discovered how much Monty wanted them and how conflicted he was about not wanting to be the stay-at-home parent. It had taken very little—nothing at all—to assure Monty that he would be more than willing to fill that role in their babies' lives. He was happy to be a stay-at-home parent.

If they were lucky enough to have children.

Our little otter is very fertile, we'll have more babies than we know how to handle.

Please do not wish that on us! Secretly, he was thrilled by the idea.

"By the number of packages in the spare room from the baby website you've been visiting frequently, I'd say you can't."

Kendrick felt the heat warm his cheeks as he gave Rue a sheepish grin. "I've no buyer's remorse, none."

"What did you buy?" Cassidy wore an eager smile.

"Rue can take you upstairs to see, if you want. Or you could wait until tomorrow, when I planned to bring it all when I came to help move the furniture in."

"Bring it all? What did you do, buy out the shop?" Trey's alarm was real.

"He did," Rue answered, eyes gleaming with mirth. "He's a baby shopper's dream. Unable to resist all the pretty things."

Kendrick sniffed indignantly at being called out so blatantly. Was it his fault there were two babies to buy for and everything was so damn cute? No, it wasn't.

"What time?" he asked, ignoring Rue, who didn't contain his laughter.

They were finally moving into the lake cabin Trey had been having refurbished after he'd bought it. "First thing, if that works?"

"I can help," Rue offered. "Take a couple of hours off." He glanced at Monty. "Monty could have the girls up at the ranch house."

"I'd love that," Monty murmured in response, staring at a droopy eyed Zinnia, whose slurping had slowed considerably.

"Are you sure you don't mind?" Cassidy had come to an agreement with Ethan about working on the ranch and bringing the babies in a stroller with chunky wheels that could manage the terrain, so Trey mentioned. Cassidy had only gone back the week before.

"Not at all. Office work... baby cuddles... it's a no brain-er. And I have to confess, I've been missing my time with Emmy."

The honesty worked its magic on Cassidy, who nodded in agreement. "It would only be a couple of hours, but I'd very much appreciate it. And if it's too much having them both, just call me and I'll come straight back to the ranch."

"I've got Ivo, Otis, Eric and Cace. They'll be more than eager to help. Heck, I'll be lucky to get a hold of the girls with how much they adore them."

"They do." Cassidy wore such a gleeful grin that, in the next moment, Trey had his arm slung around his shoulder, kissing him soundly.

When Trey pulled back, he was decidedly flushed. "Yeah, babysitters would be good."

Everyone laughed as he finally caught up with Cassidy's earlier comment.

"Should I order pizza for dinner?" Rue shifted upright, looking around the room.

"I've made meatball subs, and there's plenty for every-one." Kendrick switched his attention to Trey and Cassidy. "If you wanna stay?"

"You just want the girls to stay so you can get baby cuddles," Trey accused, with some hilarity.

"And?" Kendrick replied, not looking at all abashed at being called out so accurately. And if he considered it practice, then what harm did that do?

Epilogue
Monty

December

Monty woke disoriented and feeling way too hot for comfort. His skin felt too tight for his bones, and with it came the reality of what was happening. His womb contracted and slick trickled from between his ass cheeks as he inhaled the scent of his mates from where his face was buried in the pillows. His previous heats had never started so violently.

Was it a mate thing?

He couldn't find an answer in the fogginess of craving that was like a three day thirst. He whimpered at the force of the desire pounding through him, rolling over and running his hands over his body, undulating with need, working to entice his mates. Why weren't they touching him?

Monty reached out, touching the cool cotton surrounding him, searching for what he needed. He whined in distress, opening his heavy-lidded eyes to find the bedroom empty. He searched through the lust haze as to why that was. What day was it?

He squinted at the blinds, his brain trying to tell him something. Sunday... it's Sunday. Kendrick and Rue would be downstairs making him breakfast. They had a tradition where they'd share breakfast in bed on Sundays. Their one truly lazy day together.

Why weren't they here where he needed them? Why?

He arched into the sheet covering his cock, and whimpered louder at how much it hurt. Clutching at the bedsheets in fisted hands, he pushed it off him when the pain of its touch became too much for his oversensitive skin. He clenched his thighs together. His ass drenched the sheet beneath him as he rocked frantically, needing something to ease the ache consuming him.

"Kendrick... Rue..." he cried out.

Could they hear him?

Why weren't they coming?

He needed them.

Didn't they understand?

His fractured thoughts left tears spilling down his cheeks. He attempted to think through the cloudiness of his mind, to figure how to get what his body needed. With how his body shook with need, sitting was impossible, never mind attempting to walk.

Then, feet pounded on the stairs. He whimpered, his blurry eyes clinging to the open doorway, willing them to him.

"What is it?" Kendrick demanded, coming to a skidding halt.

"What..." Rue cursed, "Fuck!" His gaze swept over Monty's flushed body and erection, ripping the T-shirt off his body, it fell to the floor in ribbons. Shoving his joggers down his legs, he nearly tripped to get to the bed.

"Heat," Monty rasped. "Heat."

His eyes implored them both to get their asses on the bed and fuck him like he needed.

They hadn't both had their dicks in him, but with how the need pounded into his brain to have them both at the same time, he was willing to try—desperate even.

The second Rue touched him, Monty was on him. They rolled on the bed until he was on top of the warm, naked body. It was almost too much, only his desire to mate was stronger. He ground his cock against hard muscles that rippled under him. His mouth attacked Rue's in a carnal kiss that ripped at his sanity. He burned from the uncontrollable passion.

Monty's skin flamed at the press of Kendrick's chest to his overheated body. Their combined scent drove the need to mate higher. Kendrick placed open-mouthed kisses up his throat to Rue's mate mark and sucked on it.

It was as if it had a direct path to his womb and ass. Both contracted, and he begged unashamedly.

"Both fuck me... both fuck me... both fuck me... both fuck me..." he chanted between devouring kisses.

There were groans coming at him. Only one thing mattered, and that was the fingers probing his ass. He pushed back and down, never more wanton in his life. Monty would have sold his soul to get what he needed.

"Honey, we need to make sure we don't hurt you." The words floated about him, not penetrating past the craving.

"Both fuck me... both fuck me..."

Why wasn't it happening?

He cried, working to signal his need when neither mate seemed to understand his desperation.

Clinging to Rue, the fingers in his ass were not nearly enough. He sobbed and kissed Rue mindlessly.

Needneedneed.

"Fuck, honey."

He didn't understand why Kendrick sounded pained when he was the one suffering. He rutted, rocking violently, seeking to fill the burning void consuming him from the inside.

His womb contracted harder than before and everything became a blur as his ass met cock and he mounted it unceremonially, releasing a crazed groan. He threw back his head, breathing erratically. It was better, but not enough, *he needed more.*

"Both fuck me... both fuck me," he chanted, rocking on the cock in his ass, trying to make himself understood.

"He needs it, Kendrick."

"What if I hurt him?"

"Hurting now," Monty managed through the haze, desperate to make them see this was what he needed, or he'd simply fly apart into a million pieces and be no more.

"Honey, you need to hold still for me." Kendrick's hands soothed down his flanks, adding gentle pressure. His muscles rippled in agony. "Please, just for a few moments. Kiss Rue, concentrate on him for me."

Rue's hands took hold of his head and angled it, then he was kissing him with the same mindlessness. He plastered himself against Rue, his tongue darting in between the full lips to taste, too desperate to have any kind of finesse. It was wet and wild. Rue then wrapped his arms around his upper body, holding him captive. Monty's instincts kicked in and he fought to get what he wanted, then slumped against Rue when he felt Kendrick's cock press against his already full ass.

Yesyesyesyesyesyes.

Pressure, it burned along every nerve ending in his body, and it still wasn't enough. He needed it deeper. Harder. Needed to be so full that all he felt was his two mates and nothing else.

Sounds came at him through the sexual haze. He swallowed Rue's hungrily as he continued to devour his mouth. Then Kendrick's lips were next to his ear. "Push down, honey."

It took longer than it should for him to compute what Kendrick needed from him. He bore down and, not giving Kendrick any chance to stop when his womb contracted again, slick spilling down his trembling thighs, he thrust right down the hard cock, squishing it right in with Rue's.

"Argh," Rue grunted, releasing his mouth.

"Yesyesyesyesyesyes."

Rue's slick and swollen lips gaped open as Monty placed his hands on his shoulders, not giving either mate a chance to stop him, and gave in to the maddening hunger.

"God save us," said Kendrick in a hoarse groan.

There was no god here, just pure, unadulterated lust, driven by the need to mate. Driven by the two mates, his body was responding. The head of his womb opened as he fucked them hard and deep until he felt the press of their cocks at the entrance.

Sweat dripped and blinded him, not that he could see anything as he chased the need of his body. No part of him could think beyond it. It drove him into the abyss. He went willingly, despite there being no beginning and no end to what his body wanted. It was everything.

Like a pro surfer, he rode the waves as they hit with ferocious speed. He couldn't comprehend not riding the power of each wave as it rolled through him, over him, and out over his mates. There were no thoughts of how to survive when his heart knew these men would sell their souls to protect him and *their baby*. Because when Monty finally slumped over hours, maybe days later, he knew in his heart of hearts the three of them had made a baby.

Babies.

It floated around his mind, ping-ponging off his chaotic thoughts.

His body ached everywhere, but he had no regrets as he was carefully rolled onto his back. He peeled open one eye and grinned blearily up at the two men who gave him their hearts to cherish.

He placed a hand over his belly as warm clothes cleaned his skin, and murmured words of love filled his ears. If there were ever such a thing as rapture—then this was it. What else could it be when he was no longer a lonely otter? Nothing, absolutely nothing except rapture.

Other Books by the Author

Standalone Books

When Fake Changed Everything

Christmas beyond Christmas

The Elves and the Bondage Daddy)

Agrippa My Heart

His Boy to Tease

Headshot

<u>A Brat For Kinkmas</u>

Hanging With Daddy

A Little Christmas Matty Secret

A Little Christmas Terrence

Music & Dreams

A Sucker For Christmas

Sweet Haven

Cruising Right Into Love

A Little Christmas Ollie

Series

Assassins To Order With Lisa Oliver

Marvin – Marvin and Ajani in Audio

Ben – Ben, Teilo & Nico in Audio

Duron – Duron & Beaumont in audio

Conrad – Conrad & Kylo in audio

Dancing With the Devil – Wyatt & James in audio

Tangled Tentacles Series with Lisa Oliver

Alexi #1in audio

Victor #2 in audio

Todd #3 in audio

Markov # 4in audio

Kelvin # 5 in audio

Obsessions Series with Lisa Oliver

Demon's Obsession

Controller's Obsession

Christa's Obsession

Secretary's Obsession

King's Obsession

Bucket List Buddies Series with Lisa Oliver

Perilous Cuties

Ghost of a Chance

A Ballooning Display (coming Jan 2026)

Little Paws Haven Series

Little Treasure he Hides

Little & Lethal

Enforcers Little Warrior

His Littles to Love

Divergent Omegaverse Series

Alphas Divergent Omega

Taylin's Temptation

Booker's Bliss

Silas's Sweetheart

Spin off Series in the Divergent Omegaverse Darling Ranch

Unbar the Barred (book 1)

Spin off Series in the Divergent Omegaverse Vaughn Winery

Blood of the Damned – Thorn (book 1)

The Potters Creek Series

A Christmas Wish (book one)

The App Series

The App: Daddy kink (book one)

The App: Littles (book two)

The App: Puppy play (book three)

The Flamingo Bar Series

Always More (book one)

The Little Side of Me (book two)

3 Is the Magic Number (book three)

La Trattoria Di Amore Series

Puzzle Pieces (book one)

Dominated but not Subdued (book two)

Made to Submit

The Playroom Series

Mine, Body and Soul: Part One

Mine, Body and Soul: Part Two

Mine, Body and Soul: Part Three

Ferron's Journey: Damaged Part One (book four)

Ferron's Journey: Hidden Part Two (book five)

Ferron's Journey: Revelation Part Three (book six)

Mine, Body and Soul Trilogy

Ferron's Journey Trilogy

Spinoff Love's Heart Print

Dark River Stone Collective Series

The Light Beneath the Dark (Book One)

When Darkness Turns to Light (Book Two)

Running From Darkness (Book Three)

The Billionaire Playground Series

Property of a Billionaire (Book one)

Reluctant Billionaire (Book two)

Billionaire's Muse (Book three)

Heart Stones Series

Blood King

The Manx Cat Guardians Series

Where it all Began: Origins (Book 1)

Seeing Beyond the Scars (Book 2)

Destiny Collides Past and Present (Book 3)

Searching for a Soul to Love (Book 4)

The 12 Disasters of Christmas (Book 5)

Laws of Attraction (Book 6)

The Teacher's Boy (Book 7)

Boxset

Weird & Wacky Shifters

All he wants is a Fingerling

Alphas Fingerling Surprize

A Boy Called Blu

The Rhubarb Effect spin off from Weird & Wacky Shifters

Sticky For You

Rhubarb 2 Go

Ravished By the Rhubarb

Embracing The Stalk

Rhubarb Blush

Stalk of the Town

Rumble of the Crumble

Audio Books

Mine, Body and Soul, Part One: The Playroom Series

Mine, Body and Soul, Part Two: The Playroom Series

Mine, Body and Soul, Part Three: The Playroom Series

Daddy Kink: The App (book one)

Always More: The Flamingo Bar (book one)

When Fake Changed Everything

Ferron's Journey: Damaged Part One

Ferron's Journey: Hidden Part Two

Ferron's Journey: Revelation Part Three

Romance books in a mixed series of M/F and M/M by the Author under a different pen name Jayne Paton

Smith's Corner

Delilah & Dallas (book one)

Layla & Levi (Book two)

Ash & Alora (Book three)

Fox & Faith (book four)

Storm & Stone (book five)

Hunter & Holden (book six)

Crime and Thrillers by the Author under a different pen name J Paton

Headspace

Chozen: Dark MM Crime Drama (Headspace Book 1)

Chozen: Dark MM Crime Drama (Headspace Book 2)

About the Author

Eccentric cake lover who has a passion for words of all kinds. I'm Jayne or JP, I live in the Isle of Man. A tiny place in the Irish Sea where all the magic happens. I'm a confessed bookaholic, and if I'm not writing I love to snuggle with a book or two...if you catch my drift.

If you're interested in keeping up to date, then I've a few places you can do that, and they're listed below. My website is where you'll find all the different Me's there are, LOL. As I travel this path into the future, I'm going to be writing in different genres, so to stop there being any confusion I'll be writing under different pen names.

If you would like to give me any feedback or just have any questions, go ahead and friend me on Facebook, or through my website and I would be happy to answer any-thing. I hope you enjoyed this book, and if you would also like to leave a review, then I would love to read your thoughts. Even if you just want to rate it, I'll be grateful

Thank you for being a part of my dream.

www.ingramcontent.com/pod-product-compliance
Lightning Source LLC
Chambersburg PA
CBHW051538250626
47157CB00001B/96